The First Lessons

Containing:

The Hundred Year Wait

The Unexpected Coincidence

The Invisible Amateur

Amelia Price

Published by Red Feather Writing

Check out the latest about Jess Mountifield or Amelia Price at
www.jessmountifield.co.uk

The First Lesson

Containing:

The Hundred Year Wait

Text © 2014 Jess Mountifield

The Unexpected Coincidence & The Invisible Amateur

Text © 2015 Jess Mountifield

Cover art © 2015 Elizabeth Mackey

ISBN:151753030X
ISBN-13:978-1517530303

DEDICATION

To Grandma. The world's just not quite the same without you.

ACKNOWLEDGMENTS

There's always that awkward moment when getting to the acknowledgements where I panic that someone gets forgotten who should be thanked, so I'm going to start by thanking anyone I've ever forgotten to thank who has helped in some way. I didn't mean to forget you and I often remember later exactly what I wanted to thank you for and that it meant a lot to me. Writing books is never a solitary task despite how often it can seem it. From little nudges in the right direction to something as seemingly random like listening to the right song at the right time, so much goes into a book.

Thank you, Phil, for being a husband I often don't feel I deserve. For making dinner those times I didn't want to stop writing, and being gracious when I moaned because I had to stop writing to make yours.

To Bear, for always listening, even when I knew you were meant to be doing something else. I hope I haven't spoilt the plot too badly and you can still enjoy reading the stories. Just being able to say my ideas out loud makes it so much easier to get them straight and make sure there's no plot holes.

To Alex for helping polish the first story with an edit, and David for all your valuable feedback on Mycroft in the beginning. Both of you helped shape the start of this journey and I wouldn't have got very far without your help.

Thank you to my very wonderful editor, Ella, you help polish up my rough work and help it shine and it's a pleasure to work with you.

To Elizabeth, for the cover design. I always look forward to emails from you with cover concepts as you always manage to capture something unexpected that I fall totally in love with and this time was no different. You captured my Amelia perfectly on the covers of this and the ebooks. I really can't thank you enough.

Also a big thank you to the Retreat. I think I must have mentioned this series to you so many times while trying to work out the mechanics of it and you've graciously shared your wisdom again and again. Love you guys and I don't think I'd be doing so well without you all there to give me advice. Finally, to God, I really wouldn't be here without Him.

The Hundred Year Wait

CHAPTER 1

The rain pattered on the windows as Mycroft was driven through the dreary streets of London. He frowned at the typical English weather. He'd been in his house, working, for ten straight days and it annoyed him to find it raining the minute he needed to leave and see his brother. On top of splotching his tailored suit it made the traffic worse.

As the car pulled up outside Sherlock's flat he turned his nose up at the familiar sight. The number on the door was loose. It was almost never straight. No matter how many times he neatened it, by his next visit it was crooked again. Today was no different.

His driver rushed around to the side of the door with a large black umbrella and Mycroft stepped out into the cold, narrowly missing the puddle at the side of the road. An almost identical umbrella with a silver plated handle dangled from Mycroft's left hand and he realised he'd never used it to keep the rain off. After raising and lowering his eyebrow he strode through the flat door, knowing it wouldn't be locked. He paused for the briefest second to shuffle his feet on the doormat while his chauffeur shut the door behind him and went back to the shining black vehicle to wait.

Sherlock's housekeeper and landlady, the widowed Mrs

Wintern, peered around the edge of the living room door. When she noticed it was him she retreated back inside. Knowing she'd be scurrying off to make tea, whether he would be there long enough to drink it or not, he climbed the wooden steps up to the familiar flat. None of them creaked but he'd had plenty of years practice at putting his feet in the right places to ensure his arrival was unnoticed.

Three steps from the top Mycroft paused. Mixed in with the usual scent of dust, damp and body odour was the faint traces of perfume. He knew it could only mean Sherlock had a visitor, probably a client. It only took a few seconds for Mycroft to weigh up his options in light of this discovery. He needed Sherlock to begin investigating at once and couldn't let a client stop him. As he took the last few steps he searched his memory for the name his brother used now. By the time he rapped his knuckles on the door, Sebastian was floating across the back of his mind. Whoever was with his brother would know him as Sebastian Holmes.

Without waiting for an answer he twisted the door knob and strode into the room. Both occupants turned to face him and he scanned the extra person for information. She wore a black corset, styled to look like a waistcoat from the front but laced down the back, over the top of a deep red blouse. The red skirt almost touched the floor, but a slit up one side revealed size seven black boots with a small chain running behind the two inch heels. The corset took her waist in from what would have been twenty-seven inches to twenty-five and her mid-brown hair was up in a netted bun on the back of her head. As she turned he also noticed she deftly held a fountain pen in her right hand. Both hands had fingerless gloves that were made of the same material as a jacket over the arm of a nearby chair.

She smiled and the corners of her eyes wrinkled to match the upturn of her lips. Whoever she was she spent a lot of time writing; there were no ink marks on her despite the style of pen, and she was comfortable and relaxed in the odd mix of old fashioned and modern clothing.

"Myron! To what do I owe this pleasure?" Sherlock said in his usual sarcastic manner, although he knew the woman wouldn't have picked up on the disdain laced in every word. It took him a fraction of a second longer to respond as he took in the pictures of people and places on the board beside them. She had to be a client with all the information presented, although not directly involved, an observer with a vested interest.

"Let me introduce my guest, Amelia Jones." Sherlock motioned to her. "She's a writer. Amelia, this is my brother, Myron Holmes."

She swapped the pen over to her other hand and took a few steps towards him, her right outstretched to shake his. He glanced at her offering but kept his right hand in his trouser pocket and his left gripping the umbrella. Whoever she was, Sherlock had used her first name, something he'd not done since his days with John Watson. Mycroft frowned and the woman returned to her position by the board, giving no indication that she was bothered by the snub.

"I need to talk to you, brother of mine," Mycroft said when he realised the case on the board still held both their attention.

"In a moment. You'll be interested in this. This man is an undercover agent, working a case to find a stolen diamond." Sherlock pointed to the man's picture and then to the woman's, "She's unmarried, no children, parents are dead and no one else in her life, and we're trying to figure out how she was blackmailed into stealing the diamond, and how he finds out before he has her arrested."

Mycroft rolled his eyes but took a look at the information anyway. He wanted to know how this Mrs Jones was involved. If the diamond had been hers it wasn't something she was attached to. Perhaps a family heirloom she didn't care for.

"How was the diamond taken?" he asked.

"I don't know, I've not written that part yet," she said, fixing her blue eyes on him. "I was thinking she might seduce the security guard or get him drunk. She's an amateur under pressure so it can't be too difficult."

Mycroft raised his eyebrows before he noticed Sherlock grinning at him. He sneered in response. When Mrs Jones went to continue talking he put his hand up, cutting her off.

"This is a fictional scenario?" he asked, his voice dripping with disdain at the very concept.

"Yes. It's what I do for a living. Sebastian helps me get all the facts straight."

"He does, does he?"

She nodded and waited for him to continue but he had no desire to make her feel more comfortable. She glanced at his brother.

"So... Why are you here, brother. You don't visit unless you need something," Sherlock said, taking the focus back off his guest.

"I think we ought to discuss that in private." Mycroft looked pointedly at Sherlock's client, hoping she'd get the hint and hurry from the building, but she didn't move.

"Nonsense. If it's a case, Amelia can help. She's been proving most useful in my own work, and besides, she helped with the last case you gave me."

"She did?" Mycroft's annoyance grew. Somehow he'd missed Mrs Jones being a regular in Sherlock's life and he shouldn't have done.

"I did?" She raised an eyebrow and her own surprise made him feel a little better. Sherlock laughed and nodded.

"Come on, out with it brother. What do we need to investigate?" While Sherlock spoke Mrs Jones lifted the board from the two hooks it hung on, revealing a second blank white board underneath. Mycroft coughed then pulled the printout of the intercepted email from his inside jacket pocket.

"I received this coded message from a suspected terrorist

email account." Before Mycroft could begin reading it Sherlock took the paper out of his hands and wandered off with it, leaving both him and Mrs Jones standing and waiting as Sherlock read it.

"It's not a skip code..."

"It's nothing logical, I assure you," Mycroft said before Sherlock could list everything he already knew it wasn't.

"Read it aloud," Mrs Jones said. Mycroft frowned as Sherlock did just that. He would have requested one anyway but now he was sure a background check on her would be needed.

Hiya,

Totally failed today – My ringtone went off at the funeral – I've got it set to Staying Alive. :AwkwardFace: I suppose I'd already made it hard on myself, the deceased had bought me one of those ugly Christmas jumpers and I wore it to the funeral. My mother told me to take it off and I don't think she was very impressed when I told her I'd rather cry in a BMW. Then to top my day off I got rick rolled.

Thankfully my kids were cute when I got home – when I asked the eldest what she wanted for dinner she said, 'I can has cheeseburger?' and grinned. Later when I was playing a board game with the twins and I lost they came out with, 'All your counters are belong to us', their English is getting better each day. When I was a kid my dad used to swear and say 'pardon my French – I still remember when my school teacher asked if anyone spoke a foreign language and I put my hand up. :SmileyFace:

It might be a while before I communicate again, I'm staying with relatives and they don't know their own wi-fi password. FFFFFFFFUUUUUUUU. The kids are excited, they said they can get their pink unicorn back, I didn't even know they had one.

Geoff

By the time Sherlock had finished, Mrs Jones was curled up on the chair, clutching her sides and crying as she tried to stop her almost silent laughter.

"What's so amusing?" Mycroft demanded when she didn't stop as soon as the letter was over. She wiped her eyes and sat up straight again.

"It's internet memes. For example, all your counters are belong to us, is a miss-quote of all your base are belong to us from a badly translated game. I can has cheeseburger is a phrase on a lolcat, and I think there was a confession kid in there, as well as the mention of being rick rolled." She picked up the pen and wrote out the entire letter. Once she'd finished she circled phrases in the text and linked them to the names of the internet memes. Mycroft watched and waited, wanting to see where she was going with it. If it solved the email he could get back to his house and away from her.

She stood back and put both her hands on her hips, staring at the letter, now in her neat but ornamented hand-writing.

"The punctuation is strange, and not right in the slightest," she said a moment later, when no one else did anything.

"Each full stop marks the end of a coded section, that much is easy to work out," Mycroft said. His brother nodded and stole the pen from Mrs Jones, their fingers brushing past each other as he did. Mycroft sneered again, although both had their backs to him and wouldn't have noticed. He almost wished they had.

Sherlock put a line in where each sentence ended to break the message up and then she pulled the pen from his hand and wrote in another meme at the end of the letter. After a minute of browsing something on her phone she wrote in two more, completing the final paragraph with:

First World Problems
Rage comic

Invisible Pink Unicorn

Mycroft saw the message and smiled. It pleasantly surprised him that she was on the right track.

"The first letters form the first part of Friday," Mycroft said, knowing his brother wasn't paying attention and should be. He stepped closer so the whole thing was easier for him to read.

"It looks like each paragraph is a word," she replied and smiled at him. He ignored her. She was right, but that didn't mean he had to like her or praise her for it.

"The second word has an A and C in the middle and has four letters," Sherlock said.

"Four?" She turned to him, a puzzled look on her face.

"Yes, there's a fourth sentence." Mycroft pointed to the smiley face reference in between two colons. She shrugged.

"That's an emoticon gone wrong, but I suppose it might be part of the message." She put the word in brackets in the list in the two places the references appeared and then turned to his brother. "Search for, I'd rather cry in a BMW, online and see what comes up."

Immediately Sherlock obeyed and grabbed his laptop. Mycroft found himself sneering yet again. This woman was telling them what to do when she was evidently of inferior intelligence and even worse, his brother wasn't even slightly put out. He'd thought Sherlock over this sort of sentimentality after losing Watson, but it appeared he was even softer than ever.

Twenty minutes later they had one more letter and Mycroft continued to stand and do nothing but stare at the message. The entire time he'd been running through five letter words that fit with the E and N they'd already found for the first word. With the I Mrs Jones now wrote in he knew what it said. *Begin Lace Fri* was the full message, but he wasn't about to say so and be pressed to explain further. Even if Mrs Jones expressed no further interest, his brother would and with his deductive reasoning might work out more than Mycroft wanted either of them to know.

As he was trying to think of some way to get rid of Mrs Jones she pulled a pocket watch out, checked the time and gasped.

"I've got to go. I'm meant to be signing books in less than half an hour." She grabbed her jacket and shrugged into it. "Sorry to run before we're done, but I hate being late for anything."

"I'm sure we can solve this without you," Mycroft said and gave her a smile which didn't reach his eyes.

"See you tomorrow, Sebastian, and it was a pleasure to meet you, Mr Holmes." She gave him a half smile, meaning it far more than he would have, and hurried from the room. As the sound of her rapid footsteps receded down the stairs Mycroft relaxed.

"So, you've found a new John Watson." He looked intently at his brother but Sherlock remained impassive.

"She's brighter than John ever was, but she won't be around for long. She'll go write her next book in a few days. Mostly she's a recluse, like you, especially when in the middle of a book."

"You're trying to intrigue me by making me think we're similar, but it won't work. She's not as intelligent as you even, so I have no interest in her." Mycroft walked towards the door, not wanting to continue this conversation.

"She would have been as clever as me had she grown up with you as an elder brother. She's keen to learn from us and pleasant enough."

"Mrs Jones won't live long enough to ever get close."

"Miss Jones," Sherlock said, looking smug. Mycroft shook his head at what his younger brother had overlooked.

"There was a wedding ring."

"Yes, but she's not married, not anymore anyway. She uses her maiden name on her books and uses Miss in all her dealings."

"Widow." Mycroft nodded. He should have seen it in her manner with Sherlock. No woman in a solid relationship would spend time coming to London for book signings and spend so much time alone with another man. At least they wouldn't have when Mycroft had been younger. Society had changed since then. He walked out, and called back, "Don't get involved, brother of mine."

"I'll let you know when I've solved this," Sherlock yelled after him.

"No need!" Mycroft pulled the door shut. Miss Jones' perfume lingered in the stairwell even stronger than before and Mycroft found himself thinking that as far as perfumes went it could have been a lot worse. At the least it smelt better than Sherlock's flat usually did.

As he walked back to his car he messaged his assistant.

Project lace will begin on Friday. Deploy operation clean-up. Also find all information on the author Amelia Jones and forward it to me.

As soon as the message was delivered he put his phone back in the inside pocket of his jacket and stepped outside. The rain had stopped and Mycroft smiled as he was driven back to his home, his mind already focused on other matters.

CHAPTER 2

A shiver ran down Amelia's spine as she sat back in the taxi and allowed it to take her to Sebastian's. She'd barely slept since the day before when she met Myron. She'd known he was meant to be both the more intelligent, and the more arrogant of the two brothers, but she hadn't expected to be quite so intrigued by him. Ever since being a young teenager she'd found clever men the most attractive and she'd married the brightest man she could find the first time around. Fate had robbed her of a happy lengthy marriage, however, and left her to find someone else bright enough to gain her respect. A grin spread, uncontained, across her face as she realised, she'd just found him.

Myron Holmes evidently didn't think much of her. He'd sneered at her on more than one occasion but that only made the challenge of getting him to like her more appealing. Sebastian spent time with her and appeared to enjoy helping her despite his initial coldness. Myron would be another difficulty level above, but not impossible.

As she travelled through London she thought through everything she knew about Myron. If she wanted to win him over before he shut her off completely she needed to figure him, and his dislikes, out quickly.

He'd been impeccably dressed in a grey suit and waistcoat with the shiniest shoes she'd ever seen, so being well kept would be a priority. Her best clothes would be needed just to get close to his level. Thankfully she'd been smart and sophisticated in her choice of attire while in London, and, just in case she bumped into him again, she was equally groomed today.

Intelligence would also be a key factor. His level of brilliance would feel so much higher than hers so she would need to be careful not to say anything that he'd find annoyingly stupid. She suspected being silent and learning would be a safer way to handle him than speaking when unsure.

With his arrogance and commanding presence she imagined some flattery would help her case as well as a slight subservient attitude. Both would need to be subtle or she might come across as desperate or perhaps even manipulative, but she could think on her feet. On top of that she would need to show some sense of humour or wit, or she would blend into the background like a secretary or doorman at a hotel. Someone who was only meant to be ignored or talked at.

She'd spent hours already, replaying their first meeting through her head and analysing every word and gesture. So far she thought she'd probably been too keen to help and forward with what she thought the answers were, which may have annoyed him, although, Sebastian hadn't seemed to care. Before she could satisfy the obsessive desire in her to go through it all again, the taxi pulled up outside Sebastian's flat.

As usual, Mrs Wintern answered her knock on the door and ushered her inside.

"He's up and about. I've heard the floorboards creaking as he paces back and forth." She waved Amelia up the stairs, making her grin. Sebastian had only been in bed once when Amelia had arrived and only because he'd had no clients for a few weeks and hadn't been expecting her.

"You're early," he said as soon as she opened the door. He stood in front of the case board. The overlay with her characters was back in place over the one she'd written the strange email on, giving her no indication of whether he'd finished solving it or not.

"I'm always early," she pointed out and took her jacket off.

"You're even earlier than normal," He switched his attention to her, running his eyes over her, as he did every time they met, "and you barely slept. What's wrong?"

"Nothing's wrong." She went to stand beside him and stare at her characters, hoping he wouldn't pick up on anything else.

"You've done your hair differently. The French braid is very elegant, and the choker, that's new. You're making an effort, but the perfume is less obvious and you're still wearing your wedding ring so you don't want it to be too noticeable." He grinned and waited for her to react to him, as he always did when he'd figured out something she didn't want him to.

"Evidently it was *not* subtle enough." She shook her head in mock annoyance, all the while smiling.

"Well, he's a lucky fellow, either way."

"Hmmmphhh, you're assuming he'll appreciate it."

"Ah, so it is brother of mine."

She bit her lip and stamped her foot, annoyed at being so easy to read.

"It is not an obvious deduction. You mentioned you liked intelligent men and I doubt you met anyone at the book signing yesterday who you expect to see today." She nodded at his assumptions. The book signing had gone well but no one had stood out of the crowds wanting to be photographed with her.

"My effort is likely to be entirely wasted," she replied, knowing the chances of bumping into him again were slim.

"He is rather reclusive." Sebastian nodded once and fixed his gaze back on her plot notes. For now the conversation on Myron was over. With a deep breath she tried to join him in working out the best combination of motives, character traits and circumstances to make the plot gripping and unpredictable. Despite her best efforts, it only held half her attention, while Myron's personality and traits held the other half.

The two hours before her next signing slipped by in a barely registered haze. With the little they had left to work out they should have been done before time ran out but the need to move on to the bookshop came before all the details were finalised.

"You really are distracted by Myron, aren't you?" Sebastian put down the pen. She nodded.

"I don't expect that it matters much. I'm unlikely to even meet him again, let alone get him to like me, and *like* is only the first of many stages." She pulled her jacket on and neatened her hair.

"Of all the women I've met, you're the first to show an interest in my brother that I can believe in. You're also the first I've thought might interest him." He handed her the notebook she'd been jotting ideas down in.

"There is still an element of chance that may never go in my favour." Sebastian raised an eyebrow. "I may never meet him again," she explained and gave him a wry smile.

"Ah..." He scanned her face as he trailed off, making her wonder if she'd said something stupid.

"What?"

"His car has been outside for the last ten minutes."

"He's probably waiting for me to leave." Despite her brush off, every muscle in her torso tensed at the thought of him being so close to her.

"No. He would ask you to go if he wanted to talk to me. The only other possibility is that he's here for you." Her eyes went wide and she froze to the spot while her brain tried to fathom a why. "Stay calm and go on. Don't keep him waiting."

"Thank you, Sebastian." She stood on her tiptoes to give his over six foot frame a kiss on the cheek. With that, she rushed from the flat and down the stairs, only checking her pace by the front door. Rain pattered down outside but she'd not thought to bring an umbrella.

When she strode outside Myron's driver leapt up and opened the car door for her. After exhaling in an attempt to calm herself, she stooped and got into the car. Somehow she found herself sitting beside Myron Holmes while managing the potentially undignified entrance with enough grace that it boosted her confidence. A second later the car pulled off and she could only assume they were on the way to the bookstore she was scheduled to sign at.

"Good afternoon, Mr Holmes," she said, giving him her attention. Today he wore a deep blue suit and, if possible, looked even better than yesterday.

"Increased heart rate, flushed cheeks and dilated pupils. Are you nervous, Miss Jones?" Myron replied instead of greeting her.

"I always get nervous before a book signing. I'm put on show for everyone to see and fans are notorious for putting their celebrities on a pedestal that's impossible to stay on."

"Yet you chose your profession."

"For the most part my profession allows me to stay in the comfort of a familiar place and be paid to invent and solve whatever predicaments I want my characters to face. Every job has a downside." Mycroft blinked but made no response. She waited for him to explain why he'd picked her up as she definitely wasn't saying anything more about why she was nervous.

"My sources inform me that your next novel involves some, characters, of a North Korean nationality, as well as a particular incident with them that closely resembles a case my brother recently aided with."

"The storyline was his suggestion," she said before she realised Myron wasn't the sort of man to appreciate interruptions. He pursed his lips together and waited for her to stay quiet.

"I cannot allow you to publish it. Will you promise to never attempt to show it to anyone."

She looked away, thinking about her response. Writing a novel took a lot of effort and scrapping one entirely was a lot to ask of her. At the least it could damage her reputation with her fans. On the other hand, cooperating with Myron would be more likely to get her in his good graces and maybe lead to a friendship opportunity.

"If I publish it what would happen?" she asked, wanting more time to think but not wanting Myron waiting in silence.

"I will be forced to stop you. I'm sure I can find some reason to have you incarcerated, even if I have to plant the evidence."

"I don't mean to me. What are you trying to prevent by stopping me?" Her words were met with silence and she had to wait for him to process the request. She guessed he wasn't expecting it.

"At least two of our agents would be endangered as well as months of planning at best. And at worst, we would find ourselves at war with North-Korea."

"Then of course I won't publish it." She smiled at him and he nodded his gratitude. "I would never deliberately put lives in danger, especially British lives."

"Thank you."

"I do have a request, however."

"Go on," Myron replied, although the severity of his tone made her wonder if he meant it. She carried on anyway.

"Can I re-write the novel with guidance on what needs changing? It's a lot of work to discard completely, not to mention the financial implications..."

"I'm sure you can be *helped* with sales to make up for the loss," he assured her, interrupting.

"Thank you, but I'd rather know I've truly earnt my sales. I'd prefer to re-write the story. It would also give me an excuse to talk to you again." She closed her mouth around the last words, shocked she'd said them.

"My assistant will liaise with you, not me." He gave her the same fake smile as he'd given her on parting the day before. She shrugged. She'd taken one plunge but it appeared to have gone unnoticed. Something had to happen before she got to her destination or she'd always feel like she wasted an opportunity.

"Shame. Although, you can't blame a girl for trying."

"Trying what?" Myron raised both eyebrows again.

"I've decided that I like you, Mr Holmes."

"That will soon change. Most people find me unpleasant," he replied and gave her yet another fake smile. It was meant to put her off but it just made her more keen to get him to genuinely smile.

"It's too late for that. I'm a very loyal person and I've already made my mind up. I like you."

Myron turned away from her and shook his head. She bit her lip knowing she'd gone too far too soon. Now she needed to try and pull it back. Thoughts of conversation starters ran through her head but none of them came out of her mouth.

"You appear to no longer be nervous," Myron pointed out, giving her another way in.

"I have company and..." she tapped her knuckles on the window. "tinted glass. I can't be seen until I get out. I find it hard to know what to say to my fans. Most of them are smart and socially adept enough that I find them easy to talk to, but a few I struggle with..."

"Are you trying to relate to me, Miss Jones?" he interrupted.

"I was simply trying to explain my nerves. I have a responsibility to them when I do these events. When I fail to make a connection with them I run the risk of making them feel invisible, and if they already feel low... I suppose I appreciate them in their own way." She shook her head, struggling to explain and already aware she'd said far more than she'd intended to in trying to cover up the real reason for her increased pulse.

"Or your nerves were unrelated to your upcoming public appearance. You've made more of an effort about your attire than yesterday as well." He looked smug but didn't give her full eye contact for her to tell if he minded. She found herself chuckling. Both him and his brother were more observant than she stood any chance of getting around, so she decided to stop trying to fool him then and there.

"What I said is true, mostly, but you're also right," she paused to take a deep breath. "I have another request to make if I may?"

"I think you've already said enough, Miss Jones."

"Just hear me out. I think I've cooperated enough to earn that."

"All your cooperation earnt you was your continued freedom. I've already made a concession in allowing you to try and rescue your novel. I will not be making any more." His every word bit into her but she ignored it anyway.

"I want to learn from you. I know your brother isn't as clever as you and I'm not even at his level, but I'd like a chance to be, *entertaining*."

"No. You may like me, Miss Jones, but the feeling isn't mutual. I've never met a woman I've liked."

"I'm not asking you to have me as a friend, but you're the best. I'd really like to learn from you... Think of it like having a pet." As soon as she finished speaking she wished she'd thought of a better word. A pet implied more than she wanted it to.

"A pet?" He sneered.

"Yes, like a cat or dog. You can teach me some simple things for your amusement."

"So you get access to my mind, and all I get is *amusement*?" The knuckles on his left hand whitened as he tightened his grip on the umbrella handle.

"You get a loyal pet and you can teach me what you choose. If you find I'm not quick enough at picking things up you can stop." She bit her lip, hoping she'd explained herself well enough.

"A pet, also implies ownership."

"Yes, that's where the analogy falls down. I admit, it's not a perfect example of what I mean."

Her words were greeted with silence and his disdain was evident on his face.

"No, Miss Jones, as entertaining as it might be for a few minutes, I am not interested in the idea." Myron's words were said so crisply she knew it was pointless to continue. She'd done all she could and saying more wouldn't win her any more favours. She'd have to hope Sebastian put in a good word for her and tipped Myron over from a no to a maybe.

While the car wove through the last few streets, she ran their conversation through her head, hoping to glean some information from it. During this, it dawned on her that not even his brother had a copy of the newest novel. Myron or his people had hacked into her computer. He could have deleted it himself and told her she couldn't publish it. Instead he'd told her himself and given her options. Something had made him choose to see her again. The realisation made her suck in her breath and her heart raced in her ears.

The car pulled up outside the bookshop and ended any opportunity she might have to explore her most recent thought. A line of fans stood in the rain, waiting for her. She knew she couldn't keep them out there any longer. It was time to say goodbye. She turned back to Myron to find him staring at her, but not with an expression she could read.

"Thank you for not just deleting my novel, Mr Holmes, and thank you for the company." She considered putting her hand out to shake his but knew he wouldn't accept it.

"Enjoy your signing," he replied and looked away.

"I'll try to," she replied as the door nearest her opened.

After taking a second to fix a smile to her face she got out. Instantly she was met with a blast of cheering, clapping and people calling her name. The nerves dropped from her with each step towards the foyer and each splatter of rain that landed on her.

By the time she was inside she had pushed Myron from her mind and focused on her fans. Before she could want assistance a middle aged, blonde woman in a knee length black skirt, plain shoes and jumper came gliding towards her. Amelia glanced at the name badge pinned to her chest. Sue was the manager.

"Amelia, you're early. Why don't you come to the staff room for a few minutes and have a hot drink before we start?" Sue didn't wait for her to reply but took several steps towards the side of the shop. She stopped when she realised Amelia wasn't following. Instead Ameila gazed across the open foyer, taking in all the details. A table was set up to one side with a soft chair, pens and a poster of her latest book announcing the start time of the signing.

"No. It's raining and there are people outside without umbrellas. I'll get started right away." Amelia smiled to take the edge off her words, but the manager still frowned at being overruled. This wasn't according to Sue's plan and Amelia knew she would have to re-adjust the plan herself. She shook hands with the two clerks who came up to her, both realising this was their cue.

"Let's get as many people out of the rain as we can. Have them form a queue from the table and around the edge," she said to a young man barely old enough to be out of school. He hurried off so she turned to the girl who stood beside Sue, eagerly awaiting further instruction. "And..." She trailed off as Myron walked past her. She blinked and stood with her mouth open, unsure why she would see him inside the shop. Sue coughed.

"Sorry, ummm... Why don't you find the people in the queue who need to buy their books here. Get them to buy them while they wait and form a second queue I can prioritise." The girl nodded and hurried off to join her companion, leaving her with Sue who still looked like she could murder someone.

"Why don't you get back to your normal work. I have everything I need and can handle the crowds. I'm sure you'd rather be looking after your shop than having to keep an eye on me," Amelia said, giving her the warmest smile she could manage. They shook hands and Amelia found she had a few moments to survey the area while people rushed around her, enacting her suggested changes.

Almost immediately her eyes found Myron, who sat at a table in the cafe area, staring at her. She gave him a smirk and turned her back on him to switch her attention to her fans. He could watch her if he wanted.

CHAPTER 3

The waitress disturbed Mycroft as she brought him the tea he'd ordered. As soon as she was gone he looked back at Miss Jones. When he'd warned her not to publish her novel he'd expected far more resistance. Creative types didn't tend to respond well to being censored in any way. Yet she'd acquiesced, and she'd been clever enough to realise he could have deleted it and bypassed obtaining her cooperation altogether. It didn't mean she was of an exceptional level of intelligence but at least somewhat observant and rational.

Her proposal had also been unexpected. When she'd first told him she liked him, he'd thought it would lead to being asked out on a date. A request to be his student in a sort of pet like way showed more understanding of his attitude and temperament than most people grasped. Although he'd refused without hesitation, he found himself considering her suggestion. He could find out how clever she was, while keeping himself amused, and discard her when he was no longer entertained. Her pet analogy was flawed but it did hold some sensible ideas. A pet was more loyal than a normal student.

Watching her handle the booksellers and then her fans also proved interesting. She picked up on their characters with speed, using the information they subconsciously gave away to relate to them and make them feel special. He'd only ever watched his brother do it better, although both missed signs he'd picked up on.

After an hour of tirelessly greeting, signing and having her picture taken, she asked for a break. For the fifth time since he'd sat down she glanced his way and he expected her to come over and berate him for distracting her, but she didn't. Instead she walked out of the shop and into the rain.

He got to his feet, wanting to see over the tables and work out what she was up to. Outside, his car still sat, and his chauffeur stood under the large black umbrella, waiting for him to return. Amelia went right up to him, sheltering herself under the same black dome and started up a conversation. Again she'd managed to surprise him.

A few minutes later she came back inside and Daniels followed, keeping her dry all the way. Mycroft sat again so they wouldn't notice his interest in them. He assumed the gesture was just his driver being a gentleman but he came with her all the way to her table, got her to sign one of her books and then took it to the sales desk to pay for it.

It didn't take Daniels long but Miss Jones was back to her carousel of greet, sign, and pose, before his chauffeur was back by the car, the book in a small carrier bag tucked under his arm. He waited for Miss Jones to get back into her flow and decided it was time to leave. Picking a moment when she would be so absorbed with signing a book that she wouldn't notice, he got up and left. His chauffeur had the good graces to look sheepish about leaving the car unattended for a few minutes.

"Don't make a habit of it," Mycroft said. The greying man nodded. "Also, I'd like to borrow that book. I want to check something."

"Of course, sir." Daniels passed the carrier bag to him as Mycroft was getting into the car.

Once they were on their way back to his house Mycroft

pulled the book from its wrappings.

"Naive," he whispered, reading the title, "This should be interesting." Curious, he flicked to the first page and read.

Mycroft next looked up when the car halted outside his home. Forty-five pages of the novel had absorbed his attention and stopped him from noticing what was normally a chore to endure.

"I'll keep hold of this for a few hours," Mycroft said before entering the front door of his stately home. He placed his umbrella in the usual stand by the door and sat on the small stool to swap his shoes for slippers.

By the time he entered his study, a tray with fresh, hot, tea and biscuits was waiting on one side of his desk, slightly covering the green leather inlaid on the top of the oak.

Once sitting at his desk he could easily survey the whole room from the light of the large bay window to the left. It had a box seat for sitting and reading the many shelves of books that lined every other possible wall space, and dated back as far as the mid eighteen hundreds. Floor to ceiling proudly displayed the leather-bound volumes in stark contrast to the brightly covered paper book in his hands. It didn't fit in.

For the next few hours he read, only interrupting his past time to move to the dining room at the usual time of six and back again half an hour later. Once he'd reached the end of the story he sat back and stared at the front cover. The plot had been predictable and the happy ending was a little unrealistic, but Amelia Jones had been quite clever with her character's reactions. It was a murder mystery but the detective had noticed all the right details. Plenty of them had been hidden in the text to make it easy for him to pick up on the clues and solve the crime.

He found he had enjoyed reading the story. It was refreshing to read a book where the criminal was caught in a clever way, and even more refreshing for the main character to be intelligent. Mycroft wondered how much Sherlock had contributed to the plot.

Despite liking the novel it didn't help him with his decision concerning her strange request. A hundred years had passed since John Watson had been part of Sherlock's life. He'd seen the effect the relationship had on his younger brother, but he'd always been a little bit curious. Perhaps Mycroft could see what fascination Miss Jones held for Sherlock. As long as no one else knew about it, Mycroft wouldn't need to have a solid reason why, and Amelia Jones herself didn't appear to care about his reasoning as long as she got to learn.

Mycroft pulled a blank notebook from a desk drawer and wrote down this requirement, along with several others on the first page. If he was to use his time to teach her, he expected her to work through things in a sensible manner, and she definitely wouldn't be allowed to get any help.

For the rest of the evening Mycroft put together a list of basic tasks he could make her work through, starting with coded messages since she'd already shown some flair in that area. As the minutes ticked by his ideas grew more elaborate until he realised he had a six phase plan that could take years to complete. He doubted she could hold his interest for that long and knew she would struggle to solve the last few phases anyway.

With more than enough challenges thought out, he pulled a blank sheet of stationery paper towards him and wrote out the first coded message to her.

39 3 3 36   1 3 6 2 41 2 39   1 41 7 7   42 3 2 37 7 26
41   40 33 10 37   36 37 35 41 36 37 36   8 40 33 8   7 37
8 8 41 2 39   13 3 9   35 40 33 44 44 37 2 39 37 7   1 33 13
4 6 3 10 41 36 37   37 2 3 9 39 40   33 1 9 7 37 1 37 2 8   8 3
34 37   11 3 6 8 40   1 13   37 38 38 3 6 8 26   34 9 8   8 40
37 6 37   33 6 37   7 37 10 37 6 33 44   6 9 44 37 7   41   11
41 44 44   41 2 7 41 7 8   9 43 2 25   34 6 37 33 43   33 2 13
3 38   8 40 37 1 26   33 8   33 2 13   4 3 41 2 8 26   33 2 36
3 9 6   44 41 8 8 44 37   39 33 1 37   11 41 44 44   35 37 33
7 37   33 44 3 2 39   11 41 8 40   33 44 44   35 3 1 1 9 2 41

35 33 8 41 3 2 25

*15   28   13 3 9 27 6 37   2 3 8   8 3   8 37 44 44   33 2 13
3 2 37   33 2 13 8 40 41 2 39   33 34 3 9 8   3 9 6   33 6 6 33
2 39 37 1 37 2 8 25   8 40 41 7   41 2 35 44 9 36 37 7   13 3
9   8 33 43 41 2 39   33 44 44   4 6 37 35 33 9 8 41 3 2 7   2
37 35 37 7 7 33 6 13   8 3   37 2 7 9 6 37   2 3   3 2 37   37
44 7 37   38 41 2 36 7   33 2 13   35 3 1 1 9 2 41 35 33 8 41
3 2 25*

*16   28   13 3 9 27 6 37   2 3 8   8 3   6 37 35 37 41 10 37
40 37 44 4   7 3 44 10 41 2 39   33 2 13   8 33 7 43 25   8 40
41 7   41 7   33   8 37 7 8   3 38   13 3 9 6   35 44 37 10 37 6
2 37 7 7   33 44 3 2 37 25*

*17   28   13 3 9   7 40 3 9 44 36   3 34 37 13   33 2 13
41 2 7 8 6 9 35 8 41 3 2 7   33 7   7 3 3 2   33 7   4 3 7 7 41
34 44 37   11 40 37 6 37   8 40 41 7   36 3 37 7 2 27 8   35 3
2 38 44 41 35 8   11 41 8 40   6 9 44 37   15 25*

*18   28   38 33 41 44   33   8 33 7 43   33 2 36   3 9 6   33
6 6 33 2 39 37 1 37 2 8   11 41 44 44   35 37 33 7 37   33 44
3 2 39   11 41 8 40   33 44 44   35 3 1 1 9 2 41 35 33 8 41 3
2 25*

*19   28   6 37 38 9 7 33 44   8 3   36 3   33 7   41 2 7 8 6
9 35 8 37 36   11 41 44 44   34 37   7 37 37 2   33 7   33   8
37 6 1 41 2 33 8 41 3 2   3 38   3 9 6   33 39 6 37 37 1 37 2 8
25*

*20   28   41   6 37 7 37 6 10 37   8 40 37   6 41 39 40 8
8 3   35 37 33 7 37   8 40 41 7   33 8   33 2 13   4 3 41 2 8
11 41 8 40 3 9 8   37 12 4 44 33 2 33 8 41 3 2 25*

*21   28   33 44 44   1 37 7 7 33 39 37 7   11 41 44 44   34
37   4 44 33 35 37 36   41 2   37 2 10 37 44 3 4 37 7   33 2
36   7 37 33 44 37 36   11 41 8 40   11 33 12 25   13 3 9 27 6
37   6 37 7 4 3 2 7 41 34 44 37   38 3 6   33 35 5 9 41 6 41 2
39   8 40 37   2 37 35 37 37 7 7 33 6 13   7 8 33 8 41 3 2 37 6
13 25*

*22   28   1 13   2 33 1 37 26   3 6   33 2 13   3 8 40 37 6
41 2 38 3 6 1 33 8 41 3 2   8 40 33 8   35 3 9 44 36   44 37
33 36   8 3   1 37   34 37 41 2 39   41 36 37 37 2 8 41 38 41 37
36 26   41 7   2 38   8 3   34 37   9 7 37 36   41 2   33 2 13
35 3 6 6 37 7 4 3 2 36 37 2 35 37 25*

41 38   13 3 9   7 8 41 44 44   11 41 7 40   8 3   4 6 3 35

37 37 36 26   6 37 4 44 13   9 7 41 2 39   8 40 37   7 33 1 37
35 3 36 37   34 13   44 37 33 10 41 2 39   13 3 9 6   1 37 7 7
33 39 37   41 2   13 3 9 6   40 3 8 37 44   6 3 3 1   3 6   41 2
13 3 9 6   4 3 35 43 37 8   11 40 41 44 37   8 6 33 10 37 44
44 41 2 39 26   1 33 6 43 37 36   11 41 8 40   15 6   3 2   8
40 37   37 2 10 37 44 3 4 37 26   33 2 36   33 36 37 5 9 33 8
37 44 13   7 37 33 44 37 36 25
6 37 39 33 6 36 7 26   13 3 9 6   8 9 8 3 6 25

The letter took half an hour, although Mycroft sped up as his brain got used to writing it in a different sort of alphabet.

As soon as he'd finished he placed it in an envelope and melted some wax over the flap. With this done he pressed his ring into the liquid and waited for it to cool down enough that it would keep its new shape.

The moment to think almost resulted in him ripping the letter up and chucking it into the fire, but after staring at her name on the front of it for a moment he got up and called for his car.

"Going out again, sir?" Daniels asked when Mycroft met him at the front door. He gave his chauffeur back the signed book and nodded.

"I have business I need to see to. Take me to my brother's." Mycroft had no intention of explaining his real intentions to his driver or anyone else.

Once outside Sherlock's, he dismissed Daniels and told him not to worry about picking him up. If his driver thought this was odd he made no comment but drove the vehicle back the way they'd come. Knowing Sherlock liked to keep a watch by the window, Mycroft hurried inside and up to the flat. He found his brother playing the violin in his dressing gown and flannel pyjamas, with a lit pipe nearby.

"This is a late visit, brother of mine," Sherlock said as he put the instrument down and tended to his pipe. "Is it concerning this lace operation that's happening tomorrow?"

"You solved it then?"

Sherlock nodded and offered Mycroft his spare pipe.

Mycroft curled his lip up and kept his hands in his pockets.

"Don't look so disdainful. It's not like it will kill either of us."

"I need some extra eyes tomorrow at the Millennium Wheel a little before noon. I've got a full team but I want to be careful. Watchfullness from some of your discreet *friends* would be appreciated." Mycroft changed the subject before Sherlock could wonder why he was there.

"It will cost you."

"It always does," Mycroft said as he pulled several twenty pound notes from his pocket and placed them on the side table. "There's one for each person I need."

"Consider it done."

"Good." Mycroft nodded his thanks but his brother got up before he could continue with his plans.

"Anything else I can help with?"

"No, that's all I needed," Mycroft replied, knowing his brother was fishing for something.

"You sent your chauffeur away."

"I have other business to deal with."

"Oh, brother of mine, always so secretive... How did everything go with Amelia? I assume she took your decision to prevent her publishing well enough?" Sherlock's direction of enquiry resulted in Mycroft raising his eyebrows. He hoped Miss Jones hadn't been stupid enough to say anything. "She posted a message to her fans apologising for delays with her next book because of some necessary and complicated re-writes. No mention of why, but right after seeing you is evidently not a coincidence."

"She was remarkably cooperative."

"She's a clever woman."

"Next time I'd appreciate it if you didn't encourage her to use real events, especially when neither of you should know about them." Mycroft walked out of the flat before Sherlock could say anymore. He had no desire to hear Sherlock talk about Miss Jones and didn't want to give his brother any opportunity to notice the game they'd already begun to play. For the second time Mycroft considered destroying the letter and going home, but his feet led him onwards to the end of the road and he hailed a taxi cab before he could act on the alternative desire.

Mycroft didn't tell the taxi driver to take him to the hotel Miss Jones was staying at, but gave him the name of a road a few hundred metres away instead. Walking the final distance would help ensure his activities went undetected by anyone.

It had been a while since he'd had to use transport other than his own chauffeured car but the driver noticed his desire to be left to his thoughts and concentrated on his task. So close to midnight the traffic was light and only ten minutes later Mycroft stood on the pavement, alone in the dark. He walked the few streets to his destination in no great hurry. The early September night air was still warm from the summer and the later it was, the more likely Miss Jones would be fast asleep. He wanted her to be undisturbed by him dropping the letter off.

As he got closer he reached into his jacket pocket and turned on the device he always carried with him. It gave off a small electric distortion which scrambled the feed from any camera that might be looking his way.

When Mycroft strode into the lobby the female receptionist looked up from her book. She was chewing gum, resulting in an irritating lip smacking noise, and the perm in her hair didn't suit the shape of her face. He took a deep breath and decided this wasn't the sort of place where he should use his natural accent.

"Evenin'" he said as he approached the woman. "I know it's late but have you got a room goin' spare? I need a place to kip for the night." He leant against the counter and smiled.

"Let me just check," she replied, talking around her gum.

"I stayed in room three six eight recently. If it's free, I'd find it easier to sleep somewhere more familiar."

She sighed at the extra information and continued tapping

at the keyboard. Eventually she nodded.

"It's not taken. One night's ninety-five pounds."

Mycroft handed the cash over along with telling her a fake name, before taking the key-card she offered him. He hurried away to find the right floor.

As he got into the lift and heard it clank into life, the stench of cheap perfume and stale sweat hit him. Miss Jones needed to stay in a better hotel in the future and he made a note to have more internet traffic directed to her books. An increase in sales would hopefully lead to an increase in her budget.

The ting that let him know he was on the sixth floor couldn't have sounded soon enough, but instead of heading towards his own room he wandered down the hall looking for the maintenance cupboard. It only took him a few minutes to find it and another couple to pick the lock.

Inside was a little cart full of bleaches, clean sheets and the small bottles of shampoo and conditioner that they stocked the bathrooms with. Hanging up on a hook beside it was an apron. He reached into the front pocket and pulled out the master key-card for the floor.

With it in hand he made his way to Miss Jones' room, number three six seven, opposite the room he'd just booked. After checking no one was about he put his head against the door and listened. No noises came through, not even running water or the TV.

Without hesitating any longer he used the master key-card in the door and stepped through. It closed behind him with a soft-click.

The room was dark with a strip of pale light at the bottom of the curtains from the street lamp outside. It was enough illumination for him to tell Miss Jones was in bed and breathing softly. He didn't move for a minute as he concentrated on the sound of her inhales and exhales.

Once he was sure she wasn't going to wake up he moved over to the dresser and placed the letter where she couldn't fail to notice it. After taking another look at her sleeping form, curled up under the hotel duvet, he made his way over to his own room. With his work done he found a wave of satisfaction roll over him and paused to grin.

Mycroft set to work making the room look used, messing up the bed a little and pouring quantities down the sink from the shampoo and shower gel bottles. Just before leaving he grabbed the complimentary chocolate.

Once back outside he made his way back down to the ground floor, choosing to use the stairs this time. Instead of going back through the lobby he turned down a side corridor and found a fire-exit, out of the way of prying eyes. After going through it he put a small stone in against the door jam so the bar couldn't fully click back into place and it could be opened from the outside when he returned in the morning.

He walked back towards the busy roads where he would be able to get transport home, but less than a minute later his phone vibrated. He tucked himself back from the road's edge and answered the call.

"Myron Holmes," he said, in his usual business voice.

"Sir, all the preparations for monitoring the target tomorrow are in place," his assistant informed him in her well-spoken English.

"Good work. Keep me updated with any further developments." He hung up before any cars could pass him by and make it obvious he wasn't at home. Having a reputation as a recluse, he didn't want to spark her curiosity.

If he kept his arrangement up with Amelia Jones he would have to come up with an alternative way of getting the letters between them. He could post his own in several layers of envelopes and bounce them around the post offices in the country before reaching her, to make them difficult to trace back to himself, but her responses would be another matter. He would have to plan something before he sent her anything further.

CHAPTER 4

The light woke Amelia from her slumber as it streamed through the thin curtains. She yawned and stretched, trying to decide if it was worth getting up yet. The clock on the bedside table still begun with a six, although it wouldn't for much longer. Breakfast was still an hour off and she felt cosy under the duvet. On top of that her dreams had been pleasant, but now she'd opened her eyes her mind kicked in and reminded her that her short stay in London had been a mixed event.

Both her book signings had gone well and her sales were reasonable. Her time with Sebastian also meant she'd almost finished plotting her next novel, but in contrast she would need to change a large amount of her previous story and was still waiting on the exact instructions from Myron or his assistant. And it was him that had her unsatisfied with her brief excursion into the capital. Despite all the other positives, having him think so little of her, for whatever reason, bothered her. The inability to do anything about it only made it worse.

All she could do was keep writing, keep visiting his brother, and hope he appeared again. She supposed if a lot of time passed and she never got any further with Myron she could always reconsider Sebastian, but she knew that was unlikely to happen. Now that she'd decided she preferred Myron, seeing the younger brother would be a reminder that she hadn't captured the attention of the better sibling.

Amelia knew sleep wasn't going to return and gave up trying to doze off again. With a sigh she sat up. Instantly her eyes were drawn to the dressing table on the opposite wall. Propped up against the mirror's corner was a letter with her name on it. She blinked a few times, puzzled. The last thing she'd done before getting into bed was sit on the stool and undo her braided hair. Her tired expression had attracted her attention in the mirror and if the letter had been there she'd have noticed.

A shiver ran down her spine as she realised someone had been in her room while she slept and it galvanised her to get up and go over to it.

After inspecting the white envelope she picked it up and turned it over. As soon as her eyes took in the shape embedded in the wax seal a grin spread across her face and her previous concern melted from her. She'd seen the same design on a ring Sebastian always wore and a coat of arms was usually tied to the family name. One of the brothers had sent her a letter and she knew Sebastian would have no reason to.

She almost ripped the envelope off in her excitement before she stopped herself to think first. If Myron decided to teach her, she needed to be careful not to miss important details. She sniffed the envelope but no particular scent leapt out at her. Wherever Myron kept his stationery it didn't smell of anything strong. Her name was written in a reasonable sized cursive script and looked far more elegant than anything she could manage, but it could have been illegible and she'd have still been pleased with it. It was a letter and it was from the right person, or at least it was logical to assume Myron wrote it.

Unable to contain herself any longer, she broke the wax

seal and pulled the flap open. Inside was a sheet of letter paper entirely covered in numbers. There was nothing in the normal alphabet to let her know who it was from for sure and no hints on translating it. She ran her eyes over the sets of single and paired numbers, her brain too overwhelmed by her emotions to begin thinking about anything beyond the thrill of getting her way.

Five minutes passed her by and still she sat in her overly large t-shirt staring at the numbers cradled in her hands like the paper might fall apart if she moved even a fraction of an amount. Eventually she put it down and tore herself away long enough to get dressed and pack up the few scattered belongings into her small suitcase.

Cracking the letter's code would require thought and time, and she would find neither easy whilst sitting half naked and hungry in the hotel room she needed to check out of before ten. As soon as she was decent and ready to leave she grabbed the letter, her notebook and pencil, and made her way down to the dining hall. She could solve it while eating breakfast, surrounded by the noisy mass of other guests. Thinking always came easier when there wasn't silence to make her feel uneasy.

With a cooked breakfast to sooth her rumbling stomach she sat down and pulled the letter back out. She needed a starting point. Somewhere to begin trying to work out what the numbers meant. It wasn't the standard 1-26 of a basic numerical substitution as 44 appeared to be the highest number but that didn't mean it wasn't substitution. It looked like it was ordered into sets of numbers and long enough to be a full message, so she decided it was a good assumption to make. With no starting letter to substitute for a number, she chose to make a tally of the frequency each number popped up. She remembered from school that E was the most common letter followed closely by A and S. With such a long letter the tally should be clear enough that trying those three would help.

Half an hour later she'd eaten as much as she could without bursting and had a completed tally of the numbers. 37 appeared one hundred and twenty six times throughout the letter. This was considerably more than any other so she decided to begin her translation assuming it was the letter E. She had also noticed that every paragraph ended with a 25 and wondered if this might be the dot at the end of a sentence. Until she'd worked out a few words she couldn't be sure, however.

Putting in the letter she already thought she'd sussed out was delayed by her need to check out of the hotel. She noticed it was already almost nine and an hour wasn't likely to be long enough to figure out the rest.

After stuffing the letter back in her pocket, she took her belongings to her room, grabbed the already packed suitcase and transferred the letter and notebook to her handbag. With that done she made her way back to the lobby to give her key-card back and pay her final bill.

Once outside she considered getting a taxi to see Sebastian and getting his help to solve the letter but her own sense of pride stopped her. Instead she made her way to a café she wrote in when in London, and not otherwise engaged.

She was early enough that she had her pick of tables so she sat at one, tucked up in a corner where no one would bother her, and ordered a hot chocolate.

Before her drink could arrive she pulled the letter and her tally of the numbers back out. Using pencil and pressing lightly, she marked in all the letters she suspected so far and then looked at the letter as a whole again. None of them looked out of place and it gave her a couple of two letter words that ended in E. Most begun with a 34, but alone it wasn't enough to help her put in another letter.

As her drink arrived she decided to go back to her tally and work out some more letters from the more frequent numbers. 2, 3, 8, 33, and 41 all occurred a similar number of times and significantly more than most others. She also noticed that 33 and 41 were both vowels if she put the numbers in order from A to I, with 37 matching up with the E.

Fairly pleased with her logic, but unsure enough to check all the same, she glanced through the letter, trying to find a word or two where putting in A or I would give her a word so obviously right it couldn't be wrong. She soon found that the only single letter words that appeared were these numbers and therefore could only be those letters. Not noticing it sooner made her angry at herself but it gave her the confidence she needed to write them into her translation along with all the letters in between.

It took her quite some time, but once she was done she had several whole words and many partial ones. It also seemed logical to her to continue going through the numbers until the highest, moving along the alphabet, considering so far they'd been in order. 44 was the highest number that appeared so when she reached it she stopped and read what she had so far.

g 3 3 d 1 3 6 2 i 2 g 1 i 7 7 j 3 2 e 7 26
i h a 10 e d e c i d e d 8 h a 8 7 e 8 8 i 2 g 13 3
9 c h a l l e 2 g e 7 1 a 13 4 6 3 10 i d e e 2 3 9 g h
a 1 9 7 e 1 e 2 8 8 3 b e...

The first line was obviously the start of a letter, and she was pretty sure that it included punctuation and her name. If she continued down through the alphabet then the first word was good and the 10 became a V. Excitement built up within her as she realised she'd almost translated the entire thing and she got to work, filling in the rest of the alphabet from 1-14.

With those done the letter was almost complete and she could fill in the punctuation as well, guessing that 28 became a '–' the few times it occurred. It also made sense that the rest of the numbers were substituting other numbers, giving her a numbered list of instructions to follow.

After filling in the final few parts, she sat back and admired her handiwork. A letter that could only be from Myron.

Good morning Miss Jones,

I have decided that setting you challenges may provide enough amusement to be worth my effort, but there are several rules I will insist upon. Break any of them, at any point, and our little game will cease along with all communication.

1 – You're not to tell anyone anything about our arrangement. This includes taking all precautions necessary to ensure no one else finds any communication.

2 – You're not to receive help solving any task. This is a test of your cleverness alone.

3 – You should obey any instructions as soon as possible where this doesn't conflict with rule 1.

4 – Fail a task and our arrangement will cease along with all communication.

5 – Refusal to do as instructed will be seen as a termination of our agreement.

6 – I reserve the right to cease this at any point without explanation.

7 – All messages will be placed in envelopes and sealed with wax. You're responsible for acquiring the necessary stationery.

8 – My name, or any other information that could lead to me being identified, is not to be used in any correspondence.

If you still wish to proceed, reply using the same code by leaving your message in your hotel room or in your pocket while travelling, marked with 1r on the envelope and adequately sealed.

Regards, your tutor.

A grin spread across her face despite the strictness of Myron's rules. She'd translated the first message, although she suspected later ones would be significantly harder.

Holding the letter in her hands, she sat back and read through it several times, deciding to commit the rules to memory. She also felt pleased she'd not gone running to Sebastian for help. If she had, all her chances of learning from Myron would have been dashed before she'd begun.

The smile never left her face as she turned to her notebook and wrote out the uncoded reply she wanted to make.

> *Good Morning Mr Tutor,*
> *I very much wish to proceed and am happy to abide by your rules, although 6 bothers me slightly. Could I ask for a slight amendment? I'd appreciate a final message of some kind, letting me know that our arrangement is over. It would stop me from worrying that a letter had gone astray which I should have found, and, if a letter did go missing, I would know for sure to keep looking for it or inform you that someone else might have it. Of course I'd also appreciate knowing any reasons for stopping as well, but I understand you may not wish to give me those details.*
> *I look forward to my next task.*
> *Regards, your student.*

She bit her lip as she pondered over what she'd written before tweaking a few words here and there and adding in the punctuation she thought would be correct. With that done she wrote the coded version on a new sheet, taking care to get it exactly right.

After ordering another drink, she checked it through, tore the page out and folded it.

"Hmmm," she said as she realised she needed an envelope and wax to obey her instructions. She glanced at her pocket watch and frowned as she realised she only had a few minutes to spare before she ought to make her way across the London underground and get her train to Bath. Her instructions were to leave the letter in her hotel room or pocket while travelling so Amelia didn't feel comfortable waiting until she got home to find an envelope and wax.

While she was trying to think of a place she could get the required stationery on the way she noticed an unlit candle sat on her table. She looked for the nearest waitress and caught the young woman's eye.

"I don't suppose you could light the candle for me? I need some liquid wax for something I'm making," she said and gave her best hopeful expression. If the waitress thought the request odd she didn't say so but hurried off and came back with a lighter. A few seconds later the candle was burning merrily on her table and she was alone again.

Using a ripped out sheet of blank paper from her unlined, ideas book, Amelia folded it around her letter so the corners all met in the middle at the back. By this point there was a pool of melted wax in the candle, so she tipped it up sideways and let it drip over the edges, sealing the paper shut. She had no idea if normal wax would be easy to get off for Myron but it was the best she could do given the circumstances.

Before the wax could dry she used a pencil to mark an A and then gathered the rest of her stuff in her bag. With all but her pen stowed away she blew on the wax and tested it with her finger. It remained solid and unyielding so she turned over the makeshift envelope, marked it with '1r' as she'd been instructed and stuffed it in her jacket pocket. She had no idea how he would find it but she wasn't going to do anything but follow his instructions.

With that done she shouldered her bag and hurried to the nearest underground station. As she got to the platform the rounded carriage pulled up and she hopped through the open door. Very few people shared the immediate area with her, which was just the way she liked the underground.

After reaching into her pocket to check her letter was still there she sat in the middle of a row of empty seats and waited. It struck her as odd that Myron would want her to keep it on her, but she hoped that meant he would be fetching the letter himself. Any opportunity to see him again would be welcome, but no one else entered her carriage at any of the three stops before her destination.

Although there were no delays, she only arrived at Paddington with ten minutes to find the platform for her train and get on it. This station was significantly busier and she rushed through the crowds, her eyes scanning all the signs to help her find her way.

She heaved a sigh of relief as she found her allocated seat and settled into it. As soon as she had arranged her bags and leant back, her mind returned to thoughts of Myron and his challenge. She hoped he'd come collect the reply himself, but it seemed unlikely now she was on the train to Bath.

Amelia slipped her hand into her pocket again, intending to pull the letter out and look at it one last time, but found nothing.

She frowned and wiggled her fingers, wanting to make sure it wasn't there. Still nothing. Unconvinced, she pulled the edge of her jacket in front of her and looked down into the pocket. The inside lining stared back at her. The letter was gone.

The next breath caught in her throat as she tried to remember back and figure out if it could have fallen along the way, but she knew it had been nestled deep in the material and nothing could have dislodged it. Someone had taken it from her as she moved between the underground and the main Paddington station, but whoever had done it had been an expert pickpocket. She hadn't felt a thing.

She hoped it had been Myron or someone he knew who had taken it from her, but just in case she checked her phone and purse were still in place. A pickpocket was unlikely to take a letter and not something valuable. Once she'd assured herself that all her other belongings were safe she sat back in the seat again.

As the train pulled out of the station she suppressed a shiver. Not only had the first letter appeared in her hotel room while she slept but now her reply had been taken from her own pocket as she walked. The power Myron wielded and the lengths he was prepared to go to were greater than she'd expected. She could only assume Myron himself had performed both acts and that her lessons were about to begin. But for the first time she wondered if she'd found a man too intelligent for her.

CHAPTER 5

A sigh of relief escaped Mycroft's lips as he settled back into the familiar seat in his car, Amelia's reply nestled in his breast pocket.

As soon as his alarm had woken him that morning he'd headed back to the hotel and snuck back inside. He'd kept out of the way and watched Amelia as she ate her breakfast and began her translation of the letter. He'd even sat in the same cafe as her and gone unnoticed while she tried to crack his code.

Although he'd not enjoyed the interaction with people to get to that point, the look of glee on her face when she'd worked out what the letter said had been enjoyable. And her improvisation with the stationery had even made him smile. At the very least, he could be confident she would follow his orders as precisely as possible. If her intelligence matched up with her desire to cooperate, their arrangement might last longer than his initial expectations.

He'd followed her from the cafe into the underground station, changing his appearance as he went: adding a fake moustache, a hat and pulling on a jacket he slipped off a luggage bag while someone was buying tickets. By the time he was on the same tube train as her he looked different enough he could approach her, but the carriages weren't busy enough for him to make his move.

Instead he'd had to wait until they were at Paddington and pass her by while she was reading the arrivals board. She never even noticed as he plucked the reply from her jacket pocket. His skills were undiminished. Of everything he'd done to pull off his game with her it was his favourite part so far.

Despite that, he was glad to be back in his own car and heading for home. Not only was he tired and wishing to be alone but he needed to be able to monitor the events of the day. If the information in the coded message was right, something was meant to happen today.

As soon as he was back at his house, Mycroft thanked his driver and headed for his study. Once there, he pulled out the reply and ripped open the improvised envelope. He didn't even need to write in the letters to know what it said. The code was in his memory well enough that he could read it, if a little slower than normal.

His first reaction to her request was to say no but he sat back and thought for a few seconds. It wasn't an unreasonable request and she had provided a sound reason. The only real objection was her expectation of an explanation. No matter what happened he wouldn't give her any more than the basic information.

Mycroft checked his computer for information on the day but his assistant hadn't sent him anything yet, so he let his mind wander back to Amelia and how he wished to proceed. He couldn't follow her and steal the letters from her pocket each time he expected a reply. Neither could he journey to her home in Bath. After a few more seconds of thought he realised he needed to make a bigger commitment than just a few letters. To ensure privacy he needed to give her a way to communicate with him that didn't involve paper or anyone else.

Before he could stop himself he tapped the button that

summoned his staff.

"Have Daniels take some cash and get me two phones with those pay as you go things and bring them through. And make sure he gets them from somewhere busy, that's unlikely to remember him," he said as his housekeeper came through. She nodded and shuffled out again, shutting the door behind her. Over the years he'd given her stranger requests than this and she knew better than to ask questions. Daniels could also be trusted to do as asked and not query or theorise why. This was exactly why Mycroft had hired them for their positions.

With his involvement in the government, and the sort of work he did, he couldn't have staff who talked or questioned. The less they knew the safer they were, and thankfully, they were aware of this.

When it passed lunch time and he still hadn't heard anything from his assistant he pulled his phone from his jacket pocket and sent her a text.

Update on situation. Has lace happened?

He hated talking to people on the phone if it could be avoided. Within seconds he had a reply.

Nothing yet, all eyes are on target and waiting.

Mycroft frowned. The message he'd intercepted had given no indication of time but he'd hoped some developments would have occurred by now.

With nothing else to do but wait, he realised he might as well amuse himself with setting Amelia a second coded message to crack. It would need to be harder than the previous one but something along the same vein to build on what she'd already learnt.

He decided to stick with a substitution cipher for now and remain with the classic ones. He could work up to other types of ciphers once he'd run her through a few of these. While he had known all types of possible cypher by the time he was eight, he didn't expect Amelia would find it so easy to figure out which cypher had been used and he wasn't bored of her yet. So far her request was turning a dull day of waiting into something at least vaguely interesting.

After a moment's deliberation Mycroft decided to use a Vigenere square cypher with *Amelia* as the keyword. He'd have preferred to use his own name but his identity could not be so easily linked to their correspondence.

With all the important decisions made, it only remained to write out her next message and put her reply safe. After unlocking the desk drawer he pulled out the notebook he'd already begun using to detail his plans for her and, after slotting her reply in the first blank page, he pulled out his pen to write out the next message. The Vigenere cypher wasn't something he could write out instantly as he had the first message, and since then he'd mulled over the merits of keeping a log of everything, so he wrote the reply into the notebook, leaving two lines empty for every one he wrote.

After writing everything he needed to say he paused. The message wasn't particularly long and although it conveyed everything he wished it to, he hesitated to add his name and consider it finished.

Amelia herself had offered her learning up as a source of amusement for him. If he merely wrote the briefest of messages with no other sentences in them he wouldn't be getting the full entertainment value this could provide. With a slight smile he added another sentence. Teasing her was easy given her slip up with her analogy the day before.

It took him very few minutes to write out the keyword repeatedly underneath and then on the final empty lines he wrote out the coded message.

Muwd Ronqw,
Ltthayrp I waywln't zscualxc loreq xz I chmrrm in dywms I dinwgnuwp goud tzqnt mw mmins e

dmnsufwm onq. Ed auct m dpalx kcint ksfz recypat. I imwt nofmqg yog mq q chasdm to exzx oud eczansixmnt. Pspa thuw omal yevm yog qj jitol?
   Cmgadhd, goud xfbor.

Once he was satisfied with the message and the translation, he copied it out onto his notepaper and folded it, so it would fit into the smallest envelope he had. Along with it he placed a small piece of card with *Amelia* written on it. It would confuse her at first but hopefully she'd realise it was the keyword soon enough. He wrote her address on the envelope and stuck a first class stamp on it before sealing it with the wax as he had done with the first message.

Rather than posting the letter as it was, he took two more envelopes from his stationery drawer, each of a slightly larger size, and wrote the address of two different sorting offices on them, being careful not to have anything else underneath them for the writing to mark through.

As soon as they were all stamped and layered up appropriately he put it to one side to post when he next left the house. The letter would take longer to get to Amelia and go on a journey from London to Norwich, followed by Birmingham, before it reached the Bristol sorting office and then Bath to be sent out on the normal rounds. If no problems occurred it would take three working days, but four would be a reasonable estimate.

Before the weekend was over he would need to get the extra phone to her, but he wanted to take that personally and ensure she understood what it was for. He also didn't want anyone else to know she was the recipient.

Satisfied with both his precautions and the nature of his communications with Amelia Jones, he returned his thoughts to the expected terrorist attack. Several times during the last hour his assistant had sent him text messages with the same two words.

Still nothing.

He decided to look through the intercepted message again, as well as Amelia's translation of it, so he sat back, shut his eyes and allowed his brain to draw up the memory of Sherlock's case board, covered in the feminine writing of his guest that day. Assuming her concept of internet memes and his knowledge gained from two of his under cover operatives was correct, it could only indicate what he'd already guessed.

One operative had managed to find out four possible codewords to describe the operation: *lace*, *gem*, *ring*, and *rose*. The second operative had discovered another two, *clip* and *pin*, as well as finding out that the intended target was the millennium eye, so all those details could be trusted and he knew it appeared to be *lace* as the operation's codename.

Realising he could do nothing to gain more information and would have to wait for the terrorist cell to make a move, just like the team he'd convinced the government to deploy, he stopped using his mind to review the facts and opened his eyes. Daniels stood in the doorway, silently waiting for Mycroft to finish his task. The driver had seen him performing this feat of memory on many occasions and knew he didn't like to be interrupted while in the middle of it.

"The purchases you wanted," Daniels said as he removed two smallish boxes from a plain carrier bag and placed them on the desk.

"Thank you, Daniels, you can go." Mycroft gave his usual brief smile and took the top box in his hands. A reasonably new smart phone was pictured on the box and the one underneath matched apart from the colour. One had a silver case, the other black. Without hesitating he put the silver one back and pulled the other box towards himself. Silver wasn't a colour he liked and he imagined it would suit Amelia better than him anyway.

It took him another half an hour to prepare both phones and get them registered with the pre-paid cards. Before he put Amelia's back in the box he added the number of his own under *tutor* and then put her number into his under *student*. He hoped no one would find her phone, but if they did it wouldn't be enough to link him to her. If it was found, it would be her fault if they thought she was in a relationship with a wealthy elder man. He knew, given the nature of their communication and the messages he intended to send her that it would be the most likely assumption others would leap to, but any reputation loss would be her own making. She asked him to teach her.

With nothing else to do but wait for his assistant and team to report in, he loaded the files he had on Amelia. The basic details had come in the evening he'd requested them, like her age, her parents and all her exam results, as well as her finances, spending habits and political leanings.

Since then several more files had arrived, including a description of each of her novels. They'd been checked for code words already, which is how he'd known about her upcoming release and its similarity to real world events, but he now had a full synopsis for each. On top of that he had every photo of her ever taken and put on a computer or developed, every comment she'd ever posted in a forum or social network, and every email, text or instant message she'd ever sent.

Someone had already been through the raw data files and copied relevant conversation chunks and messages into sub categories, which ranged from her political opinions to her relationships and sexual interests and even her fears and dreams in life.

By the end of the evening Mycroft had scanned through it all. He had raised his eyebrows when he came across the photos of her modelling underwear, taken on an old phone, when she was still a teenager. The phone had been registered to her boyfriend at the time and the originals no longer existed. As soon as he saw them he instructed the informant to delete all copies and records of the photos from everywhere but Mycroft's own files.

He knew this was doing Amelia a service in helping her hide a skeleton in her closet but he also knew it gave him more power over her. He now had the only copies.

Since her first few weeks at university she'd been significantly more careful, probably due to the sexual assault she'd suffered on her fifth day. She hadn't ever reported the incident but she'd mentioned it to an internet friend on facebook. Given her reclusive personality, and how she'd gone from almost constantly dating to being single until she met her husband several years later, he was inclined to believe the account.

For a twenty-nine year old she'd lived through a varied amount of good and bad. She'd grown up poor to begin with before her father's fortunes had improved, so she wasn't spoilt. She had a younger brother but didn't talk to him much and she'd travelled to a few countries but nothing out of the ordinary. She'd always known she wanted to be a writer, and pursued her career relentlessly, despite doing well in the more academic subjects in school, especially maths.

Mycroft found her lack of friends interesting. She'd already mentioned she didn't enjoy the social side of her profession but she handled people well and had been an extroverted individual until her husband had died. Ever since then she'd withdrawn and kept to herself in the apartment they'd bought together, although signs of her socialising less had started to show in her years at Uni. He knew both would come down to her own feelings of hurt. It would make her guarded with her heart towards him and gave him more confidence to proceed teaching her. It also made her request to learn more genuine and increased it as the main motivation behind her pleasantness and willingness to cooperate.

Now he had the entire picture of her life, he was impressed with her. She'd reacted well to bad situations and shown she could handle emotionally stressful events without falling apart. And, despite being an artistic person with a fairly typical creative personality, she knew how to keep her emotions under control. Something he thought very important.

All the information he'd learnt would help him teach her as well as keep their game on his terms. He probably knew her better now than she did herself and he could be confident she wouldn't make a fuss when he was done playing with her.

With a smile of smug satisfaction Mycroft sat back and stared at the photos of her playing in a looped slide-show in front of him. He stayed that way for several minutes until he realised his team had still not reported in concerning the terrorist attack. He glanced at the clock on the wall. There was less than an hour of Friday left. Something had gone wrong.

CHAPTER 6

Saturday morning flew past in a haze as Mycroft attended meeting after meeting with official cabinet members and other government officials. All of them wanted to know why the information was wrong and what was going to be done about it. Ironically he'd have been more likely to give them answers if they'd stopped their pointless discussions and let him get back to work. Instead he had to text his brother and get Sherlock to re-examine the intercepted message for him.

During what he hoped would be his final meeting of the day, he received a message from his informant on Amelia.

Brother sent text to Miss Jones. She's just bought a train ticket to London and booked a hotel room. I've emailed you all the details.

He frowned and put his phone back in his pocket. The last thing he wanted was Amelia Jones getting involved. It already looked as if she'd taken them down the wrong direction and kept him from keeping the country safe. He should never have trusted her suggestions.

As soon as the meeting ended he opened the email from his informant and studied it. To make matters worse she was staying in the same hotel. At least he hadn't posted her letter and could get it to her while she was in London, although he wasn't going to sneak it into her hotel room again. If his brother had summoned Amelia then he could show up while she was there and slip it into her bag. He could also pass on the phone he wanted her to use to reply to him, assuming he still wished to. At the moment, he considered cutting all ties with her. He'd trusted her judgement and it remained to be proved wise or foolish.

"Home, sir?" Daniels asked.

"No. Baker Street." Mycroft sat back and tried to think of how he was going to sort out the mess Amelia had created. At least he would be able to point out she'd got it wrong. If he hadn't already written out the next letter he'd have told her it was over. He'd never been so furious, not even when Sherlock had been duped by that woman and lost a file of government secrets. All the hours wasted listening to people drone on had only made him angrier.

Mycroft wasn't surprised when he noticed the now familiar perfume lingering in the hallway. Both his brother and Amelia stared at him as he walked into the flat's living area. The pair stood in almost the exact same positions as they had the first time he'd discovered them working together.

She gave him a brief smile, but it vanished when he gave her his often used sneer.

"I thought we'd be seeing you soon, brother of mine," Sherlock said, taking Mycroft's focus away from Amelia and the corseted waistcoat she wore with trousers and boots.

"People want answers." Mycroft moved his gaze back to Amelia and tried not to think about the compromising pictures he'd got of her. "Nothing happened on Friday and they want to know why my information was wrong."

We've looked at the message several times," she replied, motioning to the whiteboard behind her. "We can't see any other sort of pattern."

"Which is why I am here. We shall have to look again." Mycroft walked past her and stood in front of the letter. In truth he hadn't been able to think of an alternative code yet but he wanted her to squirm for a while. He knew his agents would have provided solid information so something had gone wrong with this message and Amelia had put them on this track.

"Run me through each sentence." Mycroft directed his comment at his brother but she stepped up beside him and used the pen to point as she explained each meme, one by one.

His mind reeled at the amount of time she must have spent online to know what the possibilities were, and he didn't even feel slightly bothered that he recognised none of them. There was little point remembering such random nonsense, especially so out of context.

Once she'd finished he felt satisfied that the key to translating the message must be entirely different. If it was the wrong day then it must be something other than internet memes.

"What do you think it might be instead?" She asked when he voiced this.

"I don't know yet, but I'm sure between us we can find it." He gave her another one of his fake smiles and backed away motioning for Sherlock to follow him.

"I don't appreciate you involving her in this, brother of mine," Mycroft whispered.

"Nonsense, she's proved useful and I'm sure you'll like her when you get to know her."

Mycroft raised his eyebrows as his brother went back to staring at the letter.

After an hour of trying to find another possible key, Amelia put down her pen and shook her head.

"Is there anything else you can tell us, Myron? Something more about the kind of message we should be expecting. Sebastian mentioned you knew the target was the Millennium

Eye. Where did you get that information from?"

Mycroft frowned and kept silent but even Sherlock looked like he agreed with her.

"Two of my agents gave me several facts." She handed him the pen, brushing her fingers against the back of his hand. If she hadn't done a similar gesture to Sherlock the first time he'd seen them together he'd have thought she was trying to show interest in him.

He wrote down the names of all the different planned projects and the location.

"Are you sure you've got the right location?"

"Yes." Mycroft used the same tone of voice that he warned his brother not to argue with.

"Could each codename have a different location? So *clip* or *pin* would be the name for the attack on the Millennium Eye, but *lace* is somewhere different." Amelia said, ignoring him.

Mycroft shook his head, too angry to gather his thoughts into words. She'd misled them, not his own agents.

"Amelia has a point," Sherlock said just as he opened his mouth to begin his tirade at her. "Could it be worth looking at other locations?"

He saw her eyes flick between the two of them. She'd picked up on the anger and he'd noticed her own heart rate increase in response. Now she bit her lip and waited for him to speak. At first he didn't respond, choosing to study her instead. Until now she'd given no indication that she was affected by his presence in the room. If for no other reason than to keep his communications with her from being picked up by Sherlock, he knew he needed to move the conversation along.

"I have no more information. If there are other locations I don't know where they would be."

"That can be sorted out. If we assume the message is right and something happened yesterday we can find out what and where. Whatever happened it wasn't a big explosion."

Sherlock smiled and grabbed his maps of London from a nearby shelf. Amelia moved to his side to pore over them with him, leaving Mycroft to stand awkwardly off to one side.

After watching the two of them point out likely targets for a minute he grabbed his phone and scrolled to the email with all his agent's statements and read through everything again.

This time in the reading he noticed that the female agent who'd gained information on *clip* being a codeword had heard them mention the Millennium Eye at the same time. Amelia's theory could well be sound. He could have kicked himself for making such a bad assumption and not sending both agents back into the field to find out more. Instead of telling his brother and new student this, he wrote an email to his assistant.

Potential evidence that each codeword related to a different location. Have the agents bought in and questioned and tap the usual informants for any suspicious activity yesterday at other major locations. Have any extra information forwarded to me immediately.

M

With that done he joined his brother, still looking over a map with the underground tunnels marked on it.

"We need to know if anything suspicious happened yesterday somewhere else," Mycroft said in his brothers ear.

"It will cost you."

Mycroft rolled his eyes. His brothers homeless network did well for money some days and it was usually Mycroft's finances that took the hit. Regardless of his own annoyance he handed a stack of notes to his brother while Amelia only raised an eyebrow. Her lack of understanding made him feel a little better. She can't have been to his brother's many times if she'd not witnessed his crew of young homeless teenagers who gathered him info.

"Where are you going?" She asked as Sherlock headed towards the door.

"He has a network of people who know how to blend in. If any of them has seen anything we'll know soon," Mycroft explained. She nodded and went back to the maps, giving him the opportunity to slip her next letter into her bag while his brother wouldn't notice.

Unless there was more information from somewhere soon there was little point going through the maps trying to guess at locations. But it was all they could do at the moment, so he let them come up with a list of likely targets and write them on the whiteboard.

He was just deciding to leave his brother and Amelia to their task when she yawned and checked the time.

"I ought to check into my hotel room," she said and gathered up her stuff, "I'm not helping much here at the moment."

"Brother of mine, why don't you take Amelia over there and save her having to find a taxi. There's no point either of you staying while there's so little to go on and there's little left of today." Sherlock smiled at him while he glared back.

"I'm sure Mr Holmes doesn't have the time to do that." Amelia glanced at him and went to leave. Before his brain could stop him he stepped forward into her path.

"My car is just outside." Giving his brother another glare, he motioned for Amelia to lead the way. She swayed down the stairs in front of him and shook hands with Daniels as soon as she reached him.

"I'm enjoying the book, Miss Jones. Could barely put it down," Daniels said as he opened the door for her and helped her inside. She broke into a broad smile that was still there when Mycroft got in beside her.

He couldn't quite believe that he had her in the car with him for a second time. When he'd agreed to her request he'd expected to keep her at a distance but his brother just couldn't keep out of his affairs.

"Thank you for this," she said before he could speak.

"Blame my brother." As soon as he'd finished the sentence he wished he hadn't. To move the conversation on he took her phone package out of the briefcase he kept in the car.

"Use this to communicate with me, and only me, and don't let anyone else know you have it. Is that clear?" She nodded and took the offered object. "You can use it to reply instead of having to write messages and leave them in prearranged locations."

"I take it you had my response removed from my own pocket? And put the first letter in my hotel room?" She asked the questions in an offhand manner but he saw the tension in her hands, clasped over the phone box, and the rigidness of her jaw. He'd frightened her with his actions and the discovery pleased him. A little fear would keep her obedient in her tasks.

"Yes, both were me, and easy enough." He watched her reactions with delight as she took several deep breaths to try and keep herself calm. He considered mentioning the photos and impressing the reach of his control even further but given the implications of his other actions he decided against it. He already appeared more interested in her than he was, and he didn't want her to think there was any romantic attachment, especially with the encouragement his own brother was displaying.

"Are you enjoying it?" she asked once she had her emotions under control again. It surprised him and he had to think about his answer.

"Yes, I am so far. I enjoyed watching you try and work out the first letter." Before he'd finished speaking she'd stopped watching them pass the London streets by and fixed her gaze on him. Her mouth dropped open and he chuckled.

"You were there?"

"In the cafe and the hotel canteen." He nodded as he spoke.

"I didn't even notice you."

"I'm aware."

"So is my every move going to be watched from now on?" The sparkle in her eyes and lopsided smile showed him that she wasn't entirely bothered by the idea. He wondered what had conquered the fear she'd felt earlier.

"Of course, but you don't seem particularly bothered."

"I've had a stalker or two before. Although I've never had one sneak into my hotel room while I slept just to leave me a letter. Most of them would have other ideas if they found me in bed."

"I can assure you I'm not intending anything of that nature."

She mock pouted and he rolled his eyes in response. A second later she laughed.

"Thank you, whatever the reason. I didn't think you'd say yes to my suggestion but I'm very glad you did. I look forward to my next lesson," she said as the car came to a stop outside the hotel. He nodded but kept his thoughts to himself. Her next lesson was already in her bag waiting for her to notice it.

As he watched her walk inside he realised he should have told her to stay somewhere better and it reminded him to have her book sales stimulated. With all the information he'd been given on her he knew even affording to come to London and stay as often as she did was difficult.

Mycroft checked his email as Daniels took him home but there was still no extra information from the agents. All he could do was wait and try to focus on other issues.

A young teenager in the royal family was on holiday in Portugal and had upset the hotel owner with his late night partying. Many of the guests had complained and Mycroft was directing the process to smooth it all over. The last thing they needed right now was bad press in Europe.

As far as problems went it wasn't particularly difficult, but it kept him busy while he was waiting on Amelia to solve his most recent code, and for his brother to get him solid information to act upon.

CHAPTER 7

On the way to her room Amelia couldn't help but bounce with excitement. The day had been a rollercoaster of emotions but it was ending well. Mycroft and his games were already dictating most of her mood swings. She'd been nervous about finding the letter in her room and being pickpocketed, but he'd made her feel more at ease when he'd told her that both actions were his. At least he had been the one to see her sleeping and vulnerable. Her long term plan was to seduce him so it would be silly of her to be bothered by his actions, especially as she'd been untouched and unharmed.

During the day her biggest fear had been her reaction when he first saw her. She knew she'd directed the translation of his terrorist message and Sebastian had already told her that it hadn't delivered the right result. She'd wondered if she would be reprimanded and dismissed but he'd allowed her to continue helping. Then the conversation in the car had made her excited about their future once more.

She fell backwards onto the bed with a sigh of satisfaction. Even knowing there was an undetected terrorist attack happening somewhere in the city couldn't stop her feeling pleased with her day. If anything, knowing danger could be close made her feel exhilarated.

A few minutes later her stomach rumbled to let her know she hadn't eaten anything but a few snacks since breakfast and it was now past her usual time for an evening meal. She grabbed her handbag off the floor and headed for the canteen. Hopefully they served dinner as well as breakfast.

Relief flooded through her when she found the room open and several other hotel guests sitting in there eating. It wouldn't have been good to miss out on another meal in so short a space of time when it was likely she wouldn't eat much the following day either.

Her meal passed in peace, although she scanned the canteen several times for signs of Myron. As she pulled her purse from her handbag to pay, her fingers brushed up against something she wasn't expecting. When she glanced at it she realised she had an envelope with her name and address on. She gasped as she pulled it out, momentarily forgetting about the cashier waiting for her to pay. He coughed, dragging her eyes from the unexpected communication.

As soon as she could get away she rushed back to her own room and tore the envelope open. A piece of card with her name on fell out with a much shorter message than the previous time written on it. She stared at it for several minutes, knowing it was going to be significantly harder to work out than the first letter.

Realising she needed to learn more about ciphers and how to use them, Amelia fetched her laptop from her small suitcase and curled up on the bed with it to do research. An hour later she stopped trawling through the search information on classic cyphers and re-focused on the letter.

Based on the previous letter she was sure it began and ended in a similar manner with 'Miss Jones' being before the comma and 'Regards, Your Tutor' finishing the letter off. As she wrote these in underneath she realised not all of the letters had been changed. The M in 'Miss' and the ON in her surname were still part of the coded message. Also the GA in 'regards', OU in 'your', and the last OR were all the same and each pair of identical letters had exactly four in between.

In pencil she wrote these pairs underneath to help form the basis of her translation so far.

Miss Jones,
--th---- I w----n't ----al-- --re- -- - ch---- in ----s I
----gn--- -ou- ---nt -- --in- - --ns---- on-. -- -uc- - --al-
---nt ---- re----t. I ---- no---- yo- -- - ch---- to ---- ou-
---an----nt. ---- th-- --al ---- yo- -- -it--?
Regards, Your Tutor

Based on the information she'd just learnt on cyphers that were encrypted differently for each letter, she knew there needed to be a codeword that would match the pattern she'd already noticed. Given the pattern she also knew it must begin and end with the same letter or number and be six figures long. She'd worked out the affect the first and last had on the coded message, so she just needed to work out the others.

After scanning through what she had a couple more times she noticed the third word was likely to be 'wouldn't' and that the A needed to become an O. The process to get between these letters also needed to match up with the I in 'Miss' coming from the U and getting from a Q to an E six letters later. As soon as she wrote them out she realised they were all 14 letters apart if the alphabet started again when it finished. She then repeated the same logic on the next three letters. When she'd finished she realised she had a sort of reverse keyword to get from the encrypted letter to what it originally said using the numbers 0,14,4,11,8, & 0 and then repeating them throughout the message. She quickly worked her way through the rest of the letter filling in all the blanks.

Miss Jones,

Although I wouldn't normally agree to a change in rules I recognise your point as being a sensible one. As such I shall grant your request. I will notify you if I choose to stop our arrangement. Does this deal make you my bitch?
Regards, Your Tutor.

Amelia almost dropped the paper in shock at Myron's closing sentence. He'd been so prim and proper with her, often making a point that there was nothing more going on between them than a teacher student relationship that was very much on his terms. Yet here was a sentence that might imply a bit more, and he'd also now given her a phone to talk to him directly. If she hadn't been told nothing would happen, she'd be under the impression he was interested in more, and she knew anyone who found these letters might read more into them.

A few seconds later it occurred to her this might be his plan. He was so secretive about his involvement and helping her, he might be trying to make it look like they had a relationship contract and he was some sort of sugar-daddy she'd got herself involved with.

She supposed it could also relate to her suggestion of being his pet. Ever since she'd used those words to describe what she wanted she'd wondered if it had been a big mistake, but they might have had the impact she desired. After all, a female dog was a bitch and Myron was unlikely to use it as a slang term alone. She decided there was only one way to find out and got up to fetch the phone from her handbag.

As she moved she saw something flutter to the floor and stopped to pick it up. It was the small piece of card with Amelia written on it. She stared at it for a moment puzzled before she realised it began and ended in the same letter and was six letters long.

Counting on her fingers, she worked out that every letter was 1 more than the numbers she'd used in her reverse keyword. She laughed aloud. Myron had given her the keyword after all, she'd just forgotten about it. If she hadn't noticed the pattern she'd have been stuck for hours trying to figure out what to do.

Despite wanting to kick herself she sat back down on the bed with the phone she'd been given and turned it on. The battery was almost fully charged but nothing was on the phone except a single number in the contacts list. She pulled up the messaging service to send Myron a text.

This deal is on your terms, so I suppose it's up to you. Am I your pet?

As soon as she'd sent it she wondered if she ought to have worded it differently, and then she noticed the time. It was already the following day and she wasn't sure whether she could expect a reply.

She decided to brush her teeth and change into her nightwear while she waited but she'd barely taken two steps to the small ensuite bathroom when she heard the chime of a reply. Instantly she rushed back and picked the phone up.

It was your suggestion. If you're my bitch it's entirely because you want to be. And do I not get any gratitude for the alteration to our little game's rules?

Despite the coldness of the reply she couldn't help but grin. It was a reply with a question that invited a response and she knew she was right about his implications. If anyone found either of the phones they would assume she had herself a controlling elder boyfriend and little more.

You do have my gratitude. Thank you. And I enjoyed my first lesson. Will there be more soon?

She sent another question hoping to keep things going and

get more information from him. This time she did scurry to brush her teeth and get ready for bed, excitement flooding through her.

When she came back, ready to sleep, she had yet another reply and she couldn't help but feel delighted that her tactic was working. She curled up under the covers and read it.

There will be more when I wish there to be. It's late and you should be sleeping.

She grinned at his air of authority and thought about her reply. Being cheeky was her first temptation but she wasn't sure how he would respond to that. After biting her lip a moment she went with her initial thoughts anyway.

I'm in bed, so I'm almost there, but I'm not ready to sleep yet. And you're awake as well. Do you need my help with anything?

After snuggling down so she could lay her head on her pillow, she waited, staring at the phone. Amelia knew it was a little obsessive of her to wait for a reply like this but she couldn't help it. Now she had him talking she didn't want him to stop. It took several minutes longer for is response to come through and it made her sigh with disappointment.

It's late and you agreed to obey me. Don't make me tell you again. Go to sleep. You'll get your next lesson when I'm ready to teach it to you and not before.

She put the phone on the bed side table, before picking it up again.

As you command, I shall obey.

She hit send and turned the light out with a grin on her

face. A moment later the phone chime made her sit up and grab it.

As you should.

Her finger hovered over the reply button. He'd messaged her again when she'd expected their conversation to be over and it puzzled her slightly. Either he really was going all out on making it appear they were in a relationship or he had enjoyed their conversation as well, but she didn't know if it was wise to continue. He'd already warned her once to go to sleep and not disobey him. If she replied again he could see it as a deliberate act to break the rules and she knew that might end badly.

With reluctance she put the phone back on the bedside cabinet and placed her head on the pillow. Hopefully the following day would give her another opportunity to see Myron and might result in a further challenging message to translate.

An hour later she flicked the light back on. Tossing and turning in the dark was making her frustrated. Too many thoughts, possibilities and what-ifs ran through her head, and not just about Myron. There was a group of terrorists trying to destroy some or all of London and Myron and Sebastian were struggling to find out what their target was to stop them.

Somehow she'd managed to get tied up in all this. Normally she was a story writer who left the adventures to her characters but now she found herself on adventures of her own. One learning from a genius who, according to his younger brother, ran the entire government, and the second, helping them both keep her country safe. The adrenaline that buzzed through her was enough to keep any normal person awake, long after they would normally be sleeping.

All she could do to try and quiet her mind was write for a little while. She hoped Myron would understand she'd tried to sleep if he noticed her tiredness the following day. She knew Sebastian would.

She worked on her previous novel for a few hours, taking a look at where she could change it if she needed to. Myron's assistant had emailed her some guidelines to work with for the re-writes late on Friday but this was the first time she'd looked over them.

By the time she'd distracted herself she felt like she might be able to get some sleep but her alarm was set for less than five hours later. When it went off she felt like only seconds had passed.

She hurried to make herself presentable and wolf down some breakfast before gathering all her belongings up and getting a taxi to Sebastian's. Just in case she wasn't needed much longer she checked out of the hotel. There was almost always space if she arrived before it got too late and she didn't want to pay for another night if she didn't need it.

Mrs Wintern let her in and smiled at her, patting her shoulder on the way past. The elderly woman seemed to have a soft spot for Amelia and welcomed her into the building with a warmer greeting than she probably deserved. She wasn't there for Sebastian as Mrs Wintern wanted.

Both Myron and Sebastian were in the living room when she walked in. They turned to her.

"Have I missed something?" she asked.

"Nothing in particular yet." Myron glanced over her and frowned. "You look very tired, Miss Jones. You can't have slept much."

"Not for lack of trying. I spent plenty of time in bed, but my mind didn't want to stop." She hoped her explanation would satisfy him but couldn't be sure it would. As she'd expected, he'd noticed her tiredness right away.

"My network are only now reporting in and so far nothing," Sebastian said as he got up from the armchair and passed her a cup of tea. She took it grateful for the drink.

"Has anywhere been ruled out at least?"

"A few places." He pointed at several areas of London on

the map. "Nothing that gives us much to go on."

She sighed. With both of them working on finding answers she'd have expected more information by now.

It took them a few minutes to pass on the few findings they already had and then the three sat and tried to suggest what was the most likely target.

Thankfully, Mrs Wintern came into the room with several pieces of paper, stopping them from wasting more time.

"They said, these were the last," she explained before she handed them over and hurried away again.

Sebastian read through them before passing each one to Myron. All Amelia could do was wait, but none of them came her way. She wondered if he was punishing her for not getting enough sleep before putting the thought out of her mind. She knew it was unlikely.

"This isn't that helpful, brother of mine," Myron said a few minutes later

"There do seem to be several locations." Sherlock shook his head in frustration.

"Which ones?" Amelia asked, fed up of not being included.

"Silvertown, Teddington Lock, Dartford and near the Thames in Greenwich." Myron threw the pieces of paper down on the coffee table and stood up. "This is a waste of time."

Amelia grabbed each one and read the the information.

"No it's not," she said as her eyes fixed on the same details. "These are all the locations of the Thames barriers. The main one is in Silvertown, then there's..."

"We know where they all are, thank you." Myron rolled his eyes and pulled out his phone. A second later his call was connected to someone. He repeated the information to them and then listened for a few seconds.

"Understood." He hung up and looked at his brother. "I've got teams going out to two of the major barriers at Dartford and Greenwich. We should go to the other two."

"I'll head to Teddington. You should go to the main barrier at Silvertown, you know its construction better than I do and it's the most important." Sebastian grabbed his coat and put it on before Amelia could move.

By the time she was suitably attired he was already rushing down the stairs and Myron wasn't far behind, leaving her to trail after.

She walked outside in time to see the taxi Sebastian had hailed pull off, giving her no choice but to hurry after Myron.

"I guess that means I'm coming with you," she said loud enough that his chauffeur would hear. Within seconds Daniels was holding the door open for her whether Myron wanted her company or not.

CHAPTER 8

Mycroft almost swore as Amelia got into the car with him. He knew his brother had left her behind because she would slow him down and that just meant Mycroft now had the same problem. While they travelled she had the sense to keep quiet, however.

Just as they got out at the other end he received a phone call from his assistant.

"The first team have found evidence of tampering at the King George Lock."

"What kind of tampering?" he asked as he waited by the car. He noticed Amelia lingering nearby.

"Alone it wouldn't cause any problems and the next inspection would have picked up on it, but the gates wouldn't have held against an abnormal tide or flood waters from upstream."

"All right, it looks like a multilevel attack. Do what you can to get it repaired."

He hung up and put his phone back inside his jacket pocket.

"Stay here with the car, Daniels."

Mycroft surveyed the area, trying to remember where he needed to go to check the mechanism. He hadn't been here since they'd built it.

"We should be careful," he said and led her off towards the river. He heard her footsteps on the ground behind him and wished she'd stayed behind at the flat. "Do try to keep up."

The pattering pace increased and grew louder until she was beside him. They continued to the Thames Barrier information centre but rather than going inside he went off to the left and along a narrow walkway. The bottom was made of a metal mesh in square grids and as soon as Amelia stepped out her skirts were whipped around by the strong winds. It took her by surprise and Mycroft had to reach out to grab her arm and steady her.

"Careful." He sneered, growing even angrier at her.

"Sorry," she replied and took a step closer to shield herself from the wind behind him. His fierceness instantly softened and he let her hang onto his arm as they walked across to the nearest barrier house. The recent rains had made the metal slippery and even he wondered if he could keep his footing as they walked across. Thankfully he kept upright and protected Amelia from any further mishap.

At the other end he expected to find a locked door but he noticed the metal that normally housed the lock mechanism was cut right out of the door. He pointed at it so Amelia would notice and then put his fingers to his lips so she wouldn't make a sound. She nodded and took a couple of breaths to steady herself.

Given the time that had passed since the attack was meant to happen he didn't really expect anyone to be inside, but with Amelia at his side he needed to take more care.

The door creaked softly as he pushed it open, but the wind howled enough inside the building that no one would have heard it. He stepped inside and Amelia followed close behind. One of the barrier's weighted mechanisms towered up in front of them. He glanced around the small room but didn't see anyone lingering, so he took another few steps forward.

The wind howled around the structure so loudly he couldn't hear the sound of Amelia's booted feet coming up behind him. Wanting to make sure she still followed, he turned to her just in time to see an arm snake around her waist and a gun appear by her head.

"Don't move," a male voice said in Korean. Mycroft gritted his teeth.

"What did they say?" Amelia asked, barely above a whisper.

"Just stay calm, and don't fight them, Amelia. They won't want to hurt you." He put both hands out palms upwards and glanced between Amelia and the Korean behind her. Along the side of her neck he could see the rapid drumbeat of her pulse and knew she was afraid, but she allowed the Korean to pull her backwards out of the building.

"Come," the terrorist said. As Mycroft emerged in the light of day he saw another two burly men behind. Neither had guns out, but he wouldn't be surprised if they had them somewhere.

They walked Amelia backwards along the whole length of walkway and then waited for him to catch up. As soon as he reached them his arms were grabbed and a gun nozzle was pressed into his back.

A few seconds later both he and Amelia were marched off to one side and down a path to a small jetty floating on the higher tide. A boat waited, tied to the edge. Mycroft could only comply as Amelia, and then himself, were handed over to the men aboard. He listened as they talked to each other, catching a few words in Russian but nothing more.

He frowned at the idea of this being a joint operation and furrowed his brow as both his and Amelia's hands were bound. They were then escorted below decks and shoved into one of the cabins. Hope filled him as it looked like they would be left alone, but one of the men came in as well and locked the door from the inside. He sat down so he could see them both and Mycroft knew they were going to be there until they were identified. Whether Amelia fared the worse after or he did would depend. The brute in the room with them didn't look to want any sort of violence but that didn't mean the others wouldn't.

Being much calmer than Mycroft had expected of her, Amelia also sat down and gave him a small smile. He nodded at her and went to sit beside. The Russian lifted his hand and pointed at the other end of the bench to her. He huffed his annoyance at the arrangement but did as the guy asked, sitting as far from her as the wooden platform would allow.

A minute later the boat started to move and he and his charge found themselves heading down river to the English Channel. Even though Sherlock and Daniels had known where he was they wouldn't much longer and the boat was unremarkable. It would blend in amongst the other vessels on the water and soon be just another in the mass.

Time went past and all Mycroft could do was wait and plan. A few times he tried to engage the Russian in conversation and establish where they were and what the men wanted, but he was glared at or threatened until he became silent.

Through the small window he kept an eye on the horizon and how much of the river passed them, but hours ticked by and he could do little to help rescue them. While they were kept there and simply stared at, there was little he could do.

Several hours into their journey, as it was getting dark, they were brought water. He took the offered cup to drink, while Amelia fumbled over it, spilling a lot over herself. The Russian growled his annoyance and held the cup up so she could drink.

Before Mycroft could blink she'd lifted the palms of her hands, the ropes falling off them and shoved them up into the Russian's face. It looked like a half hearted attempt to break the man's nose but it sent him flying backwards. Instead of continuing her assault, she rushed to Mycroft, grabbed his bonds and pried one of the knots apart with already bloodied fingernails. At the same time he noticed the painful mess around her wrists. She'd hurt herself to get her bonds undone and managed to do so without letting the Russian realise. Both he and their guard had been watching each other so much neither of them had noticed her.

The Russian recovered before she could fully undo the rope binding his hands. She let out a cut-off grunt as he grabbed her around the stomach and lifted her entire body to one side. As soon as her feet were on the ground again she spun herself and brought her knee up into his family jewels. He hunched over as she brought her knee up again into his face. She then drove her elbow into the side of his back, near his neck.

While this was happening, Mycroft worked the remaining knots free with his teeth. Instead of finishing the Russian off at this point Amelia backed off, uncertainty playing over her features. She'd known some basic self defence but had evidently hoped Mycroft would have done the rest, and now the Russian got to his feet in between them.

Mycroft worked as speedily as he could as he noticed the Russian reach for a weapon concealed amongst his clothing somewhere. Although guns had been pointed at them earlier, the Russian appeared to be retrieving a bladed weapon of some sort. Amelia looked around frantically, and Mycroft realised she thought the terrorist had a gun.

Just as the Russian raised a knife, Mycroft freed his hands and leapt up. Amelia ducked as he grabbed the weapon, and the pair grappled back and forth, obviously expecting a gunshot to ring out.

The knife sliced into his side, making Mycroft flinch, but he rallied himself against the pain and grabbed the hilt to shove it back at the Russian. The burly man grunted as it cut his arm open from shoulder to elbow, spurting blood out on both of them.

A second later a plumbing pipe came out of nowhere and

knocked the terrorist out. As he slid to the floor Amelia came into view. The other end of the metal object responsible for relieving him was clutched in both her hands. A determined, wide-eyed look remained on her face, but she shook with the adrenaline.

Mycroft took the makeshift weapon from her hands before she dropped it and then got to work tying the unconscious man with the rope that had bound them. He then gagged him and hauled him into the corner. It wouldn't buy them much time but it would be better than nothing. The whole time Amelia just watched. When she recovered a little, she pointed at his side, her eyes fixed on all the blood. Already he could feel his skin healing and sealing the cut shut but he couldn't show her that.

"It's not my blood," he said in a low voice to try and explain. With that he grabbed her arm and unlocked the door with the key he'd lifted seconds earlier. He worried she'd inquire further but she followed behind without making any fuss.

"Stay quiet and close to me," he said and led her along the corridor to the back of the boat. All the lights outside were dowsed and he could just see a pair of legs further up the deck. He leant out a little more and realised the two remaining kidnappers were drinking beer and chatting while the vessel was held on course.

He turned to Amelia and grabbed hold of her hand before leading them both to the stern of the boat and helping her down the short ladder to the small platform used for diving. He joined her only seconds later and scanned their surroundings. Given how long they were on the boat he knew they were no longer in the Thames river but were at sea. Thankfully his watchfulness of the horizon let him know the English shore was off to their right and the boat had been hugging the coast. It wasn't a small distance to swim but he knew he could manage it, especially as the tide was coming in and would help sweep them closer to their destination.

He unlaced his shoes, disgruntled to need to leave them behind and motioned for her to do the same. She reluctantly copied his actions until they'd both removed everything they didn't need to be decent. He crouched with only his trousers and socks left on and she kneeled in only her petticoat, corset and tights. As soon as they were done he put all their discarded items into the water and let them sink. It would help hide their tracks, but it also reduced the chances of Amelia noticing the slit in his shirt and the injury he'd sustained. It wasn't fully healed yet but it would be by the time they reached solid ground and he couldn't risk her realising he could heal much faster than the average human. His brother and him hadn't guarded the secret for over a hundred years for it to come out now.

"Follow me," he whispered and slipped his body into the water so it wouldn't splash. The salt water stung his side but he ignored it. The pain would pass soon enough. Amelia's reaction to the pain and the coldness of the water as she joined him concerned him far more. Only then did he see her face in enough light to make out the fear. Instantly, he knew she didn't think she could manage the swim.

He motioned to her for her to follow anyway, already realising he would need to leave her if she didn't get in the water soon. Going for help would have to be weighed up against taking her with him.

After looking back up to the deck and then at the water again, he knew she was thinking similar thoughts. A second later she took a deep breath, fixed her eyes on him and slid into the water, even more gracefully than he had.

His hand immediately rose to stifle her gasp at the cold and pain, and then he put it to his lips again before motioning for her to follow. She trod water well, which comforted him but, when he went to take the first stroke towards shore and away from the boat, she didn't copy his front crawl motion. Instead she did a sort of awkward combination of a doggy paddle and breast stroke. Swimming really wasn't her strong point.

Without thinking, he put her hands together and then slid them over his head so she was behind him.

"Hang on to me and kick your legs with mine," he whispered near her ear. She nodded, her eyes full of gratitude. A large part of him wanted to leave her and get himself to shore, knowing helping her would drain him more than was wise, but she'd got them out of the locked room and he found he couldn't abandon her now.

After swimming for several minutes Mycroft stopped and trod water to give his tired arms a rest. If the tide hadn't been coming in he'd not have bothered but he knew this way he would find it easier to get them to shore. Amelia instantly let go and copied his motions beside him. Relief flooded through him that she had enough sense and focus to help him where she could.

While he was able to turn around he scanned the waters for the boat, but it was gone from view, lost in the darkness of the night. A second later he focused back on Amelia's face. The wideness had gone from her eyes but her teeth chattered as she bobbed with the waves.

"We're almost there," he said. She nodded and waited for him to encourage her to continue. When he reached for her hands again she shook her head.

"I can swim for a bit. You're tired."

He took her hands anyway and put them back around his neck.

"You'll need your strength for after." Mycroft readied himself and carried on through the water. She didn't object any further but allowed him to keep her going.

After stopping once more to rest, he managed to get them both to shore. The tide had almost fully come in so there was little mud to wade through and a pond the other side allowed both him and Amelia to wash off what little clung to their feet.

He panted for breath and she fared little better, but he

didn't allow them to rest more than a few minutes. Already her whole body shook and shivered in the wind. Stripped of so many layers and sodden from head to toe, he knew she would risk hypothermia. While he could withstand the cold and already knew he was safe, she was in as much danger as ever.

"We need to get away from here. Come," he said and took her arm to pull her to her feet again. She didn't complain but allowed him to lead her to the edge of a field and then right through it. She stumbled a few times, getting her skirts and feet caught up in the long stalks around her, but she kept walking and he kept up the pace. It was cruel to keep her moving so fast but he knew it would help keep her warm.

In the far corner of the field Mycroft spotted a farm track and knew it was Amelia's best chance of survival.

"Hurry," he called back to her and sped up yet again. He expected her to finally complain but she didn't. Instead, the sound of her stumbling footfalls and chattering teeth followed in his wake. He didn't turn around and knew he'd appear uncaring towards her, but he had to do it.

Along the dirt track was the occasional unavoidable embedded stone and he winced every now and then as one jabbed into the soles of his feet, but none were sharp enough to penetrate the socks.

The minutes dragged by but the wind didn't let up over the flat fields and even he found his body shaking from the cold. Just as he considered stopping and giving Amelia a break he saw the lights of a house up ahead. He didn't say anything but kept going at the same pace. They would be warm and safe soon enough.

CHAPTER 9

By the time Mycroft had banged on the farmhouse door enough to be heard, Amelia had caught up with him. Her shaking had only got worse but he had nothing to offer her to take the chill off.

He stopped slamming his fists into the front door as a light flicked on in the hallway.

"What time do you call this?" a man yelled as he wrenched the door open. Seeing the two bedraggled figures stopped him in his tracks.

"I need to use your phone." Mycroft put his hand out to push the door further open but it didn't move, held shut by the house occupant. Amelia stepped up beside him, doing nothing to hide her shivering.

"We were kidnapped and we had to swim to escape. Please, we need to call the police," she looked at the man with big hope filled eyes. Within seconds the door was pulled open revealing a middle-aged man in a dressing gown. Both he and Mycroft motioned for her to enter first. She just switched her gaze to Mycroft, her chin quivering.

"I can't. My feet..."

He looked down and saw the bloody footprints leading up the pathway to where she stood now. As pity washed over him he reached out for her. She swayed towards him and before she could fall he swept her up into his arms. The coldness of her skin against his almost made him gasp.

The guy led the way to his kitchen and pulled out a dining chair. Mycroft placed her down in it as gently as he could and before he'd got up the owner had a cordless home phone outstretched towards him.

"She needs a blanket or a towel," he said as he took the offered device and entered the number of the Commissioner. He answered after the second ring.

"This is Myron Holmes..." Before he could continue the man in charge of the nation's police force interrupted him.

"Good God, we've been looking all over for you."

"We were taken from the Thames Barrier." He nodded his gratitude as their host returned to the kitchen with two extra large bath towels. He helped Amelia wrap herself in one before holding the other out to him. Not wanting to appear rude he took it and nodded his thanks.

"We?" the Commissioner asked.

"Yes, I've got an Amelia Jones with me. We're..." Mycroft put his hand over the mouth piece of the phone and looked at the owner. "Where are we?"

"E End Road. CM0 7PN," The guy said. Mycroft repeated the address. "Send your nearest officers, a doctor, and...

"Are you hurt?"

"I'm fine, but Miss Jones isn't. Also have my chauffeur bring my car up here as well as my emergency kit. He'll know what that means." Mycroft tried not to get angry at the constant interruptions. The commissioner had never been a particularly patient man.

"Yes, sir."

"Finally, get someone out looking for an unlit yacht off the coast north of here. I'd assume with their speed and direction of travel that they are heading to Harwich, but they may stop and try to find us. Also there's some North Koreans in London somewhere. I recognised them from the suspected terrorists list. I'll have my brother look for them."

"Understood, sir. Anything else?"

"No, thank you. Just get those done as soon as you can."

Mycroft hung up and then put the towel around his own shoulders. At the very least it covered his chest from view, something he'd never particularly liked showing off. He glanced at Amelia and saw her look away hastily. A tear tracked slowly down her right cheek and her chin quivered with the emotions she was fighting to restrain.

By now he'd expected more fuss from her so the solitary tear came as a relief, assuming she could continue to hold herself together. He wouldn't have thought the restraint she currently showed possible if he wasn't already witnessing it.

"She's going into shock. Can you make her a cup of tea with plenty of sugar. Not too hot."

The man nodded. He evidently had no idea what else to do for the pair of them. As soon as he scurried off to obey Mycroft's request, Mycroft called Sherlock to let his brother know where he was.

It took several more rings for his brother to answer.

"Sherlock," he said before he thought about it and almost swore.

"Mycroft, where have you been? I've had to command your little team of agents for the last few hours, and your chauffeur has been phoning me every five minutes to see if I've heard from you."

"We're all right. Thank you for your concern. It's going to be a few hours until I'm back in London. Can you leave my team to ensure the barriers are in working order and find some people for me?"

"Of course. I assume you and Amelia ran into some difficulty with the North Koreans?"

"Yes. There's three of them. They jumped us at the Thames Barrier. They're on the database and armed, so be careful. Let me know when they've been apprehended."

"As you wish, brother of mine."

Mycroft hung up again and this time he put the phone down on the side and went over to Amelia. She still kept her mouth clamped down over her emotions but no more tears had shown themselves and her eyes were less wide and watery. He was also relieved to see she no longer shivered. The farm kitchen was warm and dry.

"Are you in pain?" he asked. She shook her head but didn't open her mouth to speak until the farmer came over with a large mug of tea for her. She took it in both hands and cradled it to her.

"Thank you," she said, barely above a whisper. Mycroft noticed the slight shake in her voice but doubted the guy had. He accepted the second cup the farmer had made and sat down at the table beside her.

"I'll go make myself decent, if you'll both be all right for a few minutes?"

Mycroft nodded at the man's sense. Very soon his house would be inundated with police and hopefully a doctor to check Amelia over. While they were alone together Mycroft did just that, although he remained seated and she didn't notice. He started with her hands, noticing the blood had been washed off her fingernails and none of them looked to be worse off than a few chips here and there. All of them were firmly attached.

His gaze then moved to Amelia's wrists. The sea water had washed them as well, but rather than cleaning them off, they were now swollen and red, especially where the ropes had rubbed her skin so badly she'd bled. He suspected she'd lied when she said she was in no pain.

From his seat beside her he couldn't see the soles of her feet, but noticed no drops of blood on the floor. Her thin tights were ripped and he could see the smears of blood on the tattered heals. They would need cleaning and she would struggle to walk for a day or two, but he doubted it would be any worse.

"What now?" she said as she put her empty mug down on

the table. When he didn't respond she finally looked at him. Every feature was as calm as usual.

"The police will be here soon and then you need medical attention," he explained, assuming she hadn't heard the phone calls he'd made. Considering the blunder he'd made with his brother's name, he was pleased to find she'd not been paying attention.

"After that, are we going back to London to try to stop them again?"

"My driver will take us back, yes, unless you want to go home to Bath?"

"No," she replied before he'd even finished saying her home city's name. "I'd rather come to London. I can still help."

"You can barely walk." Although he admired her determination he knew she couldn't be allowed to risk her life any more. He'd already exposed her too much.

"I know, but I'd still like to do what I can to help, even if I have to do so from a chair."

"Let's start with getting back to London, shall we? By the time we get there, my brother may have already found the culprits and solved everything." He gave her his usual smile. A part of him hoped his brother wasn't quite so efficient, while the rest of him hoped Sherlock was. Amelia had been through enough. Until he could be sure she wasn't going to break down, he had to ensure she was unexposed to more danger.

He didn't have a chance to find out whether Amelia understood his reasons or not. The farmer came back downstairs with jeans and a short sleeved shirt on and less than a minute later the police showed up. Behind them came two paramedics. They homed in on Amelia right away, allowing Mycroft to talk in a low voice with the police and tell them the events they needed to know.

The Commissioner had already passed on a small amount of information and with the other details Mycroft added, he convinced the police to give him and Amelia some space and just keep an eye on the area in case the Russians did manage to track them to the farmhouse. With that done, he could go back to Amelia.

Already the paramedics had cleaned and assessed the damage to her feet. The younger, female paramedic was bandaging them while her older colleague washed and checked over the rope burns on Amelia's wrists. Amelia gave Mycroft a brief smile when he sat back down beside her.

"There, all patched up. You shouldn't walk too much for a day or two and keep everything clean and dry. If anything starts to look infected go to your GP and get it checked out," the woman said and gave Amelia a grin.

"Thank you." As soon as the paramedics were out the door, she flicked her gaze onto Mycroft. "How long will your car be?"

"Half an hour, at most."

"Good, I'm a little tired now."

"You should have slept more last night. I do believe I ordered you to," he said, teasing her a little. She looked down, as her cheeks flushed.

"I tried, I really did."

"I'm not cross."

Now that the police and paramedics had left, the farmer hovered by the kitchen sink. Mycroft left his charge where she was to go over to him.

"It's a long journey to get her home. Do you have a blanket you wouldn't mind parting with for a few days?"

The farmer nodded and rushed off yet again. When he returned he had a patchwork woollen blanket in his hands.

"Thank you. I'll see this is returned to you and you're suitably reimbursed for your help. I appreciate your coop-eration with this... predicament."

Dismissing the man with a nod, Mycroft took the blanket over to Amelia and insisted on wrapping her in it. She tried to tell him she didn't need it but he ignored her anyway.

"Do as you're told, Amelia," he said, and looked her in the eyes.

"As you command."

He sat down again, pleased to notice the sparkle in her eyes that accompanied her words. Emotionally she appeared to be recovering already. Satisfied that he'd done all he could and wouldn't be needed until his car arrived, Mycroft sat back and closed his eyes. He knew it would appear as if he was napping, but he wanted to go back in his memories and look again at the Thames Barrier area as well as the North Koreans who had ambushed them. Any extra information he could drag up from his memory could be useful.

CHAPTER 10

Amelia fought against the waves of sleep that threatened to roll over her. She felt very warm and snug, wrapped from head to bandaged feet in a blanket and towel. It was a stark contrast from the earlier cold.

Beside her Myron sat and waited for his car to come fetch them both, and, still fidgeting in his own kitchen, the farmer tried to make himself busy, cleaning a speck here and there, and rearranging the counter-top utensils.

This day had been the most eventful of her life but she tried not to think too much about it. While Myron was with her she felt safe and it made it easier to be calm. Throughout the whole abduction, and then in their escape, he had remained stable and constant. It had helped her keep herself going when she'd wanted to just curl up and pretend none of it was happening.

She couldn't decide if the swim had been the worst part or the walk afterwards. While on the boat, she'd known as she was working herself free that no one appeared particularly interested in her and afterwards she'd been buzzed with enough adrenaline she'd functioned without thinking. It wasn't until she'd had to face the cold sea and the threat of nature that fear had found her.

To keep herself going she'd told herself it would impress Myron. Every moment since she'd first been grabbed she'd kept her mind dwelling on what she could gain by being strong. The positive focus had made it easier to keep her emotions from overwhelming her. Although, shock had caught up with her when she'd realised it was over and she was safe again. The desire to cry and wail had welled up inside her so fiercely she'd struggled to contain it. Crying had its place, and she knew she would need to do so at some point soon, but now wasn't the time. She needed to keep quiet and keep focused until the terrorists were stopped.

If she moved too suddenly pain shot through her feet and wrists, so she tried to stay still, but she'd never been much good at it. Sleep would be the best healer but her desire to know what was happening, and help where she could, kept her from succumbing to that idea.

To while away the time she allowed herself to study Myron. So far he'd been very tolerant of her curiosity and interference but she knew his patience would have worn out had she not been the one to free them while on the boat.

When he'd thought they'd missed something he'd assumed the information she'd provided had been wrong above everything else and she'd noticed his anger about having her with him that morning, so she knew he didn't trust her abilities yet. It helped that she'd studied his brother for almost a year but he hadn't really shown her any compassion until she was in the water and struggling to do as he asked. She could only put it down to her self-control and the help she'd rendered several minutes before.

Amelia had expected the bond to be set right back at the beginning when he'd seen the few tears she'd not contained but he'd ignored them and acted like he hadn't noticed. Her only fear now was that he would consider his life and work too dangerous for her. Sebastian had given her those sorts of excuses once, but she'd been persistent enough with him he'd eventually understood she would rather lead a more exciting life.

It was about time she led a life as interesting as the ones she wrote about in her books, even if it meant she had to occasionally swim in the cold sea and walk what felt like miles with bare feet and little on. With any luck the events would help a relationship grow between her and Myron. She couldn't think of much in her conduct in the last twelve hours that could disappoint him.

In the last few days she'd also decided it was time she moved on from her late husband. As much as she'd been devoted to him at the time she didn't want to be alone, and finally felt like she could stride out and face the world again. With this thought, her eyes were drawn to the wedding ring on her finger. If she'd had a pocket to put it in she'd have removed it right then, but she didn't want to lose it. Good memories were attached to it if nothing else.

A knock on the farmhouse door startled her from her thoughts and instantly Myron stood up. Feeling a little like a spare cog she didn't move, but waited for one of the two men to find out who was there.

Relief flooded through her when Daniels came into the kitchen and she could tell the feeling was echoed in the chauffeur. He evidently had a fondness for his employer. A fondness she knew she already shared. In his hands was a small case. Myron took it and disappeared into the downstairs toilet room. While they waited for him to come back the farmer offered Daniels a drink but the chauffeur declined. Amelia suspected he might have wanted to say yes but she knew Myron. He wouldn't appreciate being held up at all once he reappeared.

Daniels came and checked on her instead, asking her a few simple questions. She gave him answers using as few words as she could and felt grateful when he took the hint and stopped asking her.

"Right, time we went. Thank you for the hospitality and you have my apologies for being kept from your bed. We'll leave you now, and as I said earlier, you will be reimbursed," Myron said as soon as he was back in the kitchen. Already he looked back to his normal self, dressed in a smart suit, with his polished shoes and perfectly knotted tie.

After handing the case back to his driver he came towards her and lifted her bundled up body into his arms in such a way that she couldn't even remove her arms to hold onto him. In this state he bore her outside and to his car with Daniels hurrying to beat him to the door.

As soon as she was shut up inside with him she felt the comfort of the familiar wash over her and knew she could allow her body the sleep it craved. While Myron used the extra phone his chauffeur had also thought to bring, Amelia closed her eyes. For a few seconds the gentle drone of his deep voice lingered in her mind but even that couldn't stop her from drifting asleep.

***

As Mycroft finished speaking to the police commissioner he glanced over at Amelia. Still wrapped in the blanket, she'd fallen asleep and now rested with her face turned towards him. Although this wasn't the first time he'd seen her asleep it struck him how peaceful she was. If it wasn't for the bandages there would have been no indication of her ordeal at all.

While staring at her face he phoned his brother, but the call went straight to his answer phone service. He hung up without leaving a message. Sherlock only turned his phone off in the rare circumstances of being out on a case where being disturbed would endanger the success of his solution and that meant he had located the North Koreans and was already hunting them down. By the time Mycroft got back it would likely be over. Even the police commissioner was confident about catching the Russians on the boat.

During the journey, Mycroft ran through the events once more in his head but noticed nothing he hadn't the first time around. He knew it was pointless to try again. The memory became less accurate with each pass through.

Greater London flashed by in a blur while he thought, until the streets in Central London came into focus. About ten minutes away from Baker Street Mycroft received a text from his brother.

North Koreans all taken care of. You'll find them waiting for you at office tomorrow morning. I'll be awake if you want to come discuss it. S

Just as he'd expected, his brother had managed to follow the men and find them. London was safe again, at least for a few more weeks and, if he was lucky, maybe even months. A small amount of guilt plagued him at how caught up in the cross-fire Amelia had been, but Sherlock was the most to blame on that front. He'd summoned her back to London to join in again and she'd not known what she was getting herself into. It occurred to him that she might wish to stop their game herself, now she had some more experience of their lives.

When the car pulled up on Baker Street and Amelia still slept peacefully he decided to leave her there, under the watchful eye of Daniels, while he talked to his brother. He whispered these intentions to his chauffeur and strode inside, omitting to knock as he always did.

Sherlock reposed in his usual armchair with his violin perched nearby. Mycroft could only hope his younger brother didn't play until Mycroft had left.

"Ah, brother of mine, welcome back. I see you are no worse for wear."

"Of course not. I was stabbed, but the wound disappeared long ago." Mycroft sat down opposite. Sherlock opened his mouth to speak but he anticipated the question. "No one saw."

"Good... Where's Amelia?"

"Amelia's in my car, sleeping. How did you catch the

Koreans?"

"It was easy really. If you'd had the opportunity you'd have managed it as well. The lock they removed in the door was done with a very specific cutting device, which had a manufacturing kink. Between that and the footprints I'd found at the lock, it wasn't hard to trace them to a particular road and a quick look at utility bills provided the house number."

"You checked the address before informing the police?"

"Naturally. One can't be too careful with these sorts of criminals."

"It sounds like we're done then. Thank you, brother of mine." Mycroft got up again.

"You're not going to forbid me from seeing Amelia again?" Sherlock stood as well.

"No. Why would I?"

"Because she got hurt. You usually object to us getting civilians hurt, remember. Or is it all right when it's you leading someone into danger?"

"I didn't lead her into danger, Sherlock, don't be ridiculous." Mycroft felt his temperature rise at his brother's line of enquiry. "And it was you, who invited her to join us on Saturday."

"Yes, but it's you who is taking her home with you." Sherlock grinned in the usual smug way when he'd worked out something Mycroft didn't want him to.

"She has nowhere else to go. I'm not leaving her in this filthy flat with you and at this time of night she won't be able to get a room at her usual hotel, even if she could walk well enough to be left by herself. It's the only solution, so I will bear it." He frowned at his brother but Sherlock laughed and sat back down.

"You could send her home to Bath. You have a driver who would take her there and see she got inside. Or you could take her to a hospital. Admit it, you like her. You've had to wait a hundred years to find someone, but you like her."

"Only in the way a child likes a toy and plays with it until something bigger and better comes along or he grows bored with it. She's less dull than most."

"If you say so, Mycroft. Do ensure our secret remains that way, won't you?" Sherlock picked up his pipe and the nearby pouch of tobacco, while Mycroft frowned. His younger brother was enjoying quoting his own warnings back at him. With a roll of his eyes, Mycroft decided they'd talked enough.

"Good evening, brother of mine," he said and went back to the car, taking Amelia's small suitcase with him. He got back to the car to find she still slept.

As Daniels drove them both back to Mycroft's home he thought about the next code he would set her. After all her emotional restraint and cooperation he decided she deserved one last code to unravel, even if he did decide to heed his own words of advice afterwards and cut her off to keep her from being harmed.

Amelia mumbled in her sleep as he carried her into his house and up the stairs to the guest bedroom. Less than a minute later his housekeeper was at his side, fussing over the injured, yet sleeping, woman. The guest room had never been used before, in that regard Sherlock was right, and even his housekeeper knew this was an unexpected change.

With a great deal of patience and a good measure of frowns, Mycroft managed to calm his excited staff and get Amelia curled up under the covers so she'd be warm enough until morning. He then placed her suitcase and handbag somewhere where she'd notice it and ushered everyone back downstairs. On the way to his study he noticed the day's paper on the small table in the hall. Right in full view was a Sudoku puzzle. Within seconds Mycroft knew what he wanted his next message to be contained in and went to his laptop to design Amelia a sudoku with the numbers one to twenty-five in it.

He printed out a grid of twenty five squares by twenty five so he could write in the starting numbers for her and an extra one for him to work backwards from. An hour later he had a sudoku for her to complete and he highlighted the boxes of numbers that would make up her message. It consisted of just two words but he didn't think she'd find it too difficult to work out with a little trial and error.

18		24		10	2	4	17	6					22		7	3				5		14		
	9	13		8	7			15	■		16			25	4	2	24		21	22				6
15	19			16		14	18		21	8	2		3	10			11	9	24			25		23
5		4			1	8			25	21	10	20		23	14					11	17			9
20	23				9	16	12		19		11				18	17				15	2■			
21		5				25		14	1	2	12	16		8		18		17		4	11			
		22	19	3		18		■			11	24	17	2		4		■	23					
	20				15				25	21				12		14		22	24	1				
	23	12	18			3		16	22			10	1		21	24	20	13				2		
16			11	12	24		13			3		4	6	22	14				10	7		18		
1	■	16	5		11	24			3		19			6		22	9	4						
3		18			21	8		6			12							11	9	23				
			9	18	22	3			4				13		5	12	1							
	2	14	23					13		1		■	15	11					16				5
			9	2	10		7			15	8		23	19			12	6				14		
14		7	16			9	12	24	17		6			20		23	25	8						19
25			24	21	22	17			18	2			13	19	1			23	14	10				
2	6	8		4		16					19	21	■			7			■			17		
			13			23		10	3	1	25					6		16	15	24				
	18	1		5		19		7		16	15	3	20	14		21					11			4
	24	10		■		7	16				5		19	9	12	14						4	13	
23		19	17				1	6		18	15	21	13			25	8		12				11	
6		15		2	13	25		10	4		17	1	11		5	3		9				23	22	
9			11	14		12	22	23	6			13			17			19	7		1	10		
	21		1			17	14		12				■		23	20	22	6	25		18			3

As soon as it was complete he tucked it into an envelope and put it to one side. In the morning, once Amelia was awake and ready to be taken back to her own home, he could sneak it into her belongings so she found it when she unpacked.

Mycroft knew it would be kind to let her stay a little longer but everyone's reactions to his accommodation of her had put him off that idea. It wouldn't be good to have other people think she was more to him than the student she'd requested to be. When it no longer amused him to create challenges for her he wouldn't hesitate to cut her out of his life, if he even continued past this final test. At the moment he was seriously considering letting this be her last challenge as a reward for her conduct in the last twenty-four hours.

As he made his way to his own bedroom to sleep he passed the door to her guest room and stopped. Unable to resist the temptation, he checked she was still sleeping soundly before carrying on to the master bedroom, the only room in the house that had kept the entire original style and decoration he'd put into it just over a hundred years earlier.

While he removed his suit he realised he'd been a key part of the government on and off for over a hundred years and, just like today, had guided the British government and its agents to keep the country and its interests safe.

He glanced in the mirror on his dresser. He didn't look a day older, and he never would.

EPILOGUE

Frustration filled Amelia. She'd been back in Bath for two weeks since her kidnapping and subsequent time with Myron Holmes, and she still hadn't worked out the next coded message.

The massive sudoku he'd given her had been a nightmare to figure out. Not particularly because it was difficult. The logic was the same as the normal sized ones, just with more numbers and a lot more options to keep track of. But the time it took to explore all those options was very large.

She'd wanted to solve it quickly and have an excuse to message him again but, with the re-writes of her novel and everything that went with her career, she'd not put the last numbers into the puzzle until today.

Now she had a set of ten numbers to try and make a message with and didn't really know where to start. She didn't know what order they were meant to be in, let alone what they corresponded to. All she knew was that the numbers 2, 8, and 21 both occurred twice.

18	11	24	25	10	2	4	17	6	23	12	9	1	22	15	7	3	8	20	21	5	19	14	13	16
12	9	13	1	8	7	10	11	15	19	18	5	16	14	17	25	4	2	24	23	21	22	3	20	6
15	19	17	22	16	5	14	18	20	21	8	2	6	7	3	10	12	13	11	9	24	4	25	1	23
5	2	4	3	7	1	8	13	22	25	21	10	20	24	23	14	19	6	16	15	18	11	17	12	9
20	23	14	21	6	3	9	16	12	24	19	4	11	13	25	5	18	17	1	22	10	7	15	2	8
21	13	5	9	24	10	20	25	19	22	14	1	2	12	16	23	8	3	18	7	17	6	4	11	15
7	14	22	19	3	6	18	1	21	5	15	13	9	11	24	17	2	10	4	20	12	23	8	16	25
8	20	6	10	17	23	15	4	2	9	7	18	25	21	5	16	11	19	12	13	14	3	22	24	1
4	15	23	12	18	14	7	3	11	16	22	8	17	19	10	1	6	25	21	24	20	13	9	5	2
16	1	25	2	11	12	24	8	13	17	20	3	23	4	6	22	14	9	15	5	19	10	7	21	18
1	21	16	5	12	17	11	24	14	13	3	23	19	25	18	6	7	22	9	4	15	20	2	8	10
3	10	18	15	13	16	1	21	8	4	5	6	22	2	12	20	25	24	17	14	11	9	23	19	7
19	8	20	6	9	18	22	23	3	15	11	14	4	10	7	2	13	16	5	12	1	24	21	25	17
17	7	2	14	23	19	6	12	25	20	13	21	24	1	9	8	15	11	10	3	4	18	16	22	5
24	25	11	4	22	9	2	10	5	7	17	20	15	16	8	21	1	23	19	18	13	12	6	3	14
14	22	7	16	15	21	13	2	9	12	24	17	10	6	11	3	20	4	23	25	8	1	5	18	19
25	3	9	24	21	22	17	15	4	18	2	7	12	5	13	19	16	1	8	11	23	14	10	6	20
2	6	8	20	4	24	16	14	1	11	9	19	21	23	22	18	5	15	7	10	3	25	13	17	12
11	17	12	13	19	20	23	5	10	3	1	25	8	18	4	9	22	14	6	2	16	15	24	7	21
10	18	1	23	5	25	19	6	7	8	16	15	3	20	14	12	24	21	13	17	22	2	11	9	4
22	24	10	18	25	8	21	7	16	2	23	11	5	3	19	15	9	12	14	1	6	17	20	4	13
23	16	19	17	20	4	3	9	24	1	6	22	18	15	21	13	10	7	25	8	2	5	12	14	11
6	12	15	7	2	13	25	20	18	10	4	24	14	17	1	11	21	5	3	16	9	8	19	23	22
9	5	3	11	14	15	12	22	23	6	25	16	13	8	20	4	17	18	2	19	7	21	1	10	24
13	4	21	8	1	11	5	19	17	14	10	12	7	9	2	24	23	20	22	6	25	16	18	15	3

After several hours of trying random numbers she grabbed the phone Myron had given her and sent him a message.

Struggling with your latest challenge. I've solved the puzzle but not sure what the numbers mean, can I get a hint?

Her stomach churned as she waited for him to reply, but nothing came through within the first ten minutes so she went back to trying to work out the numbers by herself. She couldn't be sure that he would even reply. Myron could be busy or might be deliberately ignoring her until she'd worked it out. She wouldn't know for sure unless she solved this challenge.

Two hours later her phone chimed to let her know she had a message. Her breath caught in her throat as she picked it up to read the response.

No. You're my pet for my amusement. I'm not going to do it for you.

She sighed. It felt better to have him reply and gave her confidence that he'd not ignore her messages, but still didn't get her any closer to understanding. While she sat on her sofa, she remembered an old Bible verse that a woman had said to Jesus when he'd told her something similar. Something about dogs getting scraps from their master's tables.

She leapt up and hurried to her bookshelf to find the tattered old Bible someone had given her once. She scanned through the gospels until she came to the right verse, but instead of just giving him the quote she decided to set him a code to follow and work out instead.

9 780340 722190, 982, 2, 30-32

Amelia grinned and looked at the time. Somehow it was already past midnight. It would be interesting to see how long it took him to figure out he had the ISBN code from the back of the book, the page number, column number and line numbers for the quote. Just in case it didn't work she went back to her numbers to try and figure out his message to her.

Less than five minutes later her phone went off again. Her jaw dropped. He'd worked it out faster than she'd have thought possible.

'Your request is granted.' But only for code 3 – M

She bit her lip and frowned. If the message contained a hint, she couldn't see it so she waited another few minutes

The Hundred Year Wait

hoping a second text would follow, but nothing came through.

After making herself a cup of tea she looked at the text again. The hint must already be there. As she noticed how he'd ended it she could have hit herself. 3 became an M which meant 2 was likely to be an L. Assuming the alphabet was in order like the first time she turned all her numbers into letters, she had her answer.

Clever Girl

Amelia couldn't decide whether to laugh or get angry. All that work and effort for such a short message, and she knew exactly what condescending tone he'd have said it in as well. It was a message meant to irritate anyone who didn't understand Myron and his nature.

It didn't take her long to decide it was funny. Most importantly she'd solved another task and hopefully he'd had a moment of enjoyment from her indirect beg for more information. Although she'd been reluctant to refer to herself as a pet again, especially a dog, she knew it would amuse him given the way an owner might say clever girl to a dog learning to do tricks. She tapped out a response that would let him know she'd worked out the answer while also letting him know it hadn't annoyed her.

Apparently I'm rather smart, and also young enough to be thought of as a girl.

Only a few seconds later she had a reply.

Well done, you've successfully jumped through hoop one. The next stage of your lessons will begin soon. And you shouldn't be drinking caffeine at this time of night. Go to bed, Amelia, you're going to need the sleep.

A grin spread across her face as she rushed to do as he said.

THE END

The Unexpected Coincidence

CHAPTER 1

Mycroft took another sip of his tea from the delicate china cup Mrs Wintern had provided. It would have tasted perfect if it wasn't for the lingering smell of formaldehyde. Sherlock's flat never smelt normal at the best of times, but his younger brother had a case and was experimenting on some severed body parts.

"It's not that bad," Sherlock said, disturbing him from his thoughts.

"What's not?"

"Having to look over a crime scene for yourself."

"Apparently not. You seem to enjoy it," Mycroft replied, not sure whether to be relieved that his younger brother hadn't read his current thoughts or annoyed that Sherlock had figured out the real reason he was there.

It had been a week since Mycroft had realised his own people were too incompetent to do what he needed, and still he hadn't gone himself. Coming to see Sherlock was always his last resort. Most of the time his younger brother was only too eager to go take a look at a crime scene or evaluate a suspect, but Mycroft had found him in the middle of his own case.

Since Mycroft's abduction along with Amelia Jones,

Sherlock had changed his tune a little. His younger brother seemed to think it was good for Mycroft to be in the thick of the action. He, however, felt as he always had, that it was far too much effort when he could get someone else to do it for him.

"You could get Amelia to do it." Sherlock plonked himself down in the armchair opposite Mycroft. He had a smug grin on his face. He put his cup down on the nearby tray to buy himself a few seconds to compose his voice.

"And why would I ask her? She's hardly suitable for the task."

"She'd be perfect. I've taught her plenty, and I'm sure she'd love to help you catch the people who took both you and her. No doubt the event was more traumatic for her than you, even with your aversion to getting physically involved."

"Which is exactly why I would never involve her further. The last thing I need is a woman's emotions clouding a delicate situation. And besides, I've not seen her since. It's not as if we're acquainted." Mycroft rolled his eyes and hoped his brother would drop the subject. He didn't want to talk about Amelia. Every time she was brought up he ran the risk of giving something away about their arrangement, and it was bad enough that Amelia spoke to Sherlock often.

"Then I can ask her. I'm sure she won't mind." Sherlock grinned and got up again to go back to the kitchen table, which was covered in laboratory equipment.

"No, she won't have the time. She starts another book tour tomorrow and they have her signing all over the country. It seems the new book is a big hit."

"So you've been keeping an eye on her then," Sherlock said as he stared down the microscope lens.

"Of course. She's an acquaintance of yours. For her safety, I thought it best."

"Perfect," Sherlock muttered under his breath right before taking the specimen out from under the light. "Although it has nothing to do with the novel, does it, brother of mine?

The one she re-wrote for you. I suppose you feel she ought to be thanking you, considering how well it's selling."

"Nothing of the sort. I only know that part because she seems to have charmed Daniels." Mycroft let out an exasperated sigh. "Every time I come back to the car he's got one of her books in his hands."

"Well, she is very charming. But if we're done here... My case is waiting and I really have a lot to do." Sherlock put his hand out towards the door and gave his brother another brief smile.

It was fake, and Mycroft knew he'd outstayed his welcome. With another sigh that was a last attempt to sway Sherlock into helping, he got up and nodded his parting.

"Have a good day, brother of mine, and try not to cause an international incident," Sherlock said as Mycroft was part way through the door. He rolled his eyes and ignored the jibe. It was meant to annoy him, and he wasn't going to give his brother the satisfaction of seeing his success. But it wasn't the only part of their discussion that irked him. Sherlock had focused on Amelia much more than Mycroft was comfortable with, and even worse, he was going to have to look over the house himself. He'd gone to Baker Street for nothing.

When he stepped outside the sun was shining, which helped to take the chill off the late November air, but the wind had a bite to it that reminded everyone it wouldn't be long until Christmas. Not wanting to be out in such cold when wearing nothing but his favourite suit, he took several quick steps to the car and the door Daniels already had open for him.

"Back home, sir?" the chauffeur asked once he was back behind the wheel.

"No, Moffat Road in Thornton Heath. Number eighty-nine. And try to avoid traffic. I want this dealt with as swiftly as possible."

"Of course, sir."

Mycroft gazed out the window as his driver did his best to

wind through the traffic and ensure it didn't take too long to get to their destination. For a few minutes, he let the details he picked up from the passers-by go through his mind, noticing a young woman evidently having an affair and two teenagers who were about to try and rob a local shop. He knew they wouldn't succeed, or he might have got out his phone and sent a quick text to the chief of police.

When the people in the streets failed to keep his interest, he re-focused his thoughts to business. Since his little adventure with Amelia, when both of them had been abducted from the Thames barrier in Silvertown, he'd been trying to track down the terrorist group responsible. It didn't make it easier that the North Koreans and Russians appeared to be working together on this.

Of all the countries causing concern, they were two of the worst. Russia was making threatening moves in Eastern Europe, and North Korea was adapting to its younger leader. Like all people who were brought up knowing they would run a country, the Korean was a spoilt brat used to getting his own way. But all this knowledge didn't help in finding the terrorists who'd tried to flood the capital city. There was no guarantee they were acting on orders and were not simply some extreme group of mercenaries who happened to have aligned goals. Whoever they were, they had plenty of funding from somewhere.

The yacht they'd held him and Amelia on hadn't been small, and they had moved house twice since Mycroft had become aware of them. Each time, they'd sent someone into an estate agent with the deposit and several months' rent in cash. On top of that, the first house Sherlock had found had been left in such a hurry that there was technology and money left behind. Most of the computers had been wiped clean, but Mycroft had found enough information to know it was the right place. The police had completely bungled the attempt at catching everyone, alerting them to their detection and giving them time to run.

He'd been praised for saving London, despite Amelia being involved, but since then the trail had been difficult to follow. Little head-way was gained until his brother helped him track a lead to a second address. The address Mycroft was now being driven to.

Over half an hour after setting off, Daniels pulled the car over to the side of Moffat road right in front of the driveway of house number eighty-nine. It looked worse than Sherlock had said. The drive had once been bricked over, but areas had sunk while the bricks themselves had worn and crumbled. Weeds grew up in the cracks, and a large pile of rubbish filled one corner of the front yard.

As Daniels opened the car door Mycroft was assaulted by the smell of the rotting refuse. He wrinkled up his nose in disgust and hurried over to the front door. Before he made the six steps to the porch, he'd managed to fish his skeleton keys from his pocket. Pretty much every door in London opened to these.

Once inside, he paused in the hallway and surveyed the area. It smelt musty but nothing that opening a window wouldn't fix. There were a few sparse furnishings in the living room, and he expected to find the rest of the house in a similar state. A couch with old cushions sat near a coffee table. No television or music player of any kind, and no lamp shade.

The curtains were drawn in every room, but all the doors were open everywhere, including up the stairs as far as he could see to his left. Thankfully, the material hanging over the windows was thin and enough light from the shining sun still bled through into the rooms. So he could see the detail he might need, he pulled a small torch from his jacket pocket and shone it at the floor in a path to the sofa.

The carpet was yellowing and threadbare in several places, but traces of dirt from some kind of boot still lingered near the very edge of the sofa. Mycroft pulled an empty envelope and a small spatula from another pocket and scraped up some of the residue before sealing the packet and tucking it safely back. He could have his brother analyse the make-up of it and tell him where it had come from.

A glance at the sofa let him know the occupants had put a plastic covering over it. There would be no evidence for him to find. Although he didn't expect anything in the kitchen to aid his search, he put his head through the doorway all the same and looked over the appliances.

A fridge and freezer combo stood on the far wall. He knew it would be empty but he went over to it and checked anyway. On his way back to the living room he opened the oven and the few cupboards, but they were unused and dusty from neglect.

He sighed wishing this sort of process was quicker but Mycroft knew he had to be thorough. After decades of sending his little brother to crime scenes he couldn't do a worse job.

With a sigh, Mycroft padded up the carpeted stairs, using his torch to scan important locations as he went, such as the bannister and the walls at ankle height. Not even a scuff mark appeared beneath the bright light.

Each of the three bedrooms contained a single or double bed frame with a clean, barely used mattress. None of them had a single stain or blemish, although he noticed the surfaces weren't perfectly even. They had been slept on, but just like the couch, the occupants had protected them from the transference of any dirt, sweat or substance.

He took his time to look over the floor around each one, hoping to find a hair or flake of skin, but he could spot neither. The bathroom was equally as unhelpful. The shower looked like it had been hosed down and the faint smell of bleach lingered in the air. Whoever was in charge of these men, he had them being far more careful than terrorists of their type usually were.

After two hours of combing the house for clues, Mycroft gave up and headed back to his car. Other than the small scraping of dirt, he'd found nothing. It made him feel a little better about the competence of his own men, as they'd reported a similar story, but it didn't solve his problem. Somehow, the terrorist cell was staying one step ahead of him.

Once he was on the way back to his house, Mycroft thought over everything he knew and had done in response to the recent threat. He had under-cover operatives in Ukraine, Russia and South Korea, as well as several working on the case in London, but so far none of them had found anything useful. He knew if he sent his brother to one of the countries the information might be found immediately, but the British best weren't normally so ineffective. He also knew his brother disliked leaving London almost as much as Mycroft disliked being anywhere but the house or club.

He sighed and knew he would have to do some more digging himself. At least until Sherlock snapped out of whatever notion he'd got himself into over Amelia. She wasn't ready to help with the sort of work he needed - that was something he knew even she would admit.

By the time the car arrived at his house, grey clouds had pulled in and covered over the sun sufficiently to bring an early evening. It would rain, something that had happened surprisingly little for November in England.

"Have this taken to my brother," Mycroft said as he got out the car and gave the envelope to Daniels. "Be careful with the contents."

Daniels nodded and tucked it into his own pocket, ensuring it remained the same way up. It might take a day or two for Sherlock to get around to the experiment, and then another few days for him to bother passing the information on to Mycroft, but it was some progress.

Once inside, Mycroft went straight to his study. He was late for his afternoon tea, but the usual tray with a teapot full of hot water was there. The biscuits weren't. He clamped his mouth shut over the desire to yell for some, knowing he had told his housekeeper not to bring them for a few weeks. Although his supernatural abilities gave him a younger man's metabolism, he still had to be careful with what he ate. If he wanted to keep to a healthy weight he needed to manage his diet.

When he pulled open the nearest desk drawer, he noticed the thud as his spare mobile phone jerked against the edge. The light on the bottom flashed green to let him know it had a message. He frowned.

Only Amelia Jones had the number, and it was quite a large coincidence for her to be contacting him today if his brother hadn't followed through on his threat and told her about his difficulties. As he grabbed the device, he started to think of all the ways he would punish Sherlock for the betrayal. When he managed to pull the text up on screen, the lines on his forehead deepened even further.

Stage 2?

Her question gave nothing away but impatience, and definitely didn't give him an indication of why she'd decided to message him now.

Is your lack of patience the only reason you messaged? I won't reward impatience.

Mycroft pressed the send button before he thought that his message sounded angry, but he wouldn't apologise for it. If she chose to message him because of something Sherlock had said to her, it would only fuel the temper that already simmered. It didn't take long for her to respond. He flicked the screen on again, hoping she had a good answer for him.

I'm sorry. I didn't mean to sound impatient. I just noticed that it has been ten weeks since you last sent me a message. As always, I await your instructions.

He exhaled and considered the reply. If Sherlock had prompted her, she'd have said. Lying to him wasn't something she'd risk when she was so eager to learn from him.

After leaning back in his chair he thought over her request. Ten weeks was a long time to leave her without a lesson of some kind, but he'd had little time to think about it since their last communication. It would take little effort from him to begin the second stage of her teaching, and he knew just the person to start her off. He used his main phone to send instructions to one of his agents before typing a one-word reply and sending it to Amelia.

Tomorrow.

CHAPTER 2

Darkness surrounded Amelia when she opened her eyes, and the dull ache of her head soon let her know that it was still early. The combination of a message from Myron, her nerves at starting a brand new book tour, and the rain that had only stopped in the early hours of the morning, had prevented her from getting much sleep.

With a groan, she glanced at the bedside clock. It was a few minutes before six, but she wouldn't be able to get back to sleep. Her mind already whirred through the many questions and worries she had.

After rubbing the dust from her eyes, she turned off her alarm and wrapped herself in her favourite dressing gown. She padded through to the rest of the ground floor flat and her large open-plan kitchen, dining area and living room. Off to the far corner, the front door stood like a silent green sentinel in the ochre walls.

Immediately her eyes were drawn to the large white envelope on the mat. With a raised eyebrow, she wandered over to it. The postman wouldn't come for several more hours yet, and only her name appeared on the outside in a blocky but neat script. Given Myron's message, she wondered if it might be from him, but it wasn't his handwriting, and when she flipped it over there was no familiar seal holding the envelope shut. She did notice three large splotches of what must have been rain water.

Still not opening it, she wandered to the window and peeked out of a gap in the curtain. It wasn't raining and didn't look like it had been for at least an hour or so. Whoever had delivered this letter had done it at a very early time of the morning. She searched her memory of the previous night while she'd been tossing and turning in bed, but she didn't think she'd heard the letterbox clatter shut after the envelope would have been pushed through. Given the lack of sleep, she was fairly certain she'd have noticed it, and that meant it had been posted some time between one and five-thirty that morning. She shivered, not sure she wanted to open it and find out why.

To put the moment off for a few minutes, she decided to make herself a cup of tea first. She took the envelope back towards the kitchen area and placed it on the counter while she boiled the kettle and prepared the teapot.

Once she had the warm mug of hot tea in her hands, she still couldn't quite bring herself to open the letter. She stared at it while leaning against the island behind her.

It wasn't the first time she'd had strange letters from fans, and it was probably just another of those, but it was the first to be delivered by hand to her door, and the first to arrive at such an odd time. That alone made her more wary of it.

Knowing she couldn't put it off any longer, Amelia put her drink to one side and lifted the envelope up. The publishers had given her advice the first time she'd had one, and she followed it now, keeping her fingers near the edges to help preserve any fingerprints the writer might have left. She turned it over and used a knife from the cutlery drawer to slice open the flap.

After covering her fingers with a piece of cling film and making an improvised glove, she pulled the letter out. It was folded in half with no writing on the back and no distinguishing features of any kind. She sniffed at it as she brought it slowly towards her, but no particular scent came off it either. With nothing else to do, she opened the paper to read the letter.

Amelia,

I've been a fan of yours for some time now and have had the pleasure of meeting you several times. You're far lovelier than any of the other authors I've met, and I'd love to get to know you better. I am just like your character, Dalton. It's like you already know me and the way I think, and I know you like him. You've said many times that he was your favourite character.

I know you'll remember me from your last book tour. I came to several of the places you visited and I keep the photos of us from the Waterstones in Trowbridge in my wallet. I'm so pleased that you're going on tour again. I've noticed you don't write in public places very often. It's a shame. If you did, I could join you sometimes and help. I know I'd make a great muse when you're writing about Dalton.

Your biggest fan.

Amelia exhaled. This wasn't quite as sweet as some of the others she'd received. After tucking it back into the envelope, she pulled off the cling film and hurried over to her laptop. Something like this would be best dealt with by her publishers. They'd know what she ought to do in response.

Her hands shook as she typed out a quick message to them, letting them know the rough details and that she had no idea who it could be. The last time she'd been in Trowbridge to sign books was several months ago, and no one came to mind that had stood out from the usual crowd. It was also fairly common for her fans to come to more than one of her signings when she did lots of stops in one area.

By the time she was done, she realised she needed to

shower and dress or she'd be late for her first location of the day. Despite being on edge because of the letter, she couldn't let it put her off when the tour was only just beginning. It also might give her an opportunity to spot who this letter sender was. If he was too scary or obsessed, she could always tell Myron and Sebastian about it. Both of them would know what to do.

Comforted by the thought of her mentor and friend helping, she went about her morning routine as if nothing had happened. Only tiredness made her day any different, and she was a couple of minutes late walking into Bath's biggest bookshop.

Every time she started a tour she insisted it was her first location, and the fans were used to this. Despite it being early in the day, a long line of people wound inside the shop floor and then out the door and down the street. She smiled and waved as she normally would, apologising for being late to the fans nearest and the staff who were already helping organise the large queue.

It didn't take long for the manager, a greying, softly spoken man, to come over to her. They hugged and he kissed her cheek before guiding her to the familiar table in its usual location. She apologised for being late once more before stepping into her usual spot. Instantly, the normality of being in this shop made her feel better. Starting here always made it easier to go from being alone to being surrounded by people.

"Amelia!" a recognisable low voice called from near the door. She glanced in the direction of the heckle and saw two of her friends standing in the long line: James and David. They weren't too far back, but she knew it would take her quite a few minutes to get to them. With a grin, she tried to wave them over and start with them, but they wouldn't move from their position. It wouldn't be fair of her to give them preferential treatment, but she rarely let that stop her if she thought it was the right thing to do.

Instead, she had to work her way through to them,

signing, making small talk and posing for photos until they were in front of her. James launched himself at her and gave her a bear-hug so tight it squeezed what little air her corseted waist-coat allowed into her lungs right back out again. She chuckled as he put her back down onto her feet, and his friend then repeated the same action.

"We know you get nervous about the first few days of signings, so we thought we'd come be moral support. We're totally your biggest fans," James said, gushing the last sentence in an exaggerated manner.

"We even have books for you to sign." David thrust a bag under her nose and opened it so she could see two newly purchased copies of her most recent release.

"You know you guys didn't have to buy them. I'd have given you signed copies if you'd said you wanted them."

"But we're your biggest fans, remember?" James winked. "We have to pay for them."

She laughed and hugged them both again.

"How are you both doing?" she asked as she took the books from them to sign.

"You know us, we're working hard." David smiled "We've almost finished renovating the house. We'll have a proper welcome party when you're back."

"You had better. I want to see what you've both been up to for the last few months."

A cough from off to one side drew Amelia's attention from her friends. A guy in his thirties, wearing a large coat and thick-rimmed glasses, was looking expectantly at her. In his arms was what appeared to be most of her twelve published books, with several of the more recent ones in hardback. They looked heavy.

Pretending that nothing had caught her off stride, she grabbed her pen and scrawled her name across the inside title page of the books in front of her and passed them back to her friends.

"I'll let you both know when I'm back, and we'll go for

drinks."

They nodded and waved goodbye as they left the shop. Hoping she'd not annoyed the geek who appeared to be her next fan, she gave him her warmest smile.

"Sorry about keeping you waiting," she said as she held out her hands for him to pass her all the books. He hesitated and passed them to her so awkwardly that their arms and hands tangled and the top book went thudding to the floor, narrowly missing her toes.

"Oh gosh, I'm so sorry," he said, turning red.

"Don't worry, they must have been heavy for you to hold for so long."

"And I'm sorry, I didn't mean to hurry you with your friends. I... I have to get back to my mother. She has multiple sclerosis. My brother's with her, but I said I wouldn't be long."

Amelia nodded and picked up the book that was on the floor for him. In his awkward state he'd left it there, his hands wringing together in front of him. She placed the whole pile on the table she'd been provided with.

"Well, why don't I get these signed as swiftly as possible and then you can get back to her? Are they yours or hers?" She pointed to the books when he looked at her blankly.

"Oh, they're mine," he said and grabbed one to open it to the right page for her. "I like to read when she has her afternoon nap. Your books are so exciting. I often imagine I'm Dalton."

Amelia almost dropped the pen. The letter had mentioned the same character, and this fan definitely looked like the type to obsess over something.

"What's your name?" she asked, hoping he hadn't noticed her surprise.

"Thomas, uh, Guy. I'm Guy Thomas." He blinked rapidly while he spoke and continued to rub his hands together in the same odd pattern, almost as if he was constantly washing them.

Amelia Price

"Guy's a good name," she replied, focusing on the books to give him time to recover from his embarrassment. He wasn't the first socially awkward person to come to a signing of hers, and she knew he wouldn't be the last.

A few minutes later she'd signed all of them and stacked them back up in a neat pile.

"Do you want a photo?" Amelia asked when he went to pick them up again.

"I... uh... my phone doesn't have a camera. It's one of the old ones," he said and his cheeks coloured once more.

"Well, maybe another time then. Have a good day, Guy, and say hello to your mother from me."

"I will, thank you. Thank you." He backed away, a smile broadening across his face until he almost tripped over his own feet.

Not wanting to embarrass the poor man further, she quickly averted her eyes and homed in on the next person in the queue. A more elderly woman, with what appeared to be her daughter. Thankfully, they only had three books between them.

The rest of the morning flew by in a haze of faces and names she didn't have a hope of remembering. But one stuck in her mind. Guy was strange, and his allusion to Dalton put her on edge. No matter how hard she tried, she couldn't get his awkward meeting of her out of her head. It kept most of her focus over lunch, making it difficult for her to talk to the staff while they gave her an hour for lunch in the break room with them.

Whenever she spent so long in one shop she tried to give the workers some time to talk to her as well. It was a way she could thank them for their help in making the signings go well, but she was too preoccupied. She felt guilty for her behaviour when her hour was over and she'd barely said two words to the new guy, even after he'd introduced himself as a big fan. Her remorse grew even worse when she realised she couldn't remember his name either. It might have begun with a k, but even that wasn't a detail she was sure of.

The afternoon went better and was less of a blur by the time she stopped. Her wrist ached from spending so much time signing, but for the first time, there were people who were still waiting. Normally, she kept going until the queue ran out and then had a few slower hours when she signed books as people walked in with them, but she had to leave the store at four in the afternoon to get to Birmingham and check into her hotel on time.

Amelia frowned and tried to think of some way the people still waiting could get what they wanted. As an idea formed in her mind, she looked around for the manager.

"I've got to go, but could you collect the name and address of anyone who still hasn't had a book signed and keep the information for me. I'll have them all sent a signed bookplate when I get the opportunity to."

"That's a wonderful idea. I'll get Kevin on it right away."

"Brilliant. I'll pick it up when I'm home."

She smiled and said goodbye to everyone within earshot before rushing towards the door. A tour company that specialised in arranging signings for authors had already sent around the car that would take her to Tamworth. With a sigh of relief, she slipped into the back and noticed the glass was tinted, to hide her from the watching eyes outside.

Sleepiness crept over her as the driver ate up the miles along the M5. She woke up with a start as the car pulled into the hotel parking lot.

"We're here, Miss Jones," the driver said, glancing at her through the rear-view mirror.

"Wonderful, thank you. And please, call me Amelia," she replied and stifled a yawn.

The driver helped her carry her bags to the foyer, where the hotel staff took over.

"See you tomorrow," she said and smiled at the driver. He nodded and waved before walking away. Wherever he was going, he didn't seem to be staying in the hotel with her. She hoped that he wasn't sleeping in the car at his age. He didn't look to be more than a few years off retirement. The wedding ring on his finger had also told her that he was likely to have a family waiting for him somewhere. Sebastian would have been proud of her for noticing at least something about him.

"Oh," she said aloud, remembering that Myron had told her stage two would begin sometime that day. There wasn't much of the day left. The receptionist raised her eyebrows at Amelia's outburst but she didn't explain and the woman didn't ask, handing her the keycard to her room instead.

Still feeling tired, Amelia didn't bother to go to the dining room and have dinner first, but went straight to her room. The publisher was picking up the bill, so they could pay the little bit extra it cost to have her evening meal in her room.

After ordering, she unpacked the few bits and pieces she'd need for the night and her clothes for the following day to hang them somewhere they wouldn't get creased. It helped keep her awake while she waited, something she found she needed more than she ought to.

A knock on the door let her know her room service was there.

"Come in," she yelled, in the middle of putting her toiletries in the bathroom.

When she walked back into the bedroom with its small sitting area and couch by a medium sized television, the waiter was laying out what she'd ordered on the small table.

"A letter arrived for you as well, so I brought it up from reception."

"Brilliant, thank you." She handed him a few coins as he gave her the envelope. With a smile, he left her to her food and the letter she assumed would be from Myron, but as she bothered to look at the envelope, she realised the name wasn't in his handwriting. Just like the letter on her doormat that morning, this one had a blocky script that was nothing like her mentor's.

Amelia sat down heavily on the sofa and stared at it. A

second letter in so short a space of time was a bad sign, especially given that her publisher hadn't replied to her email about the first one yet. She shivered and did her best to open this one without the ease of tools she'd had in her kitchen the previous time. She used the butter knife they'd given her to go with her bread roll and pulled the letter out, covering her fingers with her jacket sleeve. A small jewellery pouch came with it.

Amelia,

I'm sorry if I made you feel awkward today. I didn't mean the declarations of my affection towards you to make your day harder. It was strange that you pretended you didn't know me when we met again, but I know you must have been worried about showing favouritism in front of the others. Especially after those two men interrupted you and took up so much of your time.

I'm not sure I liked how familiar they were with you, even if they are gay. They hugged you like they were your lovers. I'm sure you wouldn't debase yourself with men like them, however. I can only say I was relieved when you moved on to the rest of your fans and got rid of them.

Let me know if you want to meet up some time soon and have coffee, or perhaps even dinner together while you're on tour. I've taken some time off to be able to meet up with you and I've also included a token of my affection. I remember you tweeting at some point that you liked penguins. Wear them sometime in the next few days and I'm sure I'll notice them.

Your devoted fan.

With trembling hands, Amelia put the letter down on the coffee table and turned her attention to the small blue velvet bag. She opened it with her sleeves again and tipped the contents onto the wooden surface. Two silver penguin earrings fell out.

Leaving them there, Amelia got to her feet and paced back and forth. Her whole body was shaking despite the warmth of the room. Given the content of the message, she was pleased she'd opted to have dinner in her room, but the writer had known where she was staying and sounded like he was going to follow her from place to place.

After fishing her phone from her handbag, Amelia navigated to her editor's number and started the call. This late it was possible that Shane had gone home, but she could hope he was working late. If not she'd leave him a message.

"Hello?" Shane said after only three rings.

"Hiya, it's Amelia. I think I may have a bit of a problem."

"What's up? Are you all right?" Concern for her radiated out of every word and she could almost hear him sitting forward to listen. Under her breath, she thanked the room that she had such a caring editor.

"I had a bit of a strange letter posted through my letterbox in the early hours of this morning and I'm a bit concerned about the guy who wrote it."

"Yeah, I got your email. I assumed it wouldn't be much to worry about with you not being there for a few weeks."

"I just got another letter. And this time there was a gift with it. And it was hand-delivered, with details of my signing today. He says I saw him today and thinks I pretended not to know him."

"Slow down, Amelia. Why don't you read me the letters?"

"I don't have the first one. I left it at home."

"All right, tell me what you can remember and then read me this second one. Let's see if we can figure out a little more about this guy and if he's really a threat to you. It's not the first time you've had strange letters. We've dealt with them all in the past." His voice remained calm and steady, and by the time Shane had finished speaking Amelia also felt calmer. She sat back down again and closed her eyes to picture the first letter.

"That doesn't sound too bad," Shane said.

"No, it doesn't by itself."

"All right, so read me this second one."

She did as he asked and then waited for him to comment. Reading it again made her feel even worse, and it took all her composure to wait for Shane to speak.

"Okay, that does sound a little worse than normal. Why don't you take a photo of what you have there and email it to me along with all the other information you know. Things like when you got the letters. I'll look over everything and see if we can get you some extra security."

"All right. What should I do in the meantime?"

"Get some sleep and try not to worry. You're safe in your room. I'll get the driver to come get you from your room in the morning, if you want."

"Yes, please." She shuddered again despite his reassurances. The room didn't feel safe.

"I'll speak to the hotel desk and let them know to keep an eye out. Do you want to let the police know too?"

"I..." She stopped speaking, unsure of the answer. She hadn't thought about going that far. It might make her feel safer, but it might just be more hassle than it was worth.

"Or you could get a friend to join you. We wouldn't mind paying for someone to be with you, so you're not alone, until you feel safe again."

"No, I don't think that will be necessary. I know someone I can phone who can help."

"That Sebastian Holmes guy?" Shane asked.

"Yes," she replied, lying and following it with a goodbye. A few months back she would have phoned Sebastian, but not now she knew his elder brother. Who else would you phone when you had a stalker who wanted to be your controlling boyfriend but your mentor who was pretending to be your controlling boyfriend?

CHAPTER 3

Mycroft sat in his study, reading the report that some homeless teenager had delivered to his door a few minutes ago. It had cost him a twenty-pound note but it was useful enough he didn't mind. It was also early, and that let Mycroft know that his brother felt some sort of guilt or remorse for refusing to help the previous day. Although it was also possible that Sherlock had no cases and was bored.

Either way, it meant that Mycroft could progress with his problem. The dirt found around the sofa came from a mix of three different areas of London, the majority coming from a patch of the river that stretched from Rainham to Purfleet, and most notably from the Rainham nature reserve and marshland. Whatever the terrorists were up to, they visited the nature reserve a lot, and Mycroft suspected they might have been hiding something there. The rest of the mud came from places he already knew the people had visited, like the Silvertown barrier.

It didn't take him long to message the relevant officials and get a team down to the right area to have a look for signs of trespassing or other suspicious activity. His team were still keeping an eye on the other locations the terrorists had been seen in, so he knew they hadn't been to any of those recently.

He rubbed his forehead with his fingers, aware that a dull ache of some kind was settling in for the night. The meetings that morning had provided far too much stress. Government officials wanted answers, and they had no one else to grill but him. Sometimes he wished he wasn't such an important part of the system that ran the United Kingdom. It always fell to him to keep the country safe and prosperous. A task that wasn't made any easier by the many bungling prime ministers who'd ruled and the two large wars he'd had to live through.

While he was lamenting the lack of strong leadership within the country, the shrill sound of a mobile phone ringing pierced the otherwise silent evening in his house. He frowned and reached for the spare handset in his drawer. At some point he'd expected Amelia to get in contact with him, but he'd expected it several hours earlier and in message form. He'd need to reprimand her for phoning.

"Miss Jones," he said as he picked up, not doing anything to hide his annoyance at her.

"Myron! I think I need your help."

He heard the faint edge of panic in her voice and sneered. Maybe she wasn't as good at controlling her emotions as she'd displayed last time they'd been together. Not wishing to indulge her outburst, he decided to change the subject immediately. Hopefully she'd understand he had absolutely no intention of helping her with anything.

"Do you not have something to report about the second stage of our lessons?"

There was another pause and Mycroft waited.

"Are these letters from you, then?" she asked, sounding calm but confused. It was his turn to not understand. The lines on his head furrowed.

"What letters?"

"I had one posted through my door in the early hours of this morning and another brought to the hotel I'm at less than half an hour ago. I didn't think they were from you, but I..."

"They're not."

"They say they're from a fan, but I think I've got a stalker, Myron, and I'm not sure I'm safe here. I was hoping..."

"And you didn't observe anything strange today?" he asked, not interested in her fears concerning her fans. She chose her career, and any hazard it caused her was of her own making.

"I did notice this one guy."

"What did he look like?" Mycroft sat back, pleased she'd at least noticed him. Maybe all faith in her intelligence wasn't lost.

"He had dark hair, a little taller than me. Glasses, with quite wide rims."

"Go on," he encouraged, pleased she'd picked up on that much.

"He had a strange coat – although it was far too big for him – and he was a bit nerdy. He also said he was a carer for his mother who has multiple sclerosis, and he was very conversationally awkward."

Mycroft frowned again and hesitated to interrupt her. She was no longer describing the right person. He'd specifically instructed his man to wear a suit and carry an umbrella just like Mycroft's. It would have made him easier to spot, but the first challenge of this stage couldn't be too difficult if she was going to learn.

"He also said he had a brother and liked my character, Dalton, which is in the letters. He came across as the stereotypical type to..."

Mycroft gave an exasperated sigh loud enough that Amelia must have heard it. Mercifully, she went silent.

"I have absolutely no interest in your fans, although he isn't a threat to you. He couldn't possibly be the person who delivered your letters and also followed you to the hotel."

"Then why did you ask? Oh... I'm so sorry, Myron. I was so preoccupied with these letters and the strangeness of them. I've missed something I was meant to notice, haven't I?"

"Yes, you have." It pleased him that she was apologetic,

but nevertheless she had failed a task and he'd said it was grounds to end their arrangement. But now it came to it, he found his mouth firmly shut and he didn't tell her it was over. Instead, he listened as she sighed.

"I know begging for a second chance isn't going to work. Is there anything I can say that would make you consider starting this challenge again?"

Mycroft sat back and thought about her question. He hadn't expected her to fail so soon, not given how highly his younger brother thought of her. Something in the letter she received must have made her lose focus, and given how she'd behaved when they were abducted, it must be more than the usual female would be emotionally compromised by.

"Has the stalker threatened you?" he asked, curiosity overriding his displeasure.

"No, not directly. The second letter mentioned his dislike of the greeting I received from a couple of my friends at the signing today. He suggested I was too familiar with them."

"So he was there."

"Definitely."

"But you didn't notice him? Or anyone else?" Mycroft hesitated over giving her a second chance. She had calmed down while talking to him, and it was at least somewhat impressive that her response to a threatening letter was to try and spot the sender herself. Before he could continue and tell her this, she took the silence as indication that he had nothing else to say.

"I only noticed the person I mentioned, Guy Thomas. But if you don't think he's the type, then I guess I was wrong about that too."

"You sound tired."

"I am. I woke up to the first letter and it has been a long day."

"Then you'd best get some sleep. You'll need it. I fully expect a message from you tomorrow evening telling me what you've observed. Perhaps you can figure out who this man is at the same time as achieving your next challenge, and I can be *entertained* by both attempts."

"Thank you, Myron." A lighter note lifted her voice, but she still sounded weary.

"Go on, get some sleep. That's an order."

"As you command," she said in the same manner she'd used before. He could imagine the merry light in her eyes as she said it, and he found himself smiling as he hung up.,

Once the phone was tucked back in the drawer it lived in Mycroft realised he'd possibly just made the most irrational decision so far in his long life. Never before had he given anyone but Sherlock a second chance.

He frowned and got up to summon his housekeeper for some more tea. It didn't feel right to have let Amelia get away with failing, but he'd done it now. He could only hope Amelia kept her head and didn't make him regret it. Once more, he wondered if it had been a good idea to agree to teach a woman, but something had made him curious about her, and he'd followed her into that bookshop one afternoon in September. All the strange decisions he'd made had followed that one, like waves on an ocean. Maybe he needed to turn the tide.

Mycroft felt better after drinking his tea, and settled into his leather chair by the fire to read a book. He had one of his favourite classics open, and was reading the first edition in its original language, Russian.

Before he could read more than a few pages, his laptop chimed to let him know he had an email. With a sigh, he went back to it to see if it was anything important, and was pleased to find it was and he hadn't been disturbed for no good reason.

One of his men had spotted footprints in the marshes. The trail had led a small team to a cache of blueprints, food and a few Russian weapons. At least one of the men he was after had been hiding there recently.

Mycroft tapped out a quick reply telling them to keep their

distance and observe. It wouldn't help if they scared the man off. It would be better to let him come and go and give Mycroft a trail he could follow himself. It was time to take over from the amateurs and solve this problem.

CHAPTER 4

Amelia felt a lot better as she put her knife and fork down and sat back from her breakfast plate. It was now empty apart from a small smear of tomato juice left over from the baked beans. There was nothing quite like an English breakfast to start off a busy day.

With the assurance from Myron that Guy wasn't her stalker she felt a little better, and it was more than she expected for him to be allowing a second attempt at one of the tests he had for her. It encouraged her, even if she did feel nervous about the day. At some point she would need to spot the right thing and be able to give Myron the details. He'd given her no indication of what she should spot and when, but given that he also wanted her to look out for her own stalker and tell him about that, it would be wise of her to observe every little detail she could. Amelia found herself feeling very grateful that she'd slept well and was more awake and aware than she'd been in days. She'd need it.

As Shane had promised, the driver knocked on her hotel door to accompany her to the car, and when she arrived at the book shop for her signing she noticed there was a burly man watching over the queue of people there to see her. With both Myron and her publishers taking the threat seriously and lending her what support they could, she felt her tense muscles relax. She gave the people around her a genuine smile as she greeted them.

Her new bodyguard accompanied her into the building which had a similar size and layout to the Bath shop, with the slight exception of a café that sat just behind her signing table. This early in the morning it wasn't very busy, with just two women sat chatting over drinks. She could tell from the size of their handbags and the child-related objects flowing out of the top of one that they must have dropped their young children off at some kind of nursery for a few hours to themselves. Nothing unusual there, and not related to her stalker or stage two of her training, but a good start in practising her observational skills for the day.

It didn't take her long to get into the usual routine that accompanied these events, and keeping an eye out for strange people around her only slowed the ritual by a few seconds as she took the opportunity to scan the scene in front of her every time she posed for a photo with fans or said goodbye to another satisfied reader. When she was physically signing the books, she paused on her way to lean on the table to glance over towards the café. She also gave the area a more in depth sweep every time she took a drink from the bottled water she was supplied with.

It wasn't long before midday when she noticed a well-dressed man sitting in the café at a small table. He'd moved the chair to one side from the neat rows so he was angled towards her. She couldn't be sure, as his glasses had an odd tint to them, but he appeared to be gazing in her direction a lot, despite having a paper in his hands.

When she stopped for lunch and noticed him looking at her for a third time, she smiled and tilted her head ever so slightly sideways. He immediately reached into his jacket pocket and pulled something out, which he deftly folded into the paper as he closed it.

While she was still looking he got up, placing his hand on

top of the newspaper. Before he walked away, he gave her a slight nod and tapped the top of the paper with his fingers. A burst of emotion washed over her. This was either her stalker or Myron's lesson, and at this point she didn't know which.

She did know she needed to get to that paper.

"Be right back," she mumbled and walked away from her table, right over to the café. Her eyes fixed on the paper the entire way, and she breathed a sigh of relief as she got to it before anyone could try and claim it in the now heaving sitting area.

After staring at it for a moment, she lifted the paper so it held the message or small item inside and carried it back to where her bodyguard was waiting.

"I wanted to check the paper at lunch," she said, thinking on her feet. "One of my friends said they might be in it."

"Do you want me to come to the staff room with you, Miss?" he asked, not even showing an interest in what she'd just done. She smiled but shook her head.

"I'm sure I'll be fine in there. Why don't you have lunch as well, Toby?" He nodded and headed towards the shop exit, not giving her or the strange behaviour a second glance.

With her food arrangements sorted and waiting for her in the staff room, Amelia picked up her handbag. While she walked across the shop floor she rifled through the pages of the newspaper until her fingers brushed across something that had a different feel to it. Glancing down, she saw it was a small envelope. An A in Myron's handwriting adorned the outside, almost as big as the entire package.

While still out of sight among the book shelves, she pulled the letter out and slipped it into her handbag. A thrill of delight rippled through her. If nothing else, she'd managed to get Myron's challenge right this time.

She hurried through to the staff room and then beyond, to their toilet. Once she was locked in a cubicle, she pulled out the envelope and opened it up. Inside was a small piece of paper.

*What occurs once in a minute, twice in a moment
and never in one thousand years?*

Amelia frowned. Riddles weren't her strong point and
she'd not expected this one. She also knew she couldn't spend
any time right at that moment working it out. Instead, she
scanned the words, trying to commit them to memory, and
tucked the paper back into an inside pocket of her handbag.
Maybe the answer would come to her while she ate.

It didn't.

By the time she'd used up her hour and made sure she'd
talked to the workers who wanted her attention it was time to
go back out and sign. She spent another hour at this shop,
finishing up with the queue of people, despite it making her
ten minutes late on the schedule.

Toby waved her forward with his hand as she said
goodbye to the manager. He then protectively curled his arm
around her back and walked with her to the waiting car.

Once she was sat inside, she reached for her handbag. She
had about an hour before she'd arrive at a shopping centre
staying open late. There, she was doing another signing along
with a couple of other authors. An hour ought to be enough
to figure out the riddle.

While she thought over the answer and read the piece of
paper over and over again, she nibbled on her lower lip. It
didn't make any sense. And then it hit her. The letter M. Of
course it was. In her first ever coded letter, M had been the
starting letter as well. It made sense for it to be her answer at
the start of the next stage.

With a grin on her face, she typed out a message to
Myron.

M, darling, it's M.

Knowing she could relax for a bit, she took the
opportunity to think about her next novel. She needed to start

work on one soon and knew the publisher was expecting it to be in her Dalton series. Normally, revisiting her characters made her feel excited, but with the recent events she felt a small amount of nerves about writing.

A moment later she felt her jaw tensing up and realised she was gritting her teeth. Dalton was her character and she was cross at herself for letting someone put her off writing about him. As if in rebellion against the idea, she pulled out some paper and a pen and started to write the opening scene. She could work out the plot issues another time.

By the time she arrived at the next destination she'd got several hundred words she was pleased with. In a moment of forethought she pulled out her phone and tweeted a good line about Dalton. Her publisher often told her she didn't use social media enough, and letting her followers know a new book was being written was always the sort of thing that got her network buzzing.

There was no bodyguard at her new destination, but she was pleased to see the shopping centre had security staff on duty, helping to keep the masses of people in order. Of the three authors, Amelia was the least successful but there was still a cheer of appreciation when she was introduced and shepherded along to the row of tables.

Giving her no time to do anything more than greet her companions, the first few people were ushered forward and allowed to work their way along the table. Amelia sat on the far end and waited as the readers stopped at the first man's area for him to sign books. He wrote under the pen name R. Fletcher and she didn't know his real name. He was by far the most popular of the authors, with most of the horde of fans there to see him. About half then also collected the woman's next to her, Shelly Brent, who wrote under S. Brent and regularly had fans being surprised she was a woman.

Amelia had to stifle a laugh when the third reader exclaimed about the gender difference. It made her feel a little smug that she'd got her full name on her book covers and no one got her gender wrong. The feeling soon vanished when she realised over eighty percent of the people were going past her without stopping. A few of them smiled sheepishly but most pretended she wasn't even there.

Occasionally Shelly also found herself unoccupied for several minutes while the fans wandered by them both. When this happened, they would make the odd remark to each other and soon found they could converse easily. It brought some relief to the awkward waiting, but Amelia could only talk some of the time, the rest she had to sit and watch the other two authors sign.

Trying not to be defeated by the lack of interest, when someone who was curious stopped, she asked them more questions than she normally would and took longer over the signing. If nothing else, it might make fans of hers more loyal than they already were.

After a particularly long run of no one stopping to see her she noticed a familiar coat near the front of the queue. Guy Thomas stood there looking in her direction. As soon as their eyes met, he waved. A smile appeared on her face automatically, giving her mind time to process her surprise at seeing the same awkward fan two days running in two very different cities. Especially as he'd mentioned he cared for his mother. He had the newest book tucked under one arm, but was wearing exactly the same clothing as the day before.

The nearest staff member soon realised that Guy was there to see Amelia and had a quick conversation with him. She could easily figure out what had been said when Guy was let past the rest of the queue to come straight to her. There was no point in him remaining in the line when he only wanted to see her.

"Hello, Guy. I didn't expect to see you today," she said, deciding to control the conversation as well as she could. "How is your mother?"

"Not so great, actually. She's in hospital at the moment."

"I'm sorry to hear that. I hope it's nothing too serious."

She tried to sound sympathetic but it was difficult, given how strange his appearance was. If Myron hadn't assured her that Guy couldn't be her stalker, she'd be convinced he was.

"I told her and my brother about meeting you yesterday and how I didn't get a photo. They both thought it made sense to see you again and get one, rather than wait around at the hospital with nothing to do."

"Wonderful. Do you have a camera with you, then?"

He nodded and grinned as he pulled an old brick-like digital camera from one of the large pockets on the outside of his coat. The nearest shop worker offered to take it from him as Amelia got up and came around to the other side of the table.

Guy stayed where he was and looked at her, not sure where he should stand. To relieve the awkward moment, she positioned herself next to him and put her arm around his back, but it only made things worse as he fumbled with the hand closer to her and caught her side as he tried to reciprocate the gesture.

He coloured up again and didn't give the camera a proper smile, so Amelia deliberately shut her eyes as the picture was taken. By the time the girl taking the photo had checked the screen and noticed it wasn't a good shot, Guy was more relaxed and his cheeks had returned to their normal colour.

The second photo satisfied her and brought a smile to Guy's face when he saw it.

"Thank you, that's wonderful. Now I can show my mum and brother how nice you are."

"Don't mention it. Do you want me to sign that book for you as well?"

He nodded and handed it to her. She paused for a moment with the pen in her hand to think of a message to write.

To Guy, thank you for coming such a long way to see me. Having such amazing fans means a lot to me and I hope your mother is well enough to come home and return to your expert care soon. Love and Hugs, Amelia.

It didn't take her long; she just said how she felt about the effort he'd gone to. She reminded herself that Myron didn't think he was her stalker and hoped she hadn't just created a new one as she handed the book back.

As he read the message, his eyes lit up.

"Thank you," he burbled, and she saw the familiar awe-struck look fans sometimes got. Immediately, she regretted being quite so nice. She never liked it when people looked at her that way, as if she was something more than a human, something god-like. It was far too easy to disappoint someone who thought you were better than human.

Amelia was saved from having to worry about it too long by another reader wanting to talk to her about her books. Guy said goodbye and was ushered out of the way so she could focus on the woman in her fifties who wanted to know what Amelia's books were about. It didn't result in her selling anything or even signing a bookmark, but it was nice that someone hadn't just walked right past her.

The rest of the evening hurried by, despite the patches when Amelia sat alone, and by the time the shop had to shut she'd found she got along so well with Shelly that she had an invite to a dinner party that evening. Wanting to at least appear sociable, she accepted and wrote down the address of the restaurant.

No one was surprised when the line of fans had to be turned away at the end of the session. It didn't look like it had shrunk much when Amelia left a couple of minutes later and got into her familiar car to head to the hotel. The publishers had been sensible and kept the night's hotel booking close to the late signing, while also scheduling her following signing for the afternoon the next day. It meant she was only in the car ten minutes. She spent the entire time letting her publisher know she was still safe and breathing and had been successful in selling books for both of them.

Once in her room she had half an hour before the dinner booking, and now had the opportunity to see if Myron had responded to her message. She pulled out the mobile and smiled when she saw the flashing light.

Good. Anything else to report?

She had hoped for something a bit more encouraging but wasn't surprised. There was a question, and that at least meant she could reply.

Guy Thomas showed up again, but otherwise I noticed no one else. Going out to dinner this evening but don't expect to see anything there. Unless you have plans for me?

While she waited for Myron to reply, she neatened her hair and re-did her make-up, brightening the colours so they created more of a party look. She didn't have time to change her clothes after that. As she looked up the location of the restaurant and pleasantly found it was less than half a mile away, her phone buzzed with a response.

No.

Amelia laughed. It was just like Myron to be so short and to the point. After tucking the phone in the bottom of her handbag and grabbing the map she had open on her normal mobile, she headed back out into the city. The stars were out and the area around her looked well-kept, with street lamps lighting up the pavement at regular intervals, so she decided not to bother with a taxi and walked along the road.

Less than two minutes later she realised she could hear the sound of quiet footsteps behind her, heading in the same direction but not catching up to her. Up ahead, she noticed she would need to cross the road, and when she got there she paused and used the opportunity to take a look over her shoulder. Out of the corner of her eye she saw someone dart behind a hedge.

Amelia's heart rate increased, but she knew she had to keep going and stay calm. Regretful thoughts popped into her head as she crossed the road, but she pushed them away. She couldn't change the decision she'd made now, and it was better to focus on getting to her destination. Next time she would take a taxi.

After studying the map open on her phone screen for a moment, she stuffed it into her pocket. Having to look at it repeatedly would slow her down. It would be better for her to keep going at a steady pace and appear confident. If she was worried or got lost and saw another pub or restaurant, she could always wander in as if it had been her destination all along.

Straining her ears, Amelia tried to listen out for the sound of someone walking behind her again but they were either gone or were being more careful not to make a sound with their footfalls. She even tried holding her breath to keep herself quiet, but too many cars came past to make any difference. Unable to resist the temptation any longer, Amelia stopped and looked behind her.

There was no one there.

She shook her head at her own fears and chuckled. Whoever had been there must have stopped at one of the houses. They hadn't been following her at all.

Feeling lighter already, Amelia shoved her chilly hands into her jacket pockets and gazed at her surroundings. Her walk soon took her off the main road and down a quaint cobbled street with small old shops that lined both sides. All of them were shut at this time of night but she browsed the wares in the windows anyway.

She could see the bright, welcoming glow of the rest-aurant's entrance a hundred metres ahead when a car engine noise caught her attention. The deep purr of a slow-moving car came up close to one side of her, accompanied by the rumble of wheels on cobbles. She glanced at the car, but in the darkness she could only make out that it was a black Audi.

"Amelia!" Shelly's voice cut through the quiet night air and Amelia looked ahead of her to see the author standing to one side of the restaurant door, a cigarette in her fingers. With a large exhale, Amelia picked up the pace and hurried towards the friendly face.

"You're brave for walking in this cold. I took a taxi," Shelly said as soon as she was close enough to talk without yelling.

"Yeah, I think I'll get a taxi back." Amelia made no mention of the reason why. No one needed to know how scared she'd been. It wasn't the brightest idea she'd had, given the letters, but she'd made it safely.

Forgetting all her worries for an evening, she followed Shelly into the building and let her new friend introduce her to the rest of the writers there. Some she'd met at other events, but most were new to her.

They spent the entire meal talking about their careers, from contracts and advances to deadlines and genre tropes. Only one of the men there stood out to her as being particularly interesting. He wrote science fiction and had a good understanding of society's flaws, but she found herself less interested and more distant than she used to be around such clever people. The time spent with Sebastian and now Myron had spoilt her for intelligent conversation.

Despite that, she couldn't say the evening wasn't a success. She laughed, drank wine and ate plenty of good food. It was almost midnight by the time she and Shelly put their jackets on and supported each other's intoxicated bodies out to get into their taxi.

Shelly let go of her arm to get into the waiting car first just as Amelia felt someone approach her from behind.

"Amelia?" a familiar voice said as she turned. Guy stood, looking a little sheepish but with the same hero-worshipping light in his eyes. She couldn't keep her body from shivering. "Oh, are you cold? Would you like my coat?"

Without waiting for her to respond, he tugged one sleeve off, and would have done the other if she hadn't regained use of her voice in time to stop him.

"No, that's fine. I'm going back to my hotel now. Sorry, can't chat. Bye."

Hoping it wasn't too obvious that she wasn't sober and felt wobbly on her own legs, she quickly turned and followed Shelly into the car, pulling the door shut behind her. She heard a meek goodbye follow her and winced, hoping he hadn't thought her rude.

"Are you all right?" Shelly asked once the taxi had pulled off.

"Yeah, fine," she replied, checking out the window. Guy stood where she'd left him, staring at the vehicle as it pulled away. As she swept past, she also noticed the same black Audi was still sat where it had parked and scared her earlier in the night.

"Was that the same person from the signing?"

Amelia nodded, not wanting to talk about it. Although Myron had assured her Guy wasn't the stalker type, she wasn't convinced anymore. Not now that he'd shown up outside the restaurant and she'd thought someone had followed her from her hotel there. It could have been him, and he'd just been good enough at hiding from her that she'd not noticed him again. She knew she hadn't checked the road behind her as she walked inside the restaurant.

As soon as the taxi had pulled up outside her hotel, she handed her travelling companion enough money to cover her share of the cost and hurried into the building, not even hesitating in the reception area. She wanted the safety of her own room.

Once the door was shut and locked behind her, she

relaxed. It finally registered with her mind that her shoulders and neck ached from being tensed up. She was scared.

CHAPTER 5

The grandfather clock in Mycroft's study let him know it was midnight. It had been over twenty-four hours since he'd instructed his men to watch out for foreign people arriving at the site they'd found, and since then the only communication he'd received had been from Amelia.

He'd been trying not to think about her. Doubts gnawed at the back of his mind. It was more than possible she'd cause him trouble and he didn't know if the diversion was worth the mess she could make. The stalker business only made problems more likely. If anything happened to her while under his tutelage, their secret was more likely to get out, and it had been tiresome enough having to explain her involvement when the last incident had occurred. A second would create more questions about her than he wanted to answer.

Despite assuring her that Mr Thomas was safe, Mycroft had looked into the man's background. The man did spend his full time caring for his mother and had told her the truth. If his half-brother, a soldier in the British Marines, was the brother he'd referred to, he could well have left his mother with him. Although he noticed their common parent was their father, not the mother. Either way, it was still highly unlikely the man wrote the threatening letters. He couldn't have delivered them, with the type of care his mother needed, and his brother was often busy with training and had only recently come back from an overseas tour.

The final conclusion was that someone else was following her, someone she'd not spotted. He also knew he couldn't take the time to find them for her, but it would be a good lesson for her to have to protect herself and figure out who had sent the letters without his help. While she was solving her own problem, he could keep an eye on her and continue his own lessons. It was the simplest way to proceed.

As the time continued to trickle past, Mycroft considered getting some sleep, but he expected something to happen soon. The cache of food at the marshland had fruit, bread, and other perishable items that wouldn't last much longer. Whoever had left it there wouldn't stay away past the night.

Settling back in his armchair, he picked up his book again, almost hoping he wouldn't get to read many pages before someone contacted him.

When two more gongs sounded from the clock, he considered going to bed, but a few seconds later his phone let out a shrill noise from the small table beside him. He picked it up and saw what he'd wanted. A man had returned to the cache and looked like he would be there long enough for Mycroft to arrive.

He buzzed for Daniels to get the car ready and walked briskly upstairs to get changed into more suitable attire for his task. It didn't take long as he'd already had his housekeeper lay out the necessary garments for him to don at need.

Daniels already waited by the car, and the quiet noise of the running engine came to his ears as Mycroft walked out of the front door.

"Get there as quick as you can," Mycroft said as he got himself into the back of the car and pulled the door shut. Daniels was efficient enough to be behind the wheel and ready to go as soon as he was. There had been several chauffeurs in Mycroft's employment before he found Daniels, but the search had been worth it. His household ran well thanks to him and the housekeeper.

Mycroft looked over the preliminary information as it was coming in from one of the observing agents. Just before two in the morning they'd heard the sound of something rustling the grasses and reeds on the marshland. A few seconds later a tall man with a thin build had appeared, striding over the land. He'd dressed in black but the agents all had heat scanners and could see his outline as it made its way to the food.

At the moment they were watching him eat and rest, which helped Mycroft feel more relaxed about his decision to wait at home. If the man, probably a Russian, wasn't in a hurry, it would give Daniels time to get him there. At least London this late at night was nowhere near as busy as during the day.

He tried not to get impatient as he sat and waited to arrive. The agents were feeding him very little information. Hopefully, because the Russian was still eating, or even better, trying to get some sleep.

When Daniels finally pulled up in the right place, Mycroft sprang into action. Not saying a word to his driver, he headed away from his car and towards the marshlands. Daniels turned the car off and the headlights went out. The darkness wrapped itself around Mycroft and he had to wait several seconds for his eyes to adjust to the new environment.

It didn't take him long to spot the closest of his team of three agents. The light pollution from the large city helped to prevent it being totally dark, and his observant eyes did the rest of the work.

Being careful to move as silently as he could and going more slowly, Mycroft wound his way across the marshes to his agent. As he went, he kept a close eye on the area around him. Many birds roosted here and he didn't want to startle any and draw attention to his presence.

It took him another fifteen minutes to get to the agent, making his total arrival time from notification to the present just shy of forty-five minutes. Not bad, considering everything he managed. For someone well over a hundred years old, he was still in good shape.

"What's the latest?" Mycroft asked in the ear of agent Herbert.

"He stopped eating but doesn't appear to be leaving any time soon. Might be reading; hard to tell," the agent whispered back.

Mycroft nodded and took the spare heat-vision goggles, before finding a fourth spot of his own to keep watch. Just like Herbert had said, the Russian was sitting, and from the tilting back and forth of his head, appeared to be reading something.

After ten minutes the man stood up, fiddled with some items, moving them about within some kind of container or bag. When he straightened again, he took a look in several directions and then loped slowly towards the waterfront.

For a few seconds Mycroft only watched, giving him time to get far enough ahead Mycroft wouldn't be heard following. It didn't take that long with the long strides of the tall Russian, and then he was up on his feet and hurrying after.

The Russian continued a meandering pace, evidently confident he wouldn't be seen and making it easy for Mycroft to keep up. With the goggles, Mycroft could see the small animals hidden within the undergrowth, but it made it harder to see the rushes and reeds that rustled when he brushed past them.

The odd breeze or two helped to hide his movements, so he made use of them when they happened, moving faster when it blew and slowing when it didn't. With this strange method, he managed to keep a reasonable distance behind his quarry.

When the Russian reached the edge of the marshland and the bank of the Thames, he stopped. Coming down river was a boat-shaped patch of warmer colour. It was smaller than the yacht that Mycroft had been taken on only a few weeks earlier, but another person steered it towards the bank and threw what was logically a rope over to the Russian, who caught it easily.

Mycroft moved closer and removed the goggles. It would give his eyes time to adjust again before he made the last dash and got onto the boat as well. The men took a few more minutes to bring the boat in close enough that the Russian could step aboard, but as soon as his foot touched the edge of the boat, Mycroft leapt up and hurried after.

It was important they didn't spot him so he kept low and didn't sprint, but he made sure he was fast enough not to lose sight of the boat. While jogging, off to one side, he spotted another of his agents, but she sensibly remained crouched in the undergrowth. Their job was done.

By the time he reached the bank, the boat was several metres away but not travelling fast. He couldn't make the jump, but the boat moved slowly enough a quick swim would get him to the back. He put down the goggles and yanked off his shoes. Hopefully, one of his agents would have the sense to come fetch them when it wouldn't endanger the operation to do so.

The water brought goosebumps out on his skin as it seeped through his clothes. He frowned despite knowing his car always had an entire spare set of clothing. The current set would be ruined by the time his little adventure was over.

Once in the water, Mycroft could only see the back of the boat. The rungs of the little ladder glinted in the low light and gave him something to aim for. Stroke after powerful stroke, he closed the gap and latched onto the bottom rung. Pausing, he took several deep breaths to calm his heart rate. It was important to be slow and careful.

Using the strength in his arms, Mycroft lifted himself inch by inch out of the water. If he did it any quicker, the water draining from his clothing would make too much noise.

Minutes ticked by as the boat took him farther away from London and left his agents behind. His arms soon ached from the strain of holding his weight and that of his water-logged clothes, reminding him why he liked to leave this sort of thing to other people. Eventually, the majority of his body was out of the water and it was time to lift his head above the edge of the boat.

His eyes widened. There was no one there. No longer trying to be quiet, he hauled himself onto the deck and rushed towards the helm. A large piece of wood held the steering wheel in place. He swore as he put the boat in neutral. Somehow, both passengers had slipped past him while he was tailing them. It could only mean one thing. They'd realised he was following.

Hoping one of his agents might have seen something, he turned the boat around and brought it back to the marshland. By the time he got there, two of the agents were standing waiting.

"Did you see where they went?" he asked before anyone else could speak. They shook their heads. Mycroft swore again. "Get me a torch and my dry clothes. And tie this to something."

Herbert caught the end of the rope and looped it around a sturdy fence post a few metres inland, while the woman ran off. He hoped she wouldn't take too long to get back. While he waited, he kept to one section of the boat. He didn't want the water dripping off him to obliterate any of the evidence that might give him another lead.

Once he had a torch in his hands, he examined the helm area but he found nothing of interest. He would have everything fingerprinted but doubted they'd find anything. While he was looking the cockpit over, the third agent, Williams, came running up.

"Everything in the cache is gone. They must have taken it with them."

"All right. Stay away from the area and get it cordoned

off. I'm going to deal with the boat first, then I'll take a look at that. And I mean it. Don't let anyone but me or my brother near it."

Williams nodded. All of them were used to Mycroft's brusque manner and dislike of interference. If he was involved they kept back, so no one but him could be blamed if the operations went wrong. Something that had never happened under Mycroft's care. Until today.

Not even changing into fresh clothes made him feel any better. He phoned his brother, wondering if Sherlock could be persuaded to help, but the call went unanswered, and although he sent a text, he expected that to be ignored as well. His younger brother was in one of his moods and it only darkened Mycroft's further.

It took him almost two hours to check over the boat and the few cabins it had. He found nothing but a smeared muddy footprint near the front left rail. It let him know the pair had got off that way but didn't give him anything to trace. It was too smeared for an accurate print, and he already knew the man's physical make-up. Mycroft had seen him.

The boat had little equipment, and whatever the Russian had with him had gone over the front of the boat with its owner. While Mycroft had been sneaking up the back they'd snuck off the front. Once more, they had slipped through his grasp.

Having nothing more he could check, Mycroft got off the boat and allowed the forensic team to do their best at finding some evidence. They might find a fingerprint but the chances were slim. If there was anything else there he'd have found it already.

He nodded his satisfaction when he noticed the crime tape surrounding the area of bushes and reeds that the Russian had used for a hide-out. The circle had a good fifty metre radius and no one was inside it. Instead, his three agents stood around it with their torches, keeping the rest of the people well away from it. Considering how little he'd communicated with anyone since the previous day, there were over ten members of staff on top of the original agents crawling over the marshlands or boat, and they were surprisingly well informed. At least something was going well.

With this area he slowed even further, using the torch to examine every patch of dirt where a shoe print might have been left or some small item might have fallen. Given the area, the possibility of an entire print was slim, but a partial print might be enough. He worked his way back and forth over a third of the circle before he noticed a patch of mud that held a good imprint of the Russian's shoe.

Ten minutes later a small team of two people had made a reed mat path over a patch he'd checked and were using plaster to get an inverse impression. Meanwhile, Mycroft had carried on and was almost upon the centre of the area. He took even longer over the few metres closest to the cache. If anything was left behind, it would most likely be here, but he spotted nothing. A print alone wasn't enough. It wouldn't lead him to men who were being so careful. It was evidence, but not a lead.

By the time Mycroft had gone over the entire patch of land, the morning was almost upon them and the horizon to the east was no longer black. He scowled at his agents as he ducked underneath the crime tape and left the area.

"Sir, they've run checks on the boat. It was stolen four months ago but the police had no leads."

"The boat was still in the Thames. How can it have been stolen four months ago." Mycroft sighed and noticed Herbert was about to speak. "No, don't answer that. It wasn't a question. Have the police report and the victim's name and address forwarded. I'll have it looked into. In the meantime, liaise with the rest of the team on our other locations."

"What about this one?" Williams asked.

"I'll get someone more... *subtle*... on it," he said and walked off without another word. He then pulled his phone out of his pocket and messaged Sherlock.

Need one of your friends to watch Rainham Marsh for me. I'll pay, as usual. Daniels will bring the money around and some other information I'd like you to look at.

"Home, sir?" Daniels asked once Mycroft was back in the car.

"No, the club." He needed some space to think away from all the distractions. "And then take a payment and the information I'm about to receive to my brother."

"Anything else, sir?"

"No. I'll let you know when I want picking up. Get some sleep until I need you."

"Thank you, sir," Daniels said and Mycroft realised the chauffeur wasn't as young as he used to be. It often took Mycroft by surprise when the people around him got older. Being ageless had become normal, far too normal.

As the sun started another journey across the British sky Mycroft walked into the Diogenes Club. He'd been the co-founder of it well over a hundred years ago, although they were unaware of that. Just like everyone else, except Sherlock, they believed him to be a descendent of the great Mycroft Holmes and not the man himself.

Less than five seconds after stepping through the door, a butler appeared carrying his personal slippers and a tray with the day's paper. By the time he had the comfortable burgundy slippers on his feet and the paper in his hands, he was perfectly relaxed. The butler picked up the discarded muddy shoes and neither needed to say anything for Mycroft to know they would be clean by the time he left.

CHAPTER 6

The sound of Amelia's phone alarm woke her from a deep sleep. She winced as her head protested to her sitting up but she sat up anyway. Drinking so much hadn't been the wisest of ideas while on tour, but after the evening scare, she'd not been able to resist having another glass of wine before bed. It had helped calm her after her run-in with Guy and the suspicion that she'd been followed. Hotel room service was a dangerous temptation.

She tried not to think about the events contributing to the knot in her stomach as she gathered up her discarded clothes and retrieved her handbag from underneath the bed. As she reached into it to check the phone Myron had given her, she brushed up against paper she wasn't expecting. Frowning, she pulled apart the opening to get a better look and dropped her handbag.

Inside was another letter from her stalker. For a minute, Amelia couldn't do anything but shake with her mouth wide open. If she'd not regretted drinking before, she did now. At some point while she'd been out at dinner last night the stalker had been close enough to her to put the letter right into her handbag and she had no idea when.

Leaving the bag in the middle of the floor, she sank into

the dresser chair and tried to focus on the events of the previous night. She didn't think anyone had come close enough to her to slip anything inside before she walked into the restaurant, and she'd only left her handbag unattended for a few minutes while she went to the toilet, but Shelly had said she'd keep an eye on it. It could only have been when she was leaving and Guy had been waiting for her. In that moment she decided Myron must be wrong. Guy was stalking her and she'd probably made it worse with how encouraging she'd been the second time he'd appeared at her signing.

As this thought occurred to her, Amelia had to fight the urge to heave. Oddly this had a good effect on her. She mentally told herself to get a grip and fought to take command of her emotions. Nothing she'd already done could be changed, but she could think rationally from now on and act before this got out of hand and she found herself in danger. Myron had already told her he would want to know about this, so she wasn't alone in figuring this out.

Feeling braver, she got up and went back to her handbag. Using all the precautions she'd implemented on both previous occasions, she brought the letter over to the dresser and opened it.

Dearest Amelia,

Sometimes I really cannot understand your actions. After both my previous messages mentioning my desire to meet up with you for a meal or at least a coffee sometime, I thought that you'd have invited me this evening. I even told you I'd be nearby and available. Then when I did find out where you were and what you were doing, you were sat next to another man and barely spoke to anyone else. I hope he doesn't get the wrong idea about you. I also don't think you should encourage him, or anyone else. Not while I'm around.

This is so out of character for you. Normally you're

so nice. If you forgot, I can possibly forgive you, but if you do it again I won't write you any more letters to explain my feelings. I will insist upon you acknowledging my presence and talking to me in front of your colleagues.

I also noticed your tweet today and the excerpt you posted of your new Dalton book. I really don't think he would have been so mean to Cassandra, and I would know. I am Dalton. Instead, he should be considerate of her feelings. She evidently cares for him, and her worry shouldn't just be ignored. I hope you change it before you send the story to your publisher.

I'm sure we'll meet again soon. I want to tell you all my ideas for what you can do with Dalton in your next few books, and we can bond over your characters. I know you'll appreciate my point of view on your stories, and if not, I can be persuasive.

With affection.

Amelia had to read the letter twice before she could take it in. Each letter was worse than the one before and this one had more of a violent undertone. She had no desire to find out how persuasive he could be if she didn't listen to him, nor did she wish to find out how he'd act if he saw her flirting with another man. On top of all that, he seemed to always know where she was. It had to be Guy and he had to be stopped.

She rooted in her handbag for her phone and called Myron. He would know what to do, but he didn't answer, and she reached the message system. Knowing he'd not want messages to be left on the answerphone, she hung up and tried again. When it happened a second time, she left a message mentioning having another letter and being in danger. Finally, she asked him to call her back as soon as he could. It might make him a little cross, but she'd been careful with her words.

With that done, she sat and stared at the letter, trying to think of what else she could do. It wasn't safe for her to leave the hotel room unless she knew where she was going. A minute later she realised that she ought to phone her publisher as well. Shane answered after the fourth ring.

"Hi, Amelia, everything all right?"

"No, I've had a third letter."

"What did it say this time?" he asked, getting straight to business. She read him the contents, still feeling calmer than she ought to after her panic and stern lecture towards herself.

"Crap, it sounds like he's getting angry."

"Yeah. I think I know who it is, as well. He's come to both book signings and I almost walked right into him when I came out the restaurant yesterday evening."

"Can you prove it in some way? Or has he said anything?"

"No." Amelia shook her head. "It's only who I think it is."

"Do you think your friend in London would be able to prove it?"

"He might," she said, knowing Shane was thinking of Sebastian while she was thinking of Myron. "I've already tried to phone him, but I didn't get an answer yet. In the meantime I don't know what to do."

"We can postpone the tour, if you want. Or just a few days of it. I'd rather you stayed safe."

"Thanks, Shane. But don't tell people the real reason. Tell them I'm not well and I've gone home for a few days to get better."

"That sounds like a good idea. I take it you're not going home."

"No. At least, not yet."

With a plan of action and her editor making arrangements for her signings to be rescheduled, Amelia packed up all her belongings, ate a quick breakfast and checked out of her room. While waiting for her taxi to the train station in the hotel reception, she tried to phone Myron again and let him know she was coming to London, but he still didn't answer.

She tried again once she was on the train to Paddington, but again he left it to ring. Not wanting to annoy him if there was a good reason for him not picking up, she decided it would be the final time and tucked the extra phone in her jacket pocket, where she would be able to feel it vibrate if he replied in some way to her request for communication.

To keep her mind occupied and her emotions as calm as she could, Amelia wrote more on the train, but the letters kept popping into mind every time she wrote Dalton's name. After only a few hundred words, she gave up. A now familiar sick feeling settled into the pit of her stomach, and she found herself wondering if she would ever find stories about Dalton easy to write again. The longer she felt scared and the more letters she received the more she would associate the character with the stalker.

The train journey felt like it took all day, and by the time she was getting off in London she was exhausted and tense. At every stop she'd felt the nagging sensation that the next person to get onto her carriage would be him. That somehow he'd know exactly what train she was on and where she was going and he'd appear like he had the night before.

When the train grew busier and a man sat down beside her she had to stifle a squeal, but it wasn't him, just another weary traveller in a business suit. Something about his eyes looked familiar, but not enough for her to think she'd seen him before He smiled at her and she tried to reciprocate before turning to the window and finding the scenery fascinating.

Once she'd got used to him being there and showing no interest in her, it had made her feel safer. Guy couldn't plonk himself down next to her if someone else was there, but now they'd arrived in London he could appear from anywhere. The next person who rounded the corner in front of her could be him, or he could sneak up on her from behind, lost in the masses of people until he was close. Her only comfort was the audience the other passengers provided.

She spent the next twenty minutes making her way through the underground system, frightened about being alone in case Guy found her and tried to abduct her, and panicked about seeing other people in case he used them as shields to get to her. Every time she saw a coat of a similar beige to Guy's she bit down on her lip and stared at the wearer until she was convinced it wasn't him.

Once at the right stop, she hurried to the surface and found the nearest taxi. Only when she was sat in the back and the driver was already making his way to the road next to Myron's did she begin to relax. Guy couldn't get to her before she was safe with Myron now. The taxi wouldn't stop until she told the driver to.

It took another twenty minutes for the car to get the three miles from the tube stop to the neighbourhood Myron lived in, bringing her total journey time to over four hours. She checked her phone one last time, concerned that he hadn't called her back or even messaged, but it didn't deter her from her goal. Hopefully he would forgive her for turning up at his house unannounced. She'd done everything she could to let him know in advance.

Ten minutes later she was still walking down the road he lived on, confused by the houses. It had only been nine weeks since she'd stayed the night at his house, but now she wasn't sure which one was his. So many of them looked alike, set back in the trees with large gates and sweeping drives.

A few hundred metres down the road she spotted one on the other side that was wider than the others and set back a little farther. Her feet hurried her over to the front gate and the refuge she finally recognised. She'd fought back panic from so many little reasons that she was tiring from the effort, and as she stopped by the buzzer she realised she was exhausted and starving.

"Hello?" a male voice said a few seconds after she buzzed.

"Daniels?"

"Yes? Who is this?"

"Amelia Jones. I need Myron's help. He should know why," she said, hoping the chauffeur would take that as a good enough explanation. She didn't know what Myron would let his employees know. Daniels didn't reply but the gate swung open and she slipped through the gap as soon as it was wide enough to admit her, checking over her shoulder one last time.

The familiar car was sat across the front porchway of the house, forcing her to go around the back of it. By the time she got to the front door Daniels stood there, preventing her from seeing inside the house.

"Can I see Myron, please?" she asked.

"He's not expecting you, is he?" Daniels asked, frowning and not moving out of the way.

"No, but I tried to phone him, several times. He has been helping me with something and it's taken a turn for the worse. I really need to see him." Amelia gave Daniels her most pleading look.

"He's not here."

"Oh!" She furrowed her brow, not sure what to do and feeling the tightness return to her stomach. She didn't think she could simply leave again. "Where is he?"

"I don't think he'd want me to tell you that." Daniels looked away and she could tell that he wanted to help her. She bit her lip and looked more worried.

"I really need to find him. If you won't help me, I'll have to try and get to him another way. Maybe his brother will..."

"All right, get in the car. I'll take you to him." Daniels relented and walked towards the car door to open it for her.

"Thank you," she replied, barely above a whisper. With a sigh, she sank into the back seat of Myron's car. In here no one would hurt her. She was safe, and it even smelt faintly of Myron's cologne. For the first time since leaving the hotel that morning she let the tension drain from her body.

From the inside of a hidden space the world didn't seem so terrifying. The sight of a beige coat still sent a flutter through her stomach, but seeing Guy wouldn't mean she was in danger right then. No one but Daniels could see her, tucked up in the back of the large black car.

Eventually Daniels pulled up on the gravel drive of a large stately manor house. On the way in she'd seen signs proclaiming the place to be the Diogenes Club, but she'd never heard of it before.

She caught a glance at a similar sign near the entrance to the building and noticed one of the founding men had been a Holmes. Without waiting for Daniels to come around to her and let her out, she pushed the door open.

"I won't be long," she called over her shoulder.

"Amelia, I'm not sure... I should go in and let Myron know you're here."

She ignored Daniels and hurried through the massive wooden double doors that stood ajar, and had to stop herself gaping at the grand stone entranceway with its large sweeping split staircase. It was like a house from a fairy tale. A butler came hurrying up to her, his eyes wide with an edge of panic.

Not quite sure why she might be scaring him, she quickly scanned over her attire. She was dressed well, as she always ensured whenever the chance to see Myron was there.

"I need to see Myron Holmes," she said when he came closer. This seemed to only worsen the matter. He appeared to choke and his eyes grew even wider. Realising he would be of no help to her, she tried to walk right past him and called Myron's name. Daniels pulled on her arm and drew her attention back behind her but he was no longer looking at her, and he also appeared as if he was about to have some sort of panic attack. She followed his gaze and saw that Myron had appeared to one side of the staircase, by a door that had looked like part of the wall the last time she'd seen it. He motioned with one hand for her to approach. Daniels let go of her and the butler moved out of her way.

"Myron," she said with delight. She hurried over to him, her boots clicking rapidly on the marble floor. As she got closer she noticed that he was clenching his jaw and shaking with barely contained rage. She stopped in front of him, suddenly finding she couldn't speak. He was more angry than she'd ever seen him, and the way he stared at her made it obvious the reason was her.

CHAPTER 7

Mycroft pointed at the room to one side of him, hoping Amelia would hurry up and get inside before he dragged her in there. In all his years at the club, such an embarrassing incident had never occurred because of him. Not even Watson had made such a blunder.

Some level of understanding seemed to finally come to her as she walked into the room before him and held her gloved hands demurely in front of her. She stopped in the middle of the room while he pulled the door closed and made sure it made no sound.

Once it was closed and providing them with an insulated bubble to make noise within, he strode around to his side of the desk but found he couldn't sit down.

"What the hell do you think you're doing?" he said, his voice even and clipped, but full of the emotion he felt.

"I'm sorry, I didn't mean to..."

"Not only is this a gentlemen's club and you are most decidedly not male, but this is also a silent club. You've made more noise in less than a minute than is heard here in a whole year.

"I really am sor..."

"And on top of all that, I distinctly remember telling you

not to contact me in any way that could be noticed or discovered by others. Everyone here just heard you were looking for me."

Amelia finally shut her mouth again and stopped trying to apologise. He thought this would be an improvement until he saw her eyes water with the threat of tears. He let out a disgusted growl and turned his back on her. Trying to keep all the rage within him from boiling over and making him explode into an angry tirade, he closed his eyes and focused on smoothing out his breathing.

When he felt calmer he faced Amelia again and found she was doing the same thing. One tear had escaped and tracked down her cheek, but she was standing, shaking and fighting with her breathing. Impressively, she appeared to be regaining control.

He sneered as the small amount of respect he couldn't help but feel flared his temper once more.

"Explain," he said, snapping his mouth shut over the word. Her eyes flew open but she didn't speak. Instead, she swallowed and looked down at his desk.

"I found another letter this morning."

"At the hotel?" She shook her head and then nodded. He raised an eyebrow, not willing to play games. "Spit it out."

"I found it at the hotel, but it was in my handbag, and he could only have put it in there last night. It was angry, and hinted at violence."

A shiver ran through her and he felt his face sneering once more.

"You're scared," he said, not phrasing it like it was a question. He hoped his disgust at the emotion was evident.

"Yes. He could hurt me, if he tried."

"And you think I'll protect you?" He didn't hide his scorn at her assumption.

Shock widened her eyes and she took a step back as if he'd slapped her. He immediately regretted mocking her instinct to run to him, which only made him angrier. Not once had he ever softened towards someone, and he didn't want to start now.

Silence filled the room again, something normally comfortable in this place, but not while she stood there, full of emotion. While he watched her, she opened and closed her mouth several times, but he didn't want to relieve her awkwardness and speak even if he'd known what to say.

"I bumped into Guy Thomas," she said, finally speaking.

"No. I've already told you. It can't possibly be him."

"I was followed to dinner last night."

"It was my man. He said he thought you saw him." He expected this to comfort her, but her breathing only quickened.

"Then how did Guy know to be there? How did..."

"Oh, for Christ's sake, even I knew you were going to be there. Ms Brent advertised it all over her social media."

Amelia frowned but didn't back down.

"I know it's him, Myron. He's the only person who's been there every time. You're wrong, you have to..."

"Enough," Mycroft yelled.

She was stunned into silence, but it was too little too late. He fought to lower his voice to say one last thing.

"Get. Out."

For just a second, she hesitated, searching his face, but then she fled and he heard the clattering of her soles on the hard floor as she ran from the club. He faced the wall again, shaking uncontrollably.

It was bad enough that she'd been so foolish as to come straight to him, but to let her fear get the better of her so completely that she would accuse him of being wrong? Their agreement was over. He hoped he never saw her again, but he knew he also needed to reprimand Daniels.

As soon as he could be sure he would appear dignified, Mycroft followed in Amelia's footsteps outside, making no noise in comparison to her hurricane of sound.

When he stepped outside, Daniels had just shut the car

door on Amelia. He couldn't see if she was looking at him or not but he didn't care if she was.

"I'm sorry, sir. I tried to keep her in the car and fetch you but she got past me," Daniels said, knowing he was in trouble too. Although the chauffeur's actions had contributed to the problem, he knew the man had never made a mistake like it and wouldn't ever again.

"You should never have brought her here, but most importantly, I should never have let her stay in my house. You'll take her home once more, Daniels, but it will be the last time."

"Yes, sir. Of course, sir."

He watched them pull away before he walked back into the club. When he got back to his room, a brandy decanter and glass had appeared on one side of his desk. The butler knew him well.

Over the next few minutes he sipped a large helping of the drink, feeling its warmth in his stomach. When he had settled back into the calm of the club's atmosphere, he managed to turn his mind to other matters. He reached for his phone to send a message to the agent he'd had following Amelia to find his agent had already contacted him to let him know she was scared by something and on her way to London. The agent also pointed out that her publisher had postponed several events in Amelia's schedule for the next few days.

Mycroft frowned, feeling a flicker of doubt at sending her away. A moment later he'd crushed it and reassigned the agent to help locate the Russian and Korean men still roaming the capital of London. With that done, he also informed Daniels to come back to the club once he was done with Miss Jones. Only so much thinking could be done without him actively pursuing a new lead. Hopefully Sherlock would have visited the owners of the stolen boat and found a pathway or piece of information that shone some light on who was running or funding this splinter-cell of terrorists.

Neither government was claiming responsibility for the group, which didn't mean one of them or both of them were uninvolved for certain, but it did mean Mycroft had to dig further. At moments like this he wished he could clone himself. When he had to rely on others to hold meetings and keep an eye on places, he ran the risk of missing a vital clue. Only Sherlock's involvement gave him a peaceful oversight.

It took Daniels seven minutes longer than Mycroft estimated it would to take Miss Jones home and return to the club. One look at the chauffeur's face let him know that his prediction wasn't inaccurate. Daniels had talked to her about something before he left.

"I hope you didn't say anything of consequence to Miss Jones when you dropped her off."

"No, sir. I wished her well with her books and waited to make sure she was safe inside a locked house before I left," Daniels said, but they both knew he hadn't said everything and Mycroft had picked up on it. "She gave me a signed copy of the newest book, sir."

Mycroft rolled his eyes as he got into the car. In less than a second his senses were hit by the smell of her perfume still lingering near the other seat. He tried to block it out but it was no good. Four blocks from Sherlock's he had Daniels pull over.

"I'll walk from here. While I'm at my brother's have the car valeted. I want it to smell of something other than Miss Jones by the time I'm done."

Daniels nodded his assent to the command and Mycroft walked off. He could still see the black car in the distance when he regretted his decision. November was cold.

Knowing he couldn't appear indecisive, Mycroft tilted up his head and walked as calmly as he could up to his brother's front door. After putting the knocker straight, he walked in and made his way up the stairs.

Sherlock opened the door and admitted him to the warmth of the flat before Mycroft had put his foot on the top step.

"I thought I'd be seeing you this evening."

"Yes, I hoped you'd seen this couple who had their boat stolen."

"Right, yes. I did." Sherlock paused and Mycroft found himself wondering why. There was no other reason he would be visiting his brother this late at night.

"Did you find out anything useful?"

"The husband is a control freak who checks up on his wife's spending habits without her knowing. He's going to get a shock when he finds she's blown a month's wages on jewellery."

"And how is that useful?"

"Not sure yet, but I think it will be. I found this." Sherlock handed over a small coin. "A seven and a half, gold, ruble coin. It's genuine."

Mycroft examined the coin and noticed it had Czar Nicholas II on one side and the double headed eagle of the Byzantine Empire on the other.

"These were only made for one year."

"Eighteen-ninety-seven," Mycroft said, not needing his brother to tell him. In the mint condition this coin was in, it was worth a lot.

"He had more of them."

"They paid for the boat, then."

"It certainly looks that way, doesn't it, brother of mine?"

Mycroft nodded and held the coin up to the light to see it better in Sherlock's dimly lit living room.

"Oh, that looks pretty. Is it valuable?" Mrs Wintern asked as she brought in a tray of tea and biscuits.

"A thousand pounds perhaps. To the right collector, even more."

"You'd better not lose it, then." With this last addition to the conversation she left them to talk. Mycroft poured himself a cup and enjoyed the warmth it brought. He really shouldn't have walked the last few streets.

"I've already put a few friends on watch at the house, but I don't know if he'll be the best of leads. It is a little early to tell."

"It's likely to be a one-off purchase."

"Of course, when he notices he has one less, he might try to warn them."

"Perhaps. He will know you took it." Mycroft didn't say this to show concern for his brother. If Sherlock hadn't known that on stealing it, he'd be an idiot not worth feeling concern over.

"I was hoping for that. He's a control freak. He probably counted them twice a day." Sherlock grinned and flopped into the chair opposite Mycroft before picking up his pipe.

"Anyway. I'm between cases now. I solved Mrs Feltern's problem."

"The cat?" Mycroft phrased it like a question but he didn't really need to ask.

"Yes. It was making a nest to give birth in. Seemed to think her black smalls were the best lining."

"Climbed up a tree?"

"Yes, one end of the washing line was tied to an apple tree. You worked it out as well, then?"

"It was the only logical result," Mycroft said and finished his tea. He felt better than he had since Miss Jones had shown up, and knew Daniels would pull up outside with the car at the right moment if he walked out now. With a smile he got up.

"Leaving already, brother?"

"Our business is complete, is it not?"

"It is. I just thought you might have another reason for coming to see me."

"What possible other reason could I have? It's not either of our birthdays and it's still eight weeks until Christmas. Not that either of us make any extra effort then."

"No, nothing like that. I thought you'd want information on Amelia."

"Why on earth would I want information about *her*?"

Mycroft almost spat the last word, and did nothing to hide his disgust.

"The police arrested a man outside her house less than two hours ago."

"Who?"

"Some middle-aged man who was a carer for his own mother. She died recently."

"But he can't be her stalker," Mycroft said without thinking.

"No I don't think he is, but the police arrested him. I don't know any more than that. Amelia isn't answering her phone."

"Then how do you know anything?"

"Her publisher announced it not long after it happened. I assumed you'd know already."

"I've been at the club all day." Mycroft frowned. "Good evening, brother."

Giving Sherlock no time to respond, Mycroft hurried from the flat and was pleased to find Daniels waiting. In the end, Mycroft was the one who'd been late.

"Home," he said once he was settled in the back of the car. He wanted to find out what had happened to Amelia and if she was all right. The police didn't arrest someone unless they breached laws, and that meant Guy Thomas had broken into her flat. Or worse. And she'd been trying to ask him for protection against the man only a few hours earlier.

CHAPTER 8

Amelia stared at the almost empty plastic bottle in her fridge and swore. She was running out of milk. The little left wasn't enough to have tea now and have breakfast in the morning, and she had no fresh bread for toast either.

It took her another few seconds of standing with the fridge door open for her to decide to go to the local shop. It would only take a few minutes, and then she would be back in the warm. As she pulled on her coat, she checked her face in a mirror. Her eyes weren't puffy anymore, and no one else would notice all the crying she'd been doing.

Already she'd gone over the events of the day more times than she could count, yet her barely bloodshot eyes were enough to remind her and start her brain off on another loop. This time she fought it. She'd cried enough for one day. Doing it more wouldn't help. Myron and his challenges were in her past now. Something to be remembered for the good bits. She could learn from the rest and discard the unpleasant memories.

With this resolve she stepped out the front door, pulling it shut behind her and hearing the satisfying click of the lock engaging. A moment later she shoved her hands deep into her coat pockets, the fingers of her right closing over her house keys and her left over her purse.

Less than ten minutes later she walked back to her house, grasping a shopping bag with milk, bread, eggs, bacon and mushrooms. She could start the next day with a full English and hope it fuelled her into the new book.

She cut across the small patch of grass, walking near the window and past the back garden gate, to get to her front door. Just as she was pulling her keys out of her pocket she heard a sneeze. She froze to the spot, looking towards the gate, where the sound had come from. A moment later she picked up the light rustle of fabric brushing against wood.

It took all Amelia's control not to run screaming, but she managed to stay where she was, half way across her front garden, standing in the sliver of light that escaped through her curtains from the lamp she'd accidentally left on.

Acting braver than she felt, Amelia took a step towards the sound.

"Who's there?" she called, pleased her voice came out calm and steady. Silence responded. A minute later she shook her head at herself, already assuming she must have heard something else and no one was there. The sound of the gate latch creaking open stopped her.

She gulped as it swung inwards and Guy Thomas stepped out. At first she gaped at him. He didn't look at her, just wrung his hands together in that already familiar way. Then he took a couple of steps forward. Amelia stepped back, bringing her bag of shopping up as some kind of shield.

"What are you doing here?" she asked when he didn't speak.

"I needed to see you." He stepped forward again. "Do you think I could come in?"

"No, I don't think that would be..."

"Are you sick? You were so nice yesterday. I just want to talk. To tell you how I'm feeling. You're so easy to talk to." Guy came even closer.

"Stop," she said, trying to cut through his nervous talking.

"I don't know what you expect of me, but I'm not interested in what you have to say or..."

"I thought you cared. I just..." He wrung his hands and came closer to her again. Not knowing what else to do, she tried to push him away. Reacting quicker than she'd anticipated, he grabbed her arms. They grappled back and forth as he emitted a low sort of growl.

The pair rotated inch by inch as Amelia tried to keep him away from her. Uttering a final loud grunt, he shoved her. She lost her balance and flew backwards. The sound of shattering glass filled the night air and she landed with a bump on her living room floor.

"Oh, God. I'm so sorry," he said, coming to his senses before she did. She could only blink as a hot liquid trickled down from her eyebrow into her left eye, stinging as it went.

Her vision swam as Guy continued talking and his words blurred together. A moment later she saw someone else appear beside him, and had no idea how he'd got there, but he stepped gingerly through into the room.

"Amelia, isn't it?" She tried to nod, but pain flared in so many places she stopped. "I'm Andrew, from upstairs."

Staring at him, she tried to process what he'd just said.

"He pushed me," she eventually said, as much to let herself know what had just happened as her neighbour.

"I gathered that much. I'm going to call you an ambulance. Just stay still."

She nodded and raised her hand to try and clear her left eye, but it only made her eyebrow hurt more.

"Don't," Andrew said, his phone to his ear. She stopped and shut her eyes, making them sting even more. A minute later he dabbed at the skin around her eyes with something damp, and then held it against her eyebrow. It made the pain worsen at first, but then soothed it and stopped more blood flowing into her eyes.

She listened as he told someone on the other end of the phone call what had happened, while Guy continued apologising in the background. Opening one eye, she checked that he was still outside. He stood closer but still the other side of the shattered pane of glass, staring at her. Amelia closed her eye again so she wouldn't have to look at him and tried not to think about what he'd just done.

Her breath still came in ragged gasps and her chest hitched up and down, sending little ripples of pain through her each time it did. Somehow she had to slow it down and breathe normally, but it took all her focus just to listen to Andrew as he spoke to her and tried to stop the bleeding from her head.

"The ambulance will be here in a minute or two," he said, updating her again on its status. At least she thought he'd told her that already. She wasn't sure any more.

It felt like she'd only blinked when a young male paramedic appeared at her side. Andrew stepped back and talked to an older man in another green jacket and then another siren drew her attention. Two policemen leapt out of a car and came hurrying up. It didn't take them long to realise Guy had pushed her and she watched as they arrested him and took him off towards the car.

"Amelia?" An insistent voice said in her ear. She winced as she turned to look at the man. "Amelia Jones, the writer?"

"Yeah," she managed to say.

"I'm Gary. I need you to focus on me, all right?"

"Sure, Gary." As she spoke she felt herself calming more. Guy was gone and her chest wasn't so tight.

"You've got a lot of cuts from the glass and some is still in there. We're going to take you to the hospital to get it all out and, if we need to, give you more blood. Why don't you tell me where it hurts the most?"

"My head," she said, trying to think about the pain even though her instincts were doing everything they could to block it out. "I think my head hit the window first."

"All right. What about your back?" Gary asked.

"No. Bruised maybe, but not cut."

"Your hands are, and your eyebrow. Your legs?"

"I think they're fine," she replied, hoping he wouldn't ask her to stand.

"All right, I want you to sit up. Can you do that?"

She didn't answer, but tried to push up off the carpet with her arms. Pain flared in her right palm, but the recognition of it was dulled by the swimming in her head.

"Lean forward," Gary said as he put an arm around her back and helped her tilt over. "Looks like your coat kept most of the glass off you."

"I guess that's one good thing about it being so damn cold." She heard him chuckle.

"I'm afraid we're letting all your heat out."

That made her laugh, but she cut it short when her head exploded in another wave of pain.

"Sorry."

Between Gary and Andrew, she was helped to her feet and escorted into the back of the ambulance. Andrew reassured her that he'd stay in her flat and would get a mate to board up the window until she could get replacement glass. Then she was shut in and whisked off to the nearest hospital, just the other side of Bath's city centre.

***

Amelia sat down on her sofa, relieved the workmen had gone and she had a brand new window in place. They'd taken the boards with them and all the leftover debris from the change. It had cost her a small fortune, but the news surrounding the event had boosted her book sales enough to cover it in an oddly ironic sort of way. Shane had phoned her twice already today, once to check she was all right, and again to give her the happier news. She expected it was another excuse to check on her, especially as he'd cancelled her entire signing tour for now and suggested she go stay with Sebastian for a few days.

Both Andrew and his friend had been amazing. She'd come back from the hospital to find all the mess cleaned up and a large board covering the outside of the window frame, but she hadn't felt safe until now.

The hospital had kept her in overnight to monitor her, and the window company had sent someone over to assess the job within an hour of her phoning. It was late afternoon now, and the flat didn't look like it had been crashed into by her flying body. Andrew had even managed to get her blood out of the carpet. Well, mostly. She could still see a bit of an odd-coloured patch if she looked at it from the right angle, but the dark blue helped hide the stain.

The police had shown up mid-morning to get her statement and collect all the letters. She'd talked to them while people worked on the window. They'd asked a lot of questions, which made her tiredness feel worse, but having them there while so many strangers were fixing the front of the flat had helped her relax in the safety they brought with them.

Now she was alone and enclosed, she decided to take a bath. She couldn't take a shower, as she'd normally want to, thanks to the stitches and staples she had in her head, along with the stitches in the palm of her right hand. She didn't mind the ones they'd put across her left eyebrow and palm, they were neat and under a patch of gauze, but the thought of the staples in the back of her head made her stomach lurch. Not for the first time, she wished she hadn't seen them before they'd put them in.

Over an hour later, Amelia still sat in the bath. The water was going cold and she found herself struggling to resist washing her hair. With slow, steady movements, she got out the bath and dried herself off. She'd managed to keep her right hand and everything from her neck up dry so the doctors couldn't complain about her not taking care when she went back to see them.

It took her a little longer to get dressed when she couldn't use all the fingers on her right hand, but she managed to slip into jogging trousers, a sports bra, and a relatively form fitting t-shirt. Myron would have sneered, seeing her like that, but he never would, so she tried to push it from her mind.

When she walked back through to her open-plan living room and kitchen to prepare something for dinner, she stopped and fought to stifle the scream that rose instinctively within her. Another envelope sat on her doormat, with the same blocky, hand-written version of her name as the previous three.

Immediately she picked up her phone and called the number the female police officer had given her earlier.

"Hello, Officer Bryant?" she asked as soon as she heard the click of someone picking up.

"Yes, who is this?"

"It's Amelia Jones. I've got another one of those letters."

"Oh, you've found another. Could you bring it in to the station?"

"No, it's not another I found. It just came through my door. I was in the bath and I got out and there it is on my doormat." She felt her breathing increase in speed and noticed she could hear her heart pumping blood around her ears.

"Okay. Why don't I come over again and we'll open it together. I can be there in about fifteen minutes."

Bryant hung up and left Amelia standing near her coffee table, unsure of what to do. For several minutes she stared at the envelope, before she realised the door would open over it. She went to the kitchen to get cling wrap for one hand and struggled to get it out of the roll one handed. By the time she had her left hand covered, several more minutes had ticked by and she knew it wouldn't be much longer until Bryant arrived.

After taking a deep breath to help herself stay calm, she went over to the door, picked up the envelope by one corner and put it down on the coffee table. She sank into the sofa and stayed there until she heard a quick, firm knock on the wooden door.

"Miss Jones, it's Officer Bryant," the police officer said, loud enough Amelia could hear it where she sat. It galvanised her into action and she finally looked away from the letter long enough to open the door and let Bryant in.

Bryant wasted no time. As soon as she saw the envelope on the coffee table, she walked over and pulled two latex gloves from her trouser pocket.

"Where have you touched it?" she asked a moment later.

"Just the bottom left corner." Amelia waved her hand so the policewoman could see her home-made glove. She nodded her approval at Amelia's foresight.

Before Amelia could offer her some sort of letter opener, Bryant had pulled a pen knife from her pocket and was already slicing it open.

"Hopefully the writer licked the flap and we can get a DNA match on the saliva," she said as she pulled the message out of its case.

Amelia,

I really don't know what to believe any more. Your publisher said you were sick and they sent you home to rest, and then they say that it was due to a stalker threat. I really hope they don't mean me. I'm sure you wouldn't want to involve the police in our affairs. As long as you don't do anything out of character for you, you have nothing to fear.

Your publisher mentioned that you were attacked last night and were hurt. It's made me very angry. At least having time off work means I can keep an eye on you now. I'm going to take care of you.

With my love.

"Right, I'm going to need to take this," Bryant said as soon as they'd both finished reading it. Amelia nodded.

"Although I don't think the writer intends to try to break

in, is there somewhere you can go where you'll feel safer, or someone who could come stay with you? A brother, or boyfriend?"

"Uh, maybe. I'd have to ask." Amelia frowned. Her first option would have been Myron, but that wasn't possible now and she didn't appreciate being reminded of that. "You don't think it was Guy, then?"

"It can't be. We still have him in custody."

"Right." Amelia stopped again, her mind barely able to process this information. Two men threatening her was not something she wanted to think about.

"I'm going to take this into the station. It's going to affect the case we have against Mr Thomas, so the officer dealing with that will want this update." Amelia nodded and followed Bryant over to the door. "I'll call you when we have more information. In the meantime, try and get some rest."

The door shutting behind Bryant sounded too loud to Amelia's ears. Silence followed it, and she could hear nothing over the sound of her own breathing. All thoughts of food were forgotten as she went back to the sofa and sat down.

Several minutes later her mobile phone went off, vibrating along the coffee table and making her jump. She reached for it and exhaled as she saw it was Sebastian.

"Please tell me you need some help with the plot for your next Dalton novel," he said as soon as she answered. A small grin flitted across her face, "I haven't got an unsolved case. I need something to do."

"Hi, Sebastian."

"Hmmm, you don't sound good. You said you were fine in your text earlier. What's wrong now?"

"I... uh... There was another letter. The police don't think it was Guy, as they still have him locked up. It just doesn't make any sense. I thought it was him when he came to the restaurant. I know I was followed, and there was that creepy black car, but..."

"It's obviously not him. Mycr – my brother and I were

only discussing that last night."

"You discussed it with Myron?"

"Yes, I was helping him with something. He was very concerned when he heard what had happened to you. Tried to hide it, of course, but that's my brother."

"Right." Amelia frowned. She had no idea what to think. Fear gripped at her stomach and tied it in knots, and Sebastian just talked and talked.

"Well, come on, then, tell me what plot you have so far," Sebastian's voice broke through her thoughts once more.

"I'm sorry, Sebastian. I don't think I can concentrate right now. The police have said I should find someone to come stay or go somewhere else. They don't think it's safe for me to be alone. I don't... I don't know what to do."

As soon as she said the words out loud, she felt tears sting the backs of her eyes. Oddly, she also felt better, as if saying the words aloud made the fear easier to manage.

"Come here then, dear. You know you're very welcome."

"Would that be all right?" she asked in a small voice, feeling some of the weight lift off her.

"Of course. Get on the next train. It leaves Bath in twenty-two minutes. You'll have to hurry packing though."

She smiled at the information. Sebastian always seemed to know the exact train times from everywhere to anywhere.

"I haven't unpacked yet."

"Good. I'll see you in two hours and forty-three minutes, then. Your train will be ever so slightly delayed, but not by much."

At this she laughed. It wouldn't surprise her for him to be right, but it didn't matter either way. She was going to London and she realised it felt a lot like going home.

CHAPTER 9

An exasperated sigh escaped Mycroft's lips as he pulled off his tie and grabbed one of the wigs from his disguise kit. Yet again, he found himself having to leave the house to do something himself.

Now that Amelia's face was all over the news, he couldn't assign one of his agents to keep an eye on her without them growing suspicious. That meant he had to do it himself, and Daniels had just informed him that she was not only staying with his brother in Baker Street but that she had decided to leave the house to go get food.

Mrs Wintern had felt concerned and told Daniels, who'd passed it on to him. Most irritatingly, Sherlock was inside the flat. If he was meant to be keeping her safe, he was doing a crap job of it.

Once Mycroft looked like a street cleaner, he had Daniels bring the car round. In the back, Daniels had already placed a see-through bin bag with bits and pieces of rubbish and a stick designed to grab litter without the user needing their hands.

He wouldn't need to do much of the job, just enough to get close to Amelia. It would give him a chance to keep an eye on her, and if the male who'd sent her threatening letters happened to be there as well, Mycroft knew he would notice.

After sending Amelia away and insisting Guy Thomas was no threat to her, he felt a small pang of guilt that the carer had pushed her through a window. Sherlock said she was fine, but he'd seen her medical records. With that much glass and the way she'd gone into it, it was only luck that resulted in the damage not being worse.

As soon as he'd found out about her state, he'd demanded the police records. Mr Thomas was pleading guilty, but saying he never meant her to go through the window. Just that tempers had flared. In his case, he'd just found out his mother had died. And Amelia had admitted to pushing him first because she felt threatened. Given that another letter had come through while Thomas was held in a cell, the police had decided to let him go with a verbal warning to leave Amelia alone.

Finally, Mycroft had asked for the letters. At first the chief of police had been awkward about handing evidence over to him, but they both knew having Mycroft on the case would solve it more swiftly.

The original letters had arrived by courier that morning. He'd already identified the ink and where it would have been bought from, as well as the month the stationery was purchased. Given that it was likely to be in the Bath area, there was already someone looking through the shop records of all the suppliers of the envelopes and matching those with names. If Mycroft could find even a little more information, they would figure out who the imbecile was.

Daniels pulled into a small alleyway so Mycroft could get out where no one would see him and turned the car off to wait for his boss to come back. In only a few seconds Mycroft adjusted his posture and manner of walking to look more like a poor and slightly grumpy cleaner, but a bit of a stoop, an odd mutter and a ruffle of his wig hair helped finish the transformation.

It only took him a minute to work his way up to the shop

and spot Amelia. She was paying at the self-checkout near the window and focused solely on her task. He picked up a few cigarette ends as he kept an eye on her, trying not to wrinkle his nose in disgust at the smell.

Before stepping out of the shop she buttoned up her coat and took a good look at the street outside. The buttonholes were stiff and fought back against her deft fingers, another sign that it was new. The old one hadn't survived its encounter with the window glass.

He tried not to appear too obvious when her eyes came in his direction. It made him feel a little better that she was trying to be careful and see any potential threats, but it made her more likely to spot him. He wondered if he should have put more effort into the disguise, but hiding in plain sight was more Sherlock's sort of thing and he'd wanted to be quick.

Letting her walk ahead, Mycroft followed Amelia along the street towards Sherlock's flat. Every few hundred metres she took a good look around her, flicking her hair or pretending to look for a shop to cover her actions. When a guy almost bumped into her, coming out of a clothes shop, she bit back a scream and he saw the wild haze of panic in her eyes before she managed to contain it and move on.

As she turned the corner at the end of the road, he hurried to catch up. Mycroft didn't want her out of his sight for longer than necessary, even if no one else seemed to be following her.

It didn't take him long to get to the end of the road, but a few people gave him odd looks as he loped down the pavement. He knew they expected him to pick up litter, but it didn't matter if they were confused.

He paused at the end of the road to pick out his quarry from the crowds of people, but when he looked left to see where Amelia was, he realised she was gone.

A cough came from the doorway just behind him. Amelia stood, half in the shadows, a slight grin on her face. They stared at each other for a moment. He took in all the damage to her body. She'd removed the gauze patches and had an assortment of cuts and several stitches on her eyebrows. The shopping was also hanging from her left hand, despite her being right-handed.

"Hello, Myron," she said, a hint of pleasure in her voice. "Not your *usual* attire."

He gave her a fake smile as she eyed him up and down, and then came up closer so they could talk without being overheard. He was impressed. Not many people would have noticed him, even considering his lack of practice.

Once he was beside her, he turned to face the road so they were side by side, but not looking at each other. He then took her right hand and gently inspected the wound.

"Very neat stitches," he said to break the silence.

"Yes, but it will probably scar and in the meantime I can't write – not by hand, anyway."

Mycroft let go of her and looked away. He wouldn't say sorry, even if he was glad she wasn't more hurt.

"My brother sent me a message to tell me that you were fine, but staying at Baker Street with him."

"I suppose it depends on your definition of fine. I'll heal. But yes, I'm staying with Sebastian. He offered when he heard I'd had another letter and the police recommended I wasn't alone. They released Guy as well. He's gone missing since. No one knows where he is."

"I'm aware."

"Of course you are." She shook her head and he picked up on her annoyance. It only served to flare up his.

"Given our arrangement, I'm surprised you didn't ask *me* to find you somewhere safe to go."

"I did, don't you remember? About five hours before Guy shoved me through a window."

Mycroft coughed as a woman walking by stared at them. It was evident she'd heard Amelia's outburst.

"I assumed our arrangement was over anyway," Amelia managed to say in a calmer tone. He knew it was a question despite how it was phrased, and he knew she was providing him with a way to apologise. It was an easy way out of a situation he didn't feel comfortable in, and he found himself impressed with her skills for the second time in only a few minutes. He was starting to understand why Sherlock liked her. Somehow, she had a way of getting what she wanted.

"If you can refrain from turning up at my club unannounced in future, I think I can be magnanimous enough to allow our arrangement to continue."

"Thank you for your most gracious leniency." Every word she said oozed sarcasm and he found himself raising his eyebrows at her. A smirk flitted across her face. She was mocking him. He wasn't sure anyone had ever mocked him, except Sherlock.

"I'm still not happy you're staying at Baker Street," Mycroft said, changing the subject.

"Why ever not?"

"My younger brother is more easily charmed, especially by someone of such intelligence. I would hate for him to think you have more of an interest in him than you do." His words were met with laughter. He frowned at her lack of seriousness. As soon as she saw his face she stopped.

"Myron, your brother is in no danger from me. He knows where my interests lie and has even encouraged me in them. It's quite amusing, really." Mycroft raised an eyebrow, not entirely sure he wanted to know what she found entertaining. "This conversation is the first time you've expressed a sort of jealousy over my intentions. I didn't expect you to be worried I might prefer another to you."

He hmmphd his distaste at the idea, but she didn't stop talking.

"There really is no need to worry, Myron. Sebastian is well aware of my feelings. I consider myself to be yours. Claiming me is entirely up to you." She smiled up at him, but he avoided her gaze.

"Now. I should get this shopping back before the milk

gets too warm and the ice-cream melts. Thank you for your concern, Myron. Have a good evening."

Without so much as a backwards glance, Amelia wandered off, leaving him standing in a stranger's doorway. Despite the brush-off, he kept his under-cover act and followed her at a distance back to Baker Street. The whole way, she continued her obsessive checking, even though their eyes met a couple of times. He wasn't sure if he felt pleased she was being so careful and trying to observe the people around her, or annoyed that she wasn't leaving it to him.

It was evident that she knew he was there. When he stopped on the corner of Baker Street, she walked up to the flat door, smiled and mouthed a thank you in his direction, but she'd been checking for her stalker anyway.

He was just as wary as he headed back to his car, on the slight chance her stalker was clever enough to notice Mycroft and hang back, but he saw no one suspicious. The streets were filled with people as normal as London usually was.

Daniels knew better than to ask how the trip had gone when Mycroft got back into the car. A frown was fixed on his face until he sat down behind his desk and found his housekeeper had pre-empted his desire for tea. She'd even placed two of his favourite biscuits on a plate beside it.

While he munched, he put his awkward conversation with Amelia aside. It wouldn't take much longer to figure out who her stalker was, even though he hadn't shown up that afternoon. His analysis of the letters, combined with the research he had the police doing, would pinpoint the man in a couple of days.

In the meantime, he had a watch out on the Russian ruble coins. Apparently a whole cache of them had gone missing two years before. The Russians had hushed it up. Mycroft had noticed it at the time, but they'd resurfaced in a container in a US dock about six months later.

He'd forgotten about it and assumed they had been returned to Russia, but it had recently been brought to his attention that the crate had been put on a very interesting ship. The Lyubov Orlova was misplaced in February on its way from Newfoundland in Canada.

At the time, the Canadians had assured him it was deliberate. They wanted to monitor Ireland after some interesting remarks they'd made at a previous diplomatic meeting. A storm conveniently helped cover the Canadians' tracks, and the newspapers focused on the rats aboard rather than any possible cargo.

Knowing he had to find out what had happened to the ship, Mycroft put his best research agent onto the task. Wherever that ship had travelled after, it wasn't Ireland. He suspected it was deliberately sunk and then divers smuggled the contents out over the next few months. This operation had been in planning a long time and he'd interfered.

This time, he wouldn't miss any of the information. He read through everything he had, and then once more to make sure. Someone by the name of Delra, no gender specified, but given the nature of the operation, probably male, had hired a yacht. Rumours abounded that he wanted to look for sunken treasure, but after three weeks had turned up empty-handed. At least that was the rumour. He didn't believe one word of it.

Less than ten minutes later Mycroft had sent out enquiries for more information on the yacht, which ports it had docked at on its voyage and the description of Mr Delra.

He sat back, satisfied with the day's work. Amelia was a small hiccup, and he finally had enough information that he would get to the bottom of this strange alliance between the Russians and the Koreans.

To stretch his legs, Mycroft got up and wandered over to the bay window overlooking his garden. Darkness had set in and the sky was dark overhead but clear enough to see the North Star and a crescent moon on its way to becoming full.

The sound of an email arriving disturbed him from the rewarding view and brought him back to his desk. Hoping it was information from one of the many sources he was waiting on, he eagerly clicked on it. One sentence in, he frowned.

Mycroft,

It has come to my attention that you are looking into certain events involving the missing ship Lyubov Orlova. If you value your position within my government, you will desist immediately.

There was no email address in the sender field, but he knew who it was from. She'd emailed him before, and he didn't need the little, but perfectly drawn, crown in the signature to know it was an order he shouldn't disobey.

CHAPTER 10

Frustration filled Amelia as Sebastian lolloped over his armchair. He'd been playing the violin, badly, for over an hour. He needed a case and she needed to have at least ten minutes to herself.

The most exciting thing that had happened that day was a police conversation to let her know they'd found Guy. His brother had been hiding him to give the neurotic geek some time out of the limelight. One of the people in the police had leaked his name to a local paper, and he'd been hounded ever since attacking her. Something not even she wanted.

After everything that had happened, she felt sorry for him. He'd been caught up in events of a bigger nature than he was used to handling. If she'd not been receiving strange letters, she suspected their last encounter would have ended differently. Now the poor guy had no job, no mother and a police record.

On the more positive side, there had been no more letters, and Myron had sent her a message to let her know no one else had followed her back to Baker Street the last time she'd left. But three days had passed since then and Sebastian Holmes appeared incapable of stocking his own fridge.

With a sigh she grabbed her coat and handbag.

"I'm going to the shop," she said. Sebastian didn't stop his odd droning with the instrument. It definitely couldn't be called music. Although she didn't think he'd heard, she walked out of the flat anyway and hurried down the stairs. Mrs Wintern was out, so she took the front door key off the little hook on her way past.

The outside chill nipped at her fingers, making her shove them into the large pockets. She sighed and stepped down onto the pavement.

"Amelia!" an unfamiliar voice called from behind her. She turned and paused, not placing the guy's face at first. A moment later she twigged, but couldn't remember his name.

"Hi," she said, "How are you?"

"You don't remember me, do you?" He took a step closer and she frowned.

"You were at my signing a few days ago."

"Yes, but you don't remember my name, and I thought you and I had connected."

Amelia's eyes went wide and a chill ran through her torso, numbing her insides, stopping her breathing and rooting her feet to the spot.

This was her letter sender.

"I think you and I should have a talk, don't you?" he strode towards her and grabbed her arm. A second later she felt something hard pressing into her side.

"Why don't we chat over coffee," she replied, her mind finally kicking in. "There's a great place just up the road."

Pretending she hadn't noticed the weapon he held against her, she tried to walk towards the café she'd thought of, but his grip on the top of her arm tightened until it was painful.

"No, I think we should go somewhere more private, don't you? This way." He jabbed the weapon into her ribs and steered her towards a waiting car. As he opened the door and pushed her inside, she tried to think of his name, but she couldn't. At most, she thought it might begin with a J or a K, but that was the closest she could get to it.

He pushed her over into the farther seat, pointing the gun directly at her now, and got in beside her, shutting the door. With one hand he reached forward and picked up a pile of items on the passenger seat of the car.

"Here, put this in your mouth." He passed her a slightly squishy plastic ball as he pulled a strip of gaffer tape off a large roll. She hesitated and gulped. "Don't make me ask you twice."

"You know you don't have to do this," she said.

With an exaggerated sigh he moved closer to her. She leant back as he came forward, but the seat and edge of the car gave her little room to get away. He grabbed her chin to pull her head closer to his.

"Put it in your mouth."

Amelia stared at him and then gently shook her head. Pain exploded across her face as he backhanded her, catching her stitched-up eyebrow. A hot liquid welled up and trickled slowly downwards. He grabbed her face again, took the gag from her and held it up to her mouth. This time she cooperated.

As soon as her mouth had closed around it as best it could, he slapped the gaffer tape over the top. Once he'd used more tape to bind her hands together, he strapped her seatbelt over her body and arms, pinning them at her sides. Finally, he pulled a nightmask over her eyes, this time being careful to miss her eyebrow. Her only relief was the knowledge that it would keep the blood out of her eyes for a little while.

"This won't take too long," he said and moved away. It didn't make her feel any better. The longer this took the more time she had to think of his name, or even better, escape. A shiver ran through her as it occurred to her how this might end if she didn't. It would be ages before Sebastian noticed she was missing, let alone have any idea where she'd gone.

Waves of fear rippled through her as she thought about the words in the letters she'd received. He had somehow convinced himself that there was a spark between them, and the first few moments of him spotting her had shown it wasn't true. His reaction let her know that it wasn't going to go well if she couldn't think of his name or convince him that she knew he existed.

Pinned into her seat with her hands fixed in one position, she slid across the leather with every turn. Just as she'd seen in a film, she tried to remember the direction they drove in, but there were too many lefts and rights for her to remember after only a couple of minutes.

Her stomach tightened into a painful knot when the car drove into a parking space and stopped. A few seconds later, he pulled the mask off her face. She blinked in the parking lot light, but barely had time to look at the area around her before he hooked his arm around her body and hoisted her out of the car.

"Almost there, baby."

Amelia grunted her response and immediately found herself glad she hadn't been able to say it properly. Calling him names wouldn't help her situation.

As he pulled her through the car park and into a lift, she didn't dare struggle. He had what looked like a gun in his pocket, but it was still pointed at her and she had no idea if he would use it. The lift took them up into the block of flats and he walked her quickly along past several doors, stopping in front of thirty-four.

"Reach into the right pocket of my jeans and hook my keys out," he said, turning her and holding her up against the doorway. When she didn't move, he pulled a four-inch switchblade out of his pocket and raised his eyebrows at her. She hid her shock at finding it hadn't been a gun but a knife. If she'd known, she'd never have let him take her from outside Baker Street, but it was too late to fight now.

Feeling her heart rate increase, she focused all her effort on her bound hands and slid the fingers of her left hand into the pocket. When they brushed against the cool metal of the key ring, she grasped a hold and pulled them out.

Once she'd opened the door for them, he pushed it open and gave her a shove forward. She tripped over the metal strip that divided the room from the hallway, landing hard on one side. Her hip flared with pain, taking her mind off the dull throbbing on one side of her face.

"Get up," he said in a low voice. She tried to push herself up with her hands, but his impatience led to him grabbing her shoulder and yanking upwards. A few seconds later, she was stood unsteadily on her feet.

The hallway was empty, and as he walked her through to the living room, she noticed there was very little furniture there as well. Just a camping chair and a small stove with discarded take-away containers scattered here and there.

"Do you like my flat? I rented it especially to be near you."

Amelia stopped walking when they reached the middle of the room, and almost went sprawling across the floor for a second time when he pushed her again.

"Keep going. I think we should go somewhere more comfortable, don't you?"

This time she managed to refrain from trying to answer him. She knew he didn't want to hear her opinion, and it would be good practice to keep her mouth shut rather than saying what she was thinking.

It didn't take long for him to manoeuvre her through to the bedroom. In here there was a large but low bed, neatly made, and a wardrobe, making it the most furnished room of the flat. He pushed her down onto the bed and she flicked herself over onto her back.

After grinning at her, he locked the door behind them. As he pocketed the key, she noticed it was a newly fitted lock and hadn't been an original feature of the door. It wasn't well done, but it looked sturdy enough to give her problems.

"DIY isn't my strong point," he said when he noticed what she was looking at. Keeping the blade in his hands, he came closer to her and sat beside her. She didn't dare move away, but felt her heart rate increase even further.

He used one hand to pull the tape off her mouth, making her skin tingle where it had been stuck. She spat the ball out.

"That doesn't taste very nice," she said, hoping it would be odd enough to defuse some of the tension in the room. Now it was gone, Amelia also focused on keeping her breathing steady. If she wanted to survive this, she needed to keep calm and get plenty of oxygen to her body and mind.

When he stared at her, she lifted her hands to see if he'd take the tape off those as well, but he must have decided against it because he ignored the gesture.

"Have you remembered me yet?" he asked.

"You work in the shop in Bath. I spent lunch with you and your colleagues."

"And my name?" He didn't sound impressed with her reply.

"It begins with a K."

"Well, I suppose it's better than nothing. It's Kevin, although you can call me Dalton if that makes this easier for you."

"No, it's okay, Kevin is a good name." She tried to give him a small smile, but it made the pain in her cheek flare up again and she involuntarily winced.

"Hmmm." He got up and went through to the en-suite bathroom. A moment later he came back with damp toilet paper and dabbed at the cut near her eyebrow. She hissed her breath through her teeth at the sting, but savoured the moment of him being kind. It was impossible to tell how long it would last.

"That's better," he said and threw the bloodstained wad through the door to land on the bathroom floor.

"Thank you," she replied. Silence followed as he stared at her. He then reached up with his hand and stroked her cheek.

"I've dreamt of this moment a lot of times. Being your Dalton. Charming you into bed the same way he does your heroines. We're a lot alike, although I think I'm a little more settled. I've settled on you." He lent forward to kiss her but she pulled back. This needed to slow down.

"Well, why don't we discuss my next book? You can tell me what you think of my idea. I'm struggling with it, and you said you'd always wanted to do that." Amelia tried to keep her fear out of her voice but wasn't sure how well she'd managed it when the lines on his forehead deepened.

"Are you trying to slow me down? Dalton doesn't do this sort of thing slowly. He tends to take what he wants."

"I know, but I prefer to go one step at a time. Even Dalton likes a willing partner. Slower would get us both what we want." She watched his face for a reaction, hoping she could talk her way out of this or at least buy herself some more time.

"Do you want it?" he stroked her cheek and gazed at her lips.

"I'm not sure yet. I'd like to get to know you a bit. This has been rather... rushed."

He almost snarled, and she realised she'd said something wrong.

"I already told you, I'm just like Dalton, and I know you like him."

"You have a different backstory," she blurted out. He raised his arm to strike her once more, but stopped as she flinched and tried to protect herself with her arms.

"All right, I'll be patient with you. After all, we have plenty of time together. And I'm sure you *will* make the right decision in the end, and if you look like you'll make the wrong one I can help *persuade* you."

"As I said earlier, I'm sure we can both get what we want. As a writer, I know the backstory of all my characters, whether I put it in my books or not. I'd love to know yours. Why don't you tell me where you're from? The sorts of things you liked to do as a kid?"

He moved to sit beside her on the bed and put his arm around her. After giving him another warm smile, she leant back against the headboard and let him talk about himself. Several minutes ticked by as he told her about the village he'd grown up in. Wanting him to talk as much as possible, she asked questions. She even laughed when he told her a funny story about his cat.

She estimated that fifteen minutes had passed while he talked, but it felt like no time at all when he stopped. Immediately, he focused on her again.

"Now, I think I've talked enough. You know everything you need to know. I'm your Dalton and I'm going to protect you. You're safe from that Guy Thomas while you're here with me, and I intend to keep it that way."

Leaning forward, he pressed his lips tenderly against her stitched eyebrow. If she hadn't been brought there against her will, the gesture and accompanying words would have seemed sweet, possibly even romantic, but in light of what he'd done to her they were more possessive.

As she felt her pulse quicken again, her mind frantically searched for something else that might distract him, but she couldn't think of anything before he crushed his lips against hers. He used his body strength to hold her against the bed and pushed his tongue into her mouth.

Without thinking, Amelia bit down on it. As he pulled away from her, he cried out in a mix of fury and pain. Seizing her moment, she wriggled her body back towards the edge of the bed, pushing with her hands where she could, but Kevin recovered quicker than she expected.

Another explosion of pain and momentum erupted on one side of her face. The force propelled her the rest of the way off the bed and onto the floor.

"Now, that wasn't nice. It seems I'm going to have to persuade you after all," he said as he pulled the switchblade back out of his pocket.

CHAPTER 11

A shrill buzzing sound disturbed Mycroft from his afternoon tea. When he saw that it was Sherlock calling he almost didn't answer, but his younger brother almost never phoned him.

"What?"

"Did you just pick up Amelia?"

"Of course not. Why would I want to speak to –"

"Mycroft, she's gone." The panic in Sherlock's voice was evident.

"Tell him I saw her," Mrs Wintern's voice came out the speaker pressed to his ear as if she was on the phone instead of his younger brother. Mycroft wasn't sure he could cope with the annoying voice.

"Can't you send her away?" he replied. His younger brother ignored the comment.

"She saw Amelia outside talking to someone as her taxi pulled up, but by the time she'd paid the driver and gathered her bags, Amelia and the man were both gone."

"Does Mrs Wintern know –"

"No, I'd estimate that it was only four minutes ago, but she can't confirm."

"It's a good estimate. They'll be in a car."

"That's why I'm phoning you. Can you access the cameras?"

"Of course," Mycroft said, forcing his voice to sound as bored and unconcerned as it usually was when Sherlock asked him to use his powers to help solve some crime. "Not that they'll do any good if we don't know which car. Baker Street is busy enough it could be one of many taxis or private vehicles."

Silence greeted his statement. Sherlock would know it was true. At this time of day the cameras were focused on the traffic and not the pavement. He could follow a car across the entire city, but he had to know what car to follow. The muffled sound of Sherlock talking to Mrs Wintern started up in the background while Mycroft waited. He knew he still sounded calm and reasonable, but he'd detected the slight increase in muscle tension around his jaw and shoulders as well as the few extra beats per minute of his heart. He felt concern for Amelia. Not as much worry as he'd feel for his brother if his brother was in danger, but he'd known his brother for more than a century and he was the only other person who came close to Mycroft's level of thinking. That many years of companionship made a person fond.

The sound of Sherlock yelling at Mrs Wintern to get out interrupted Mycroft's reflection upon his reactions and brought him back to their predicament.

"She didn't see anything. It could be any car."

"Not even a colour?" Mycroft asked, knowing women seemed to notice that first when it came to vehicles.

"Wait... Oh... the clue was there all along. Urggh, I'm such an idiot."

"Sherlock?"

"Amelia mentioned that there was a car that followed her and waited outside her restaurant the night she got the third letter. The one slipped into her handbag."

"Then I can find it. I'll call you." Mycroft hung up and immediately dialled the agent who'd been following her that night. Less than five minutes later he had the car registration. A black Audi under the name Kevin Merton. A minute after that his personal assistant was running a check on the name and car registration while he surveyed the video footage of Baker Street.

It didn't take him long to spot the car on screen, and he moved through the camera feeds until he had enough of an idea where Merton was taking her that Sherlock could get going. While watching the next few cameras along the road, he called his brother back.

"He took her north-west, towards Warwick Avenue and Abbey Road."

"So you're sending me after her, then?" Sherlock said, but Mycroft heard the sound of the flat door slamming shut and Sherlock's feet hammering out a quick step down the stairs.

"Need I remind you that you had offered to take care of her? And you know footwork's not my sort of thing."

"It never has been, brother of mine."

Mycroft heard Sherlock get into a taxi and tell the driver to head for Warwick Avenue. Knowing his brother was on the way, he relaxed a little and concentrated on watching the Audi on the CCTV footage.

"Manor House Court, Warrington Gardens," Mycroft said when the car pulled over. Here the camera was set back far enough that he could see the vehicle drive into the garage underneath the block of flats.

"I'm going to need a flat number," Sherlock said after relaying the information to the taxi driver.

"I'm aware."

Although it was normally the sort of thing his brother did, Mycroft searched the database of residents for any who might be related to Kevin but out at work or on holiday. Most were young workers who had no connection to the young man from Bath, but a few raised possible flags. As he was trying to narrow them down, he received an email from his secretary.

Kevin Merton has recently put down a deposit on flat 34 Manor House Court, Warrington Gardens. He also recently purchased the car, with cash.

Pleased at the speed of his assistant, Mycroft gave Sherlock the number.

"Good. I'll talk to you later." His younger brother hung up, leaving him sitting in his study wondering what might be happening. He felt a little disgruntled that he'd been exploring the wrong path of enquiry concerning the likely flat, trying to find it through connections rather than the man himself, but knew he'd asked the assistant to help to ensure no angle was missed. She'd done her job well and he didn't normally have to perform under such pressure.

While he waited for Sherlock to inform him of Amelia's state, Mycroft paced back and forth across the study floor. Each time he came towards his desk, his eyes fixed on the letter Merton had sent Amelia.

The man evidently sought to control Amelia out of his own deep-seated insecurities and desire for power. He was the exact opposite of what a man should be when presented with power, and Mycroft spent almost every day combating men just like him. Admittedly, they normally had significantly more power, but they were the same.

While men of honour, like him, used their control and power to protect people and better society, men like Merton used their control and power to intimidate and get their own desires, bending the will of others until they broke under the strain. Mycroft would see him stopped and Amelia protected.

***

Fear rippled through Amelia as Kevin stepped closer. Her eyes never left the knife in his right hand.

"I'm your Dalton. The man you've always wanted in your life, and you're going to be my Amelia and be a good girl. But you've pushed me too far and right now I need to teach you a lesson. This is for your own good."

She tried to pull back from him as he came closer, but the wall wouldn't give, no matter how much she dug her feet into the carpet and pushed herself back into it.

The sound of a door crashing open stopped Kevin's advancement.

"In here!" Amelia yelled, hoping it was one of the Holmes brothers. In that moment she didn't care which. Kevin growled and lunged at her with the knife. As she pulled herself to the side, she screamed. A hand clamped down on her shoulder and he used his body to try and hold her still, but before he could do her any harm two strong arms wrapped around his middle and pulled him off.

Kevin flew onto the bed, but not before he'd brought the knife down into Sebastian's arm. The younger Holmes brother grunted in pain but pulled the weapon out and threw it to one side as Kevin recovered and found his feet again.

Trying to stand, Amelia scrabbled against the wall and floor. Eventually, she'd levered herself upright and watched as Sebastian tackled Kevin, sending him into the wardrobe, which broke under the force of the impact and revealed the few sets of clothing and other items.

Several growls and grunts filled the room as the pair wrestled until a well-aimed right hook from Sebastian sent Kevin down for the count, right in front of the wreckage of the wardrobe. She watched as he checked her stalker's pulse and nodded in satisfaction.

"I think the police can deal with him from here," Sebastian said and smiled at her. She nodded gratefully and wobbled as her legs and head protested. Less than a second later Sebastian's arms were around her and she was resting her head against his chest.

"It's over now. You're safe again."

Tears stung her eyes and she let out a deep breath. After being worried and nervous for so long she felt weightless now she knew who her stalker was and that he wouldn't be able to hurt her anymore.

As her relieved mind kicked back into gear she remembered that Sebastian had been stabbed, but she could see his arm while he held her. The skin was smooth, and only a small amount of dried blood showed where the knife had gone in. Her eyes went wide, but she didn't say anything. Adrenaline still pumped through her quick enough to keep her mind one step ahead of her mouth.

"I'm sorry I didn't get to you sooner," Sebastian said as he let her go.

"It was quicker than I expected. How did you know where to find me?"

"My brother. He found the car and followed it on all those cameras he has access to."

"Wow," she said, trying not to stare at his arm and let him know she'd seen him heal.

Thankfully, the police came hurrying in, followed by two paramedics, and distracted both of them from each other. Sebastian went into his official mode, something she'd only seen him do twice before, and told the police what they needed to know while both she and Kevin were seen to by a paramedic each.

When Kevin showed signs of coming back to the waking world the police read him his rights and took him away. He didn't look at her and she ignored him.

Only the wound on her eyebrow and the bruises Kevin had caused on her face needed seeing to, but her stitches were still in well enough that the woman tending her didn't think she needed to go get them done again. The police then asked her a few questions, mostly to confirm that events had happened the way Sebastian had already told them. They must have been used to handling cases where he was involved, because they didn't question how he knew what had happened while he wasn't there. Once she'd confirmed that Kevin had hit her twice and threatened her with the switchblade after taking her from Baker Street, they let Sebastian take her home.

Mrs Wintern came rushing out of her flat as soon as she heard the door open, and Amelia gave the elderly landlady a small smile.

"Oh my," she said as she saw the swelling bruises on the side of her face. "I'll make you some tea, and get some painkillers."

Sebastian chuckled as she hurried away again.

"Tea solves everything," he whispered in Amelia's ear as he followed her up the stairs. A smile flitted across her face until the pain of moving her cheeks made her wince.

Once she was sat in the extra armchair in the living room, Sebastian fetched her a blanket and arranged it over her lap. Before either of them could do anything else, Mrs Wintern returned with the usual tray.

"None for me, thanks. I'm off out again," Sebastian said as she set it down beside Amelia and poured the tea.

"You can't go out and leave her like this! She's just had a scare."

"It's all right, Mrs Wintern, really, it is. I'm in the mood for some television, and it's not really Sebastian's thing, is it?" Amelia took the offered tea. "Would you mind having some company while you watch your evening programs?"

"No, not at all, love."

"There, you can watch them up here on my television. Amelia won't be alone, and you can bond over the dramatic lives of fictional, larger than life, characters," Sebastian said with as much fake enthusiasm and sarcasm as he usually used when talking about anything on the TV.

Amelia and Mrs Wintern smiled, knowing that was the way he was. If Amelia was honest, the soaps were a bit too much for her as well, but they could be on in the background while she thought about what she'd seen and waited for the painkillers to dull her headache.

If nothing else, going over the strange occurrence with Sebastian's arm would keep her from thinking about the rest of the events of the day. While the memories were fresh, it would be harder to be emotionally rational.

At first she'd wondered if Kevin had missed Sebastian's arm with the knife, but she knew he hadn't. Not only did he have blood on his arm, but the knife had some on as well; she'd seen it when the policeman had taken it as evidence. The blade hadn't been used on anyone else, so it had to be Sebastian's blood.

The more she thought about it the more she realised something similar had happened with Myron when she'd been kidnapped with him. A large, blood-soaked gash had appeared in his shirt. He'd told her it wasn't his blood but that of the Russian he'd fought. Now she wondered if that had been a lie as well.

Whatever the explanation for it, she knew without a doubt, the Holmes brothers were hiding something, and she intended to find out their secret.

**

A message from the police had finally allowed Mycroft to relax and know Amelia was safe once more. It didn't surprise him that his brother hadn't said anything. Sherlock only informed him when something wasn't satisfactory, not when it was.

Despite that, he hadn't expected his brother to visit him and almost dropped his tea cup when the younger Holmes strode into his study. Without saying a word, Sherlock sat in the nearest armchair.

"I assume Miss Jones is safe?"

"Oh, of course. She's got quite a bruise on her, going to ruin her looks for a week or so, but she'll recover."

Mycroft nodded and waited. Something wasn't right, and it would come out in due time. If it was time-sensitive it would have been said already. After a minute of sitting there with his eyebrows bunched forward together and his head rested on his arched hands, Sherlock seemed to remember he was in Mycroft's company. He reached into the inside pocket of his coat and threw something small and shiny at Mycroft.

Raising his eyebrows, Mycroft caught the coin. He didn't really need to look at it to know it was another seven and a half ruble coin.

"The boy?"

Sherlock nodded. Mycroft closed his eyes for a moment. It was the only outward sign that he'd received bad news.

"Many?"

"Enough. They were in the wardrobe. Noticed them when his body broke the side. I'd say it was a rather unexpected coincidence, but neither of us believe in coincidences."

"Where are they now?"

"Safe."

"Good. Keep this between us, brother of mine."

"And Amelia?"

"We'll *both* keep her safe."

Sherlock nodded at this reassurance. They both knew it might not be possible. Neither of them knew enough about what they were up against. But he also knew his brother was asking him to protect a person caught up in their affairs and he'd just promised to do it, something he wouldn't normally have done.

Now it seemed he had an agreement with both of them to teach her as much as she could learn, but he knew when she'd requested to be taught she'd not expected her life to depend on her results.

Just as Sherlock had shown himself in, he saw himself out, leaving Mycroft once more alone in his study. There was nothing more to be said.

Mycroft sat there for several more minutes staring at the Russian coin. The same person behind the terrorist attack on London had funded Amelia's stalker. Whoever they were, he had put the young author on their radar and now they wanted to hurt her.

When the email from the most powerful voice in the UK had come through and told him to drop the matter, he'd considered doing so. And as long as the UK itself was safe, that would have been enough, but now he had a conflict. Did he follow the monarch and country as he always had, and keep his promise to the crown, or did he break that promise and do what he needed to keep Amelia safe and keep his word with his brother?

After an hour of deliberating, Mycroft made his mind up. It would be done outside of official channels, but by morning he would know all the information there was on Mr Delra.

'

EPILOGUE

A sigh escaped Amelia's lips as she finished the first draft of her next novel. It had taken her six weeks of effort and hard work, but the next Dalton story was told and nothing had ever felt quite as satisfying as writing the last words of a tale and knowing it was told and done, at least for a little while.

To reward herself, she ordered another hot chocolate and sat back in her favourite writing café to people-watch. She'd been in Bath since Sebastian had declared her recovered enough to be on her own. The care he'd shown had been sweet, but even she had craved coming back after three days stuck in his flat with him, especially once her hand had healed well enough to write again.

While processing her emotional response and preparing for Christmas, she'd decided to write another novel and she'd finished the three tasks at about the same time. Not only was she ready for the chaotic season of the year, but she felt like she could face Myron and danger again. And now the book was complete. If nothing else, Shane would be pleased.

As she drank she noticed the other people around her. A couple of mums, laden with shopping bags full of toys, were taking a break over coffee, while a couple of students huddled in one corner with their laptops, trying to concentrate in the hustle and bustle around them.

When her eyes caught those of an elderly gentleman who'd been sitting a table over reading a newspaper for the last hour, Amelia smiled. He returned the gesture, the corners of his eyes wrinkling up in a way men seemed to manage with more dignity than women. Just as she was finishing up her hot chocolate, he decided he was leaving and packed away his things. After taking up his walking stick and leaning on it, he hobbled in her direction.

He pulled an envelope out of his pocket and threw her a wink as he gave it to her. She had to stop herself from laughing as she realised it was the same man who had passed her a letter before. Myron was up to his usual tricks.

"Merry Christmas, pet," he said and then hobbled off. Knowing he wasn't old only made her more impressed. One day, she hoped to be as good at disguising herself.

Once she'd watched the messenger leave, she tore open the sealed envelope and pulled out her next letter.

My first is in soccer, my second in polo, hockey contains my third, and the equestrians have my fourth, while my fifth lies in tennis; what am I?

Some of these are soft and some of these are full of nuts. Everything has one, even the world, but you can't journey to it, despite the story.

We like hot T and tolerate cold C, we're adrift in the water, but not alone, with a castle for every man. What are we?

I am no fearsome beast, but my thin teeth are bared. I can't befriend the bald, but find love with the haired.

Realising it would take her a little while, Amelia ordered another drink. Staying a little longer wouldn't do her any harm.

Of all the riddles, the third was the easiest, so she scribbled the answer beside it on the letter. She used pencil just in case she'd got it wrong, but she knew that one without a problem.

Out of the other three, the first one looked easiest. It also appeared like the first, second and so on meant a letter in each of the words. She used the envelope as scrap paper and wrote the words out one under the other with plenty of space between the letters, not bothering to repeat any if they occurred twice in a word.

She eliminated the Q immediately, as there was no U to follow in tennis. After eliminating a few other letters she found only two words jumped out at her and only one made sense, given the context of the lines. She wrote in the first word still using pencil, and then tried to work out the other two riddles.

For several minutes, she nibbled on the inside of her lip and tried to work out what the second riddle could mean. Eventually it came to her. The classic book, Journey to the Centre of the Earth.

She then turned her attention to the fourth, but she agonised over it far longer than the rest had taken her combined. Eventually, she went back to the three words she had already.

Sport, Centre and British

A frown flitted across her face. The words didn't make much sense. The first two appeared to be telling her something about a sports centre, but with British as the next word, it didn't make enough sense on its own.

When Amelia realised the mistake she'd made she hit her forehead with the palm of her hand. She then crossed out British and wrote English instead. A grin spread across her face when she remembered there was a sports centre on Englishcombe Lane nearby. The answer to the fourth riddle dawned on her. Bald people didn't need a comb but someone with hair did.

After picking up her phone, Amelia tapped the type of building and the road into the map section and soon had directions to the Baskerville Fitness and Gymnastics Centre.

Less than a minute later she was outside the café and walking towards it. It wasn't far up the hill from where she was, so she didn't bother getting a bus or calling a taxi. It would be quicker to walk.

Breathless and a little sweaty underneath her coat, Amelia arrived at the building and walked into the reception. Before she had time to think about where to go, a well-built male in what looked like a martial arts gi came up to her.

"Amelia Jones?" he asked. She nodded. "Brilliant, you're early. It gives us plenty of time to get your training under way."

THE END

The Invisible Amateur

CHAPTER 1

Tension filled the muscles in Mycroft's neck and shoulders. He sat at his usual desk in his study trying to process the report in front of him. One of his agents had delivered it to the new drop-off point only an hour ago.

The information he'd been provided with regarding Mr Delra was unhelpful at best. More than ninety percent of it, Mycroft had worked out himself over the last two weeks, and the rest was bizarre.

Mr Delra lived either in his house in St Petersburg or on his yacht. He didn't often travel between the two and didn't go out much in public, but he had a female assistant who did much of his public business for him. He'd inherited wealth but had plenty of it invested and it was multiplying.

No one could confirm where the yacht was. It was one of the largest yachts in the world, and all three of Mycroft's personal agents told him they'd seen it. One off the west coast of Ireland. Another in Norway, where Mr Delra kept his yacht when he wasn't on it, and the third in the Mediterranean, where he normally spent his summer. With only two weeks between the first and last sightings, being seen at those separate locations was impossible.

At the time of the Lyubov going missing, the yacht was

also apparently in more than one place. The most logical explanation was that there were several identical yachts and Mr Delra owned only one of them, but neither Mycroft nor his agents could find any reference to another yacht of the same design being built. It was a one-off custom design supplied by the owner himself.

Somehow, the recent events with Amelia Jones, the terrorists in London and the Russian ruble coins no longer in circulation were related to this man and his yacht, but Mycroft couldn't find the connection or any reason why he might want to harm the UK and her citizens.

Mycroft's only relief was the lack of activity from the terrorist group over the Christmas period. While London was in full celebration mode and packed with people, the terrorists had stayed out of the way. Not even a coin had shown up anywhere.

Since his emailed warning, Mycroft had been very careful about who he had working for him in the field. All three of the agents were trusted men who knew to keep their information out of official channels.

It wasn't the first time Mycroft had hidden his actions. Sometimes a country needed to be protected from itself. Those occasions had been rare, much to his preference. It never felt entirely comfortable to move behind the protocols he himself had set up.

In his entire life, this was only the fifth time he'd acted against his reigning monarch, but this was the first time the subterfuge made his task difficult. Previously, he'd been able to move people into the right positions and act as he needed, but in this day and age it was harder to move unseen.

He knew his own activities were being watched, and his brother had noticed strange people in the dark and shadows wherever he went. While either of them could give their tails the slip, it would arouse suspicion and so would need to be carefully planned. And he couldn't go to three different countries to try and verify the accuracy of information in the little time he would gain.

For now, he had to wait and trust his agents would gain him the information he needed, and hope Sherlock didn't get too curious about the people watching. Mycroft hadn't told him about the warning, or Mr Delra.

With a sigh, Mycroft filed the information away and ordered some tea. Patience would win out. It always did, and until then he could always focus on his protégée, Amelia Jones. The Wing Chun lessons he funded on her behalf were proving a good investment.

She attended sessions at the Baskerville fitness centre in Bath three times a week and received solo tuition. The dojo area even had a small security camera that gave him access to footage of her training. Whenever his mind was clouded, he found himself watching it.

Amelia moved with grace and already showed signs of aptitude at the techniques. For her safety, it was pleasing progress. She would always lack the main advantages he and his brother had, and would need much more training if she were to survive in their hidden realm, but it was a start and she learnt with an enthusiasm students rarely mustered.

While he was watching her spar with her teacher, he heard the sound of gravel crunching under tyres and the low growl of a car engine. With a frown creasing the lines on his forehead, he looked towards his study door expectantly. Someone other than his brother was visiting him, and he couldn't think of many people who knew where he lived.

A few seconds later he heard his housekeeper knock on the study door and show in two well-dressed men in suits. He recognised both at once. They worked for the royal family at Buckingham Palace, and both had been hired by him. He raised his eyebrows at them and saw the nearest gentleman's finger on his left hand twitch. They were nervous.

"You're needed," the man said when Mycroft still didn't respond or move.

At first Mycroft remained sat where he was, but he knew

he couldn't be aloof for long. He rang the bell to summon his housekeeper back.

"I'm going out," he said, when she came back. The woman nodded, knowing it wasn't something he'd have normally bothered to tell her, but having enough sense not to say anything to betray whatever had caused the difference. When Mycroft was satisfied he looked like he was leaving on his own terms, he got up and fetched his coat and umbrella. It might be considered petty by some for him to act that way, but the most likely reason for being summoned to the palace was Mr Delra, and that meant this was a wrist-slap, or worse. His pride wouldn't allow him to show even the slightest amount of any emotion but indifference.

The men accompanied him out to the car. He noticed the letters on the number plate, and they confirmed his suspicions. They'd sent the highest numeral in the series of number plates bearing their particular reference. It made the nature of the summons clear. They were displeased and he had been relegated to their least important car.

Both men sat in the front, leaving Mycroft alone in the back with his thoughts. Outwardly, he was the usual picture of calm patience and control, but the inside of him was a little different. No matter the conversation that followed, Mycroft would act in the best interests of his country and the people he had sworn to protect over a hundred years earlier. If the royal family were acting in a manner unfitting for their station, it would make that task more difficult, but not impossible.

The task left to him would be figuring out the why of their interference in his work. Although he tolerated their belief that he answered entirely to them and the accompanying delusion of thinking they knew best, he wouldn't give them reason to think otherwise, but he would need to know why.

Through the traffic of London, it took the better part of an hour for the car to make its way to the palace. The number plate afforded no special treatment on the road. The biggest difference between this vehicle and the ones around it was the armour plating built in and the bulletproof glass in every window. His own car was made the same way. When working for the government you could never be too careful.

When they did finally pull up in the courtyard of the palace, Mycroft was escorted into the building. They needn't have done so. He knew where to go and how to get there, but it was one more part of the message for him. This time in the palace, he didn't have free rein to go where he pleased.

While he walked he pretended to admire the décor. In truth, he didn't like all the crystal and shiny metal gilding everywhere. Not to mention the elaborate paintings of scenes and people. He much preferred wood of deep soothing hues, and the only things made from metal should be functional, like weapons or door handles. The bright metals and crystal reflected light in too many directions. One wrong glance when the sun was out and you were momentarily blinded. A metal should only shine enough to give off a dull reflection; anything more reduced its helpfulness.

"Good afternoon, Mr Holmes," the butler said from his position on the couch. Mycroft sat down opposite him. The lack of royalty in the room boded well. If he was being relieved from his position, it wouldn't be done by a lackey.

"I hope her majesty is well," he said and smiled. The warmth never reached Mycroft's eyes, as always.

"Health-wise she is as well as can be expected for someone of her age, but she has a concern that she's asked me to mention to you."

"I believe I have an idea what that might be."

"Then you are probably aware that her majesty doesn't like having to repeat herself."

"Of course." Mycroft lifted his chin a centimetre higher.

"She feels that it would be unwise to look into matters concerning the Russian and North Korean people you recently... met, especially concerning their out-of-country support." The butler paused and gave him a look to emphasise his point. "Since your initial encounter with them, which we understand was beneficial for us, and of course thank you for, we've come to an agreement."

"What sort of agreement?" Mycroft almost spat. Less than a second later he was calm once more. Thankfully his vocal tone had changed so little, the butler wasn't clever enough to have noticed his anger.

"I was not privy to the details, but I believe they wish to finish one last small task, some unfinished business, which will pose no threat to the country as a whole, and then leave unhindered." The butler smiled but Mycroft didn't return the gesture.

"So I am to do nothing?"

"Correct. The problem is already resolved. London is safe."

Mycroft picked up on what he wasn't being told. Amelia's life had been traded for the rest of the country, but he still didn't know exactly why. Why would they want Amelia dead, and why would a woman who prided herself in doing what was best for her citizens allow even one of them to be sacrificed without their knowledge? Nothing about this meeting was right, and he wouldn't be swayed from his task. It would be even more difficult, but he couldn't allow this arrangement to stand.

"I understand the situation perfectly. Please reassure her majesty that I would never endanger the citizens of London."

"I'm sure she'll be grateful to hear that. The alternative would be quite distressing." The butler stood and offered out his hand. Mycroft took it. "For all of us."

Ending the meeting and taking back control of the moment, Mycroft walked away, back down the hallways and corridors to where the car waited. He took long strides, making it difficult for the shorter men to keep up without quickening their paces. It seemed, for now, that these little things would be his only victories.

By the time he was sat back in his study he already knew

exactly what he wanted to do. From the moment the butler had explained, he'd known he had to stop it. No matter what the missing factor in the agreement was, it wasn't worth someone innocent dying. Mycroft would need to do two things. Find out why the arrangement had been made, and protect Amelia until he could prevent it from going ahead.

When he'd agreed to teach Amelia he'd never expected to get far before she became boring or too much of a liability, but she'd been anything but dull. This was just another interesting development that he couldn't have expected.

Although she'd made him angry enough on several occasions to want to stop their games, he'd found her impossible to ignore and she'd even proved her own intelligence to be far better than average in a couple of situations. Spotting a man as a threat to herself when not even Mycroft had seen it coming, and helping solve several tasks of his through her own knowledge, after he'd passed them to Sherlock, were not easy achievements.

Most of the time, he told himself he was still teaching her because of Mr Delra's interest in her. She'd been battered at the hands of a kidnapper because the tycoon had decided she was part of the threat to the Russian and North Korean efforts. But it was more than that, and he knew it. After so many years, he was taking an interest in the way someone learnt. Within him, he knew there was the hope that she could learn. That someone else might understand at least a small fragment of his world.

Using the spare phone normally reserved for contacting Amelia alone, Mycroft booked a hotel and train tickets from Bath to London and paid with one of his aliases. It took him only a few minutes. When he was done, he sat back and smiled. It was only the first of many tasks before him, but it was the most satisfying. Surprising people always gave him a buzz of delight.

The rest would be satisfying in another way. It was a game of wits. Who could outsmart the other? Not once in his adult life had he lied. He'd told the butler he'd always do what was necessary to protect the citizens in London. Within twenty-four hours, that's exactly what Amelia would be, and he would make sure nothing happened to her.

CHAPTER 2

After placing the last decoration in its space in the box, Amelia stopped for a moment and stared at them. The same routine, year after year. She took the same items out at the beginning of December and put them all away again a month later. In between, she was just as alone in her flat, just as lost in her writing. Except this year she'd done something different, more adventurous. She'd gone to the fitness centre and learnt something new.

This was a new year and full of the possibility of new adventures. Maybe next Christmas wouldn't be spent alone or with a few neighbours. The next might be in London, or perhaps even farther afield than that. Wherever it was, she would make sure she had company, and interesting company at that. Someone like Sebastian or Myron, if not one or both of them.

After gazing at the decorations in the box a little longer and trying to work out how long she'd had some of them, she closed the flap and took it to the spare room. It took a little effort to get it to the back at the top of the wardrobe, but with some pushing and shoving while standing on a chair, it slid back into its old spot.

When she came back to the living room to do the same

with the small fake Christmas tree, she noticed a packet on her doormat. Amelia felt a familiar tug in her stomach and the muscles down her back tensed in expectation, but the moment soon passed. Her stalker had been dealt with and she was safe.

The outside was unmarked and there was no name. With two raised eyebrows, she walked to the sofa and sat down to open it. Out fell a letter, train tickets, two small knives and a pouch to keep them in.

Amelia,

When you have finished reading this letter, destroy it along with the envelope and never mention it to me or anyone else. The knife holster will fit along the bottom of the corsets you wear and give you easy access to use them. Tomorrow morning at eight you have an extra lesson with Tom. He'll teach you everything you need to know.

I'm sure I don't have to tell you that knives like these are illegal to carry. I expect you to keep them concealed in public.

After your lesson, you'll pack your bags for two weeks and go to the hotel listed on the back of this letter. Memorise the address. If anyone wonders why you're in London, tell them you are here for business – doing research for a book you are ghost writing, all expenses paid, and that you cannot talk about it.

In your hotel room you will find further instructions. Do not be late.

M

For a minute Amelia could only gape at the message. It seemed her adventure was going to start sooner than she'd thought. Once she'd read the letter again, she picked up the leather holster for the twin blades and inspected them. The handles had grips that fit neatly in her palms and the metal shone, reflecting the light at her.

She'd never held a weapon before, and it felt strange now. It also seemed odd that Myron would give them to her. He frowned upon any kind of illegal activity; at least, Sebastian had told her Myron did. Without a license to carry a weapon it was very illegal, and she didn't know where someone would start trying to get a license for something like these.

With the holster, she noticed, were several sets of clips that could be sewn into whatever garment they would attach to, and then the holster could be moved to whatever corset she was wearing to sit neatly against her back, underneath the material and hidden from sight.

Amelia inhaled and exhaled slowly to try and calm the more rapid breathing that had snuck up on her while inspecting the weapons, and then went back to the letter. It wasn't mentioned but she had a feeling that disobeying his commands or not getting them entirely accurate this time might mean more than losing her teacher. He'd never been so serious with her.

Over the next five minutes she memorised the hotel address like he'd asked, saying it out loud under her breath several times with her eyes closed to check she remembered it. With shaking hands, she then took the paper to the sink and set light to it. Once the message was gone, she repeated the address again a few more times, as much to convince herself that she would remember it as to help aid her memory. If she forgot it now she would have a lot of trouble working out where to go.

The rest of the evening was spent working out the best place to sew and attach the clips to several of her corset waistcoats so she could wear the concealed knives while in London. She doubted Myron would have sent them to her now if he didn't intend her to start using them right away. It took her several hours, but by the time she was done she stood in front of her full height mirror, wearing her best outfit and having the satisfaction of knowing the knives were nestled against her lower back. She couldn't see a difference, and only knew they were there from the warm hardness pressed against her.

As she'd been instructed, she went along to her lesson in the morning and took the small weapons with her. Tom said nothing about the oddness of the extra lesson, but put her through the warm up routine with more haste than usual, encouraging her to stretch a little further and focus more than she ever had.

During her lessons, there was usually light conversation. He was an interesting man who had travelled much of the world and enjoyed talking about the countries and cultures he'd experienced. Although he never said one way or another, she suspected he only lived in Bath now to teach her. His nomadic lifestyle and unattachment to any woman made him a likely candidate for some kind of agent in the British secret service. Either that or he owed Myron, because she was his only pupil and he lived in Bath nearby, something not cheap to do.

When she'd stretched every muscle she knew of in her body, as well as a few she hadn't known she had, he pulled two almost identical knives from somewhere underneath his gi. He spent the next hour teaching her how to disarm him without getting hurt. Then he spent another hour on how to attack with her own blades and keep hold of them. During most of the first hour her little blades went flying across the dojo again and again and Tom grew more stony and silent. When she was exhausted and covered in sweat, he stopped her and allowed her to breathe.

"You need to bring your reaction times up. At the moment, you're not flowing from one move into another, and the hesitation in between each move is where I can disarm you."

She nodded. The assessment was true. She was being so careful not to hurt him that she was hesitant about which move to do.

"Practice combining different moves into groups of attacks and parries. Try to get used to holding them as well, building the strength in your wrists. They need to be extensions of your arms. Part of you."

"I'll try," she said, not sure what else to say. The seriousness of the lesson and the letter the previous night were making her wary. She found herself biting at the inside of her bottom lip, deep in thought, wondering what could have caused this change, but neither Myron nor Tom spoke of it.

"You should take off your gi. A taxi to take you home will be here in five minutes," Tom said before she could ask him if something was wrong. He came up to her and gave her a hug. "I'll see you when you get back. If you see him, tell him I said hi, or sent my regards. Yes, tell him I send my regards, that's the sort of way he'd say it."

Amelia laughed, relieved that Tom's normal sense of fun was still in there somewhere.

"I'll tell him. I'm sure I'll see him; I'm practically at his beck and call."

"Aren't we all? Now go on. He hates it if people are late."

She gave him a wry smile and hurried to the changing rooms to change tops and dry off some of the sweat before the taxi arrived. Tom must know Myron well.

As she got into the taxi to head home and pack, she exhaled and tried to relax the knot of tension building in her stomach. She couldn't decide if she was in danger or not. This could just be the next stage of whatever scheme Myron had devised to teach her, or it could be something more real. Unless he told her himself, it would remain a mystery, however. She hoped the instructions waiting for her at the hotel made the situation clearer.

"See you in an hour, love," the driver said as he pulled up outside her front door. "It's the station you'll be going to then, right?"

She nodded and reached for her purse to pay the man for the journey. As he glanced back at her in the rear view mirror, he noticed.

"It's already been paid for, and the next one too."

"Ah, brilliant," she replied and stuffed her purse back into her handbag. It seemed Myron had thought of everything, except how long it took a corset-wearing woman to change clothes. He'd given her an hour to shower, dress and pack before being picked up again.

Having no time for anything else, she hurried inside, dropped her handbag on the coffee table on the way past and rushed around the flat to gather everything she needed to finish her packing. Half an hour, later she'd never been more grateful for being organised enough to pack some of her clothing the night before.

She yanked off the clothes she'd worn to the gym and got into the shower to have the quickest wash she could manage. Rushed dressing wasn't something she was used to either, but she did her best. No part of her wanted to be late. She'd already angered Myron too many times.

When the taxi driver beeped the horn to let her know he was back again, she swore. Her hair was unbrushed and she'd only managed to dry it a little. Her only solace was knowing everything else was ready.

After making sure her hairbrush was in the top of her handbag, she yanked on her boots and wheeled her case outside. The driver helped her put it in the back and gave her a grin when he noticed her hair.

"Not quite enough time, then, love?"

"Not when you like to wear corsets," she replied. He laughed but didn't ask her about the odd wardrobe choice. Most people grew curious about anyone choosing to wear such an old item of fashion, but Amelia wanted time to think and observe. Myron had summoned her to London and that meant she had to be on the watch and on her guard.

Normally, Amelia had a book to read when on long journeys, but she had opted against that form of entertainment this time around. Without knowing why she was going to London, she preferred to keep an eye out for potential threats and knew a book would absorb too much of her attention. If she read, it would suck in all her focus until she forgot the world around her. As a teenager she'd even missed a stop and had to backtrack once. To keep herself from being tempted to read, she hadn't even brought anything with her.

By the time she got to London the only result was her boredom, over-brushed hair that hung in neat lines down her back, and a far too intimate knowledge of the woman across the carriage's love life. Nothing of any importance had happened, and Amelia regretted her decision.

The pit of her stomach still felt tense and uncomfortable, but she was bored of that as well. It made no sense to be this nervous when it could easily be Myron's way of testing her. In both his and Sebastian's line of work it was useful to be calm. The seriousness could be designed to teach her to manage her emotions and responses to potential threats without there being one to her physically. But, of course, it could equally be any number of other tests. In reality, she was clueless.

As she exited the station she looked for a road name to get her bearing. She soon saw one, but realised it didn't help. She couldn't remember the name of the hotel. A gasp escaped her lips as she tried to search her mind for the information. Not once that morning had she thought about it or how to get there.

In the middle of the street, she closed her eyes and tried to picture the map she'd looked up. She remembered something about a marble archway just off to her right and needing to head away from it, so she walked to the junction and turned to put it behind her. As she past the Cumberland, she began to piece together the rest of the directions, although the hotel name still eluded her.

She kept walking past several roads and then past a semi-circular road to her right with another land mark she recognised. The Marble Arch Synagogue was her cue to turn right at the next junction and head down another road that took her in front of the hotel. At least, she hoped she'd remembered that much correctly.

When she got to the next junction, she saw a large amount of green trees a few hundred metres away and hoped that was the square just beyond her hotel. Keeping her head high and her jaw firmly shut, Amelia kept walking, hoping she appeared to know where she was going.

A hundred metres on she exhaled in relief when she realised the canopy on the other side of the road was her hotel. The sign saying '*Radisson blu*' welcomed her into a bright and shiny foyer with several reception desks at the far end. A man stood to one side with a name plaque in his hands. It had her character, Edward Dalton's full name written on it. She raised her eyebrows a moment before walking over to him.

"Mrs Dalton?" he asked.

"I think so," she replied, knowing that sounded vague and hoping he wouldn't take it the wrong way. Myron hadn't said anything about her being booked in under a different name.

"You're here to do research for a book, I understand, Mrs Dalton?"

"Yes, I'm looking forward to getting started," she said and gave him a relieved smile as he summoned a bell-boy to take her case for her.

"Brilliant. Your first client is already here, sitting out on the garden terrace. Why don't you go straight out to him and we'll get your room sorted and bring your key to you in a moment."

"That sounds wonderful." She headed in the direction he'd indicated with his fingers and tried to look like she knew what she was doing and had expected this from the beginning. Inwardly, she was hoping this was Myron and she'd get some answers.

CHAPTER 3

As Mycroft drank his tea and waited, he continued to organise his small team of retired agents. Not everyone he'd approached had answered his messages requesting their assistance, but he didn't want to ask too many people. The more who knew what he wanted them to do, the more chance the wrong people would find out. He did know his current field agents couldn't be trusted, so he was asking men who'd retired but still felt loyal to him. Very few of them would be loyal to anyone else now they were out of the game. Mycroft had looked after them well over the years.

If he could, Mycroft would work alone on every situation that required his expertise, but he couldn't keep an eye on Amelia, investigate Mr Delra, and find out why their monarch was making deals with terrorists alone. Someone would need to help him and his younger brother.

For now, he'd left Sherlock looking into the Russian coins. It was an inconspicuous way his younger brother could find out more about Mr Delra, and Mycroft could deny knowledge of it. It wouldn't be the first time Sherlock had disobeyed him and looked into a situation without Mycroft stopping him. That meant other people would need to keep Amelia safe.

Tom had already updated him on her morning's progress and it hadn't been as swift as he'd have liked or expected from her earlier advancement. Most of the time, Amelia was an amazing example of a human being, especially when he considered what most were like. However, every once in a while she displayed the exact feminine characteristics which he abhorred. The emotional clouding of judgement and a caring attitude that made her hesitant in acting.

Tom had picked up on this caring attitude and how it had held her back. She'd been unwilling to risk hurting him and therefore made herself less effective in combat. It was yet another reason that right now he wished he'd never agreed to teach her.

Just as he was thinking this, he realised she was late. Her train had pulled into the station on time. Mycroft had checked. It would have taken her exactly six and a half minutes to walk from the Marble Arch tube station to the hotel and another two to be sent through to the terrace by the hotel staff. By now she should be sitting in front of him.

He arched his hands together and considered the possible events that might have delayed her, other than her own stupidity. If he needed to act to keep her safe already, he couldn't afford to delay working out what might have happened and assessing the options for their likelihood.

Just as he was deciding someone must have picked her up in a car between the tube station and the hotel, movement from the doorway caught his eye. He blinked a couple of times, the only outward sign that he was struggling to process the feelings within.

Every time he'd seen her she'd had her hair tied up out of the way in a bun or braid of some kind. Today the chestnut locks tumbled, yet still neatly, around her face and the shoulders of the deep green outfit she wore. Her cheeks were flushed from both the cold and exercise, and she had a little sparkle in her eyes that appeared the moment she saw him. The combination made him pause for breath. She'd have fitted neatly in his study and not looked out of place, in either colour or style, and the thought stopped all other threads in his mind. A few seconds later he had gathered the dropped pile back together again, and the blip was in his past.

"My, my, what a surprise to see you here," he said, getting up and shaking her hand. She smiled and allowed him to steer their meeting. "Why don't you join me for tea, Mrs Dalton?"

"That would be wonderful." She sat in the seat opposite him and gave the waiter, who'd swiftly appeared, her order. The over-excited greeting had been for the benefit of the few other guests within the terrace area more than anyone else, so he dropped the pretence now she was sat.

"I think I need to learn my way around London," she said, before he could speak. Her eyes flicked up to his face while he watched her, but they couldn't remain on him while he stared. It made him feel a little better. She knew she was late and was aware it displeased him.

"You followed all the other instructions precisely?" he asked, although he knew she had. She nodded to confirm.

"But I do have a question." Now she looked at him, and Mycroft knew she was studying him for a reaction, as he would study her, but he gave her nothing.

"Not now. Maybe at the end." He hoped she was intelligent enough to realise the maybe had a condition. It would depend on her performance over the next half an hour. She had some redeeming to do.

"Tell me what you see out there," he said a moment later and motioned to the people in the small garden nearby. She raised her eyebrows at him and then turned her body to look outwards. He rolled his eyes at her lack of subtlety but didn't expect her to notice.

For several minutes she remained quiet, studying the people. She didn't even notice when the waiter brought her drink. As this continued, he wondered if she was going to tell him anything, but she eventually looked back at him.

"The couple on the left. They've had an argument. Not a big issue, more a sort of bicker over a small detail. I think it's more important to her than him. She's more angry and he's more worried about looking after their small child." She looked to him with slightly wider eyes, and he recognised the unspoken question. She wasn't confident she was right. Hoping she would get going a bit quicker, he gave her a slight nod.

"The woman by herself who is feeding the birds is sad about something. Either her childhood or something attached to it. She keeps getting a wistful look."

He nodded again when she glanced his way but frowned at the same time. These were only snippets of the whole picture and not quite the things he'd wanted to know.

"Over there," she said, pointing and speaking before he could tell her she wasn't doing it right. "Business man in the dark suit. He just got a promotion and probably a raise. He's phoning someone to let them know the good news."

Mycroft snorted at this and she stopped. Immediately, the interested and excited look vanished from her face to be replaced with the same worried, unconfident, wide eyes she'd had earlier. She rotated her body to face back in his direction.

When he shook his head and sighed his disapproval she lowered her eyes and took a sip from her tea. An awkward minute ticked by in silence as he felt the familiar regret well up within him. No one had ever come close to his level of intelligence.

"Will you tell me what I missed?" she asked, breaking through his angry thoughts. "That way I will know what to look for another time."

If he hadn't needed to continue, Mycroft would have got up and walked away, but she needed to learn or she wouldn't survive what was coming. Out of necessity, he opened his mouth and told her what he'd seen.

"The couple have argued over what to feed the girl. The father is feeding the girl chips and the mother is not happy about it. Personally I don't blame her. He's very unintelligent, you can tell by the way he controls the girl and simply ignores his partner instead of having a conversation. They're unmarried but engaged. See the ring on her hand, but none on his."

While he spoke about them Amelia looked at them again, trying to see what he saw, her eyes darting to every feature he mentioned and drinking it in. There might be some hope for her to learn, but he knew his patience would be tried by the attempt.

"The woman on her own recently miscarried a child. In between throwing bread she occasionally strokes her stomach, which is a shape befitting someone who was pregnant. She hasn't lost all the baby-weight yet and her skin hasn't tightened where it was stretched. Frankly, she could have covered that up better."

"It must have been recent, then," Amelia said. He could hear the sadness in her tone.

"It was," he snapped.

"Sorry, please continue." She looked outside again.

"She's married to a soldier and he's not here at the moment. The bag she has the bread in is from a shop on one of the bases, but you're right that this is attached to her childhood. It's not a shop in London. She grew up here and is staying with her parents until her husband is back. She's also left-handed, probably creative. That's harder to tell from this distance."

He paused a moment and then looked at the business man Amelia had pointed out. She followed his gaze.

"He's a lawyer, and did not get a promotion, but he provided a colleague with evidence that won a case. He was too concerned at the start of the conversation for it to have been a possibility without risk. Too young to be a fully fledged lawyer and taking cases of his own, and if he was winning his own case he'd have been in court to find out if he won or not."

Mycroft snapped his mouth shut as soon as he'd finished saying the last letter.

"Wow, that was amazing." She looked at him with wide-eyed wonder and he blinked in surprise. His anger seemed to have melted off her entirely. "Can I try again?"

He blinked at her, not quite believing what he was hearing. Most people, when confronted by his anger and disappointment, didn't ask for a second opportunity to make it worse. He nodded and motioned to another man who'd just sat down at the far table.

This time, as she studied, she flicked her eyes over a lot more, trying to do more than read his body language. It took her longer than it had the first time, but on this occasion when she turned back to him, she had a brighter look and rattled off what she knew without hesitating.

Once she'd finished speaking, he put down his tea cup and sighed.

"I missed something?" she asked. Mycroft nodded. "Tell me, please?"

Amelia looked up at him through her eyelashes, and he had no doubt that the glance normally charmed men into giving her what she wanted. He rolled his eyes and she chuckled.

"You missed the small item of clothing hiding in his pocket. He didn't go home last night." Mycroft saw the surprise on her face and felt a small thrill of delight when she whipped her head around to see what he meant. She gasped and looked back to him. He nodded.

"Practice," Mycroft said and got up. The meeting had gone on long enough and she'd drawn more attention to both of them than he felt comfortable with. "And keep it discreet."

"What about my question?" she asked as he walked away. He smirked but kept going. If she improved, he'd let her ask him another time.

After walking out of the hotel, Mycroft continued down the block and then around the corner into Portland Square, where his car and Daniels waited.

"Home, sir?" the chauffeur asked. Mycroft nodded, deep in his own thoughts. Amelia had done as she predicted and amused him. She'd been slow and infuriating at first, but somehow she'd managed to break through his anger and impress him.

It reminded him of how he'd taught his brother to see the world when they were children. There was a time when Sherlock had been learning from him in the same way she had, and the same way John Watson had learnt from Sherlock all those years ago. Today he'd caught a glimpse of what had existed between John and his brother. The admiration, the desire to learn and understand, and then finally the delight at making progress. She'd bared all her emotions for him to see and it had pleased him.

On top of that, her appearance had relaxed him. He'd never before seen a woman who would have looked at home in his house. Natural, graceful and with the air of someone who belonged in a time long forgotten, but still here and still very much alive. He knew it didn't mean he loved her. Those sorts of emotions were far from him, and he didn't intend to let them in. He wasn't even sure he respected her; after all, she was still female and prone to emotional irrationality. But his opinion of her had been different this afternoon. There was metal on the inside of her, and with the right persuasion it might be moulded into something he could appreciate.

CHAPTER 4

Amelia exhaled once Myron had left the terrace area. That hadn't been what she'd expected from the man. He was almost impossible to read unless he was angry with her, and that was far too frequent for her liking. No matter how much she tried to be endearing and make the most of the charms and personality she had, he seemed to rebuff her. His interest really did seem fixed on only one thing. Although she hoped her intelligence was up to the task of impressing him, she was starting to wonder if it was. She'd never thought it possible for a human brain to process and remember so much.

A few of the times she had been with Sebastian, she'd seen him do what Myron had just tried to get her to do, but Myron himself was on another level above. He'd seen information about these people that she wasn't sure Sebastian would even notice, and she'd had the opportunity to have him explain it as well. The whole experience had sent wave after wave of exhilaration and adrenaline through her, even with Myron's evident disgust at her first assessment.

It hadn't given her an answer to her worried assumption that she was in danger, and the knives nestled against the small of her back had gone entirely unmentioned, but she couldn't be disappointed. They'd had afternoon tea together and she'd had another lesson. It was progress, even if it wasn't as fast as she'd have liked. Being an amateur at anything was always an unpleasant feeling.

Now that her heart rate was calming down, she realised she had barely touched her drink. After sipping the tea she grimaced. It was cold.

"Would you like me to bring you a fresh tea?" the waiter asked, noticing her plight. She nodded gratefully and allowed him to take her discarded one.

It didn't take him long to reappear and place a steaming cup down in front of her.

"Thank you. Do I pay you here or can you put it on my room bill?" she asked, not sure if Myron would have paid already for the other two.

"Mr Holmes has taken care of that. One of the perks of owning the hotel."

"He owns this hotel?" She sipped her tea and tried not to look too surprised by the information.

"Yes, although he doesn't like too many people to know. His great-grandfather invested in a few, I believe. Mr Holmes is almost identical to the man."

"How do you know?" Her curiosity was piqued, especially as she'd found no pictures of either Holmes boy or any of their family on the internet. They were difficult to track down, and what little research she had managed to do had turned up little but some old fictional stories about a man called Sherlock Holmes who might or might not have also been a person alive at the time they were written.

By the time she'd left Sebastian's care, gone home and finished her own novel, she'd forgotten the name of the club Myron had been in and the name of the person who'd founded it. Searching for a club founded in London by a Holmes also turned up nothing.

"There's a picture over the mantelpiece in the main office."

"Could I see it?" she asked, not hesitating. It could be the clue she needed.

"I'm sorry, miss. It's not somewhere I can take a guest."

"That's all right. I'm sure I can ask him myself sometime. What's his great-grandfather's name?"

"Sir Mycroft Holmes," he said and moved off to serve other customers.

With a smug grin, she finished her drink. That was the name of the man who'd founded the club. She shouldn't have forgotten it, given how similar it was to Myron.

Amelia didn't know whether to hope Myron was Mycroft and something out of a fiction novel was happening or it was just a good likeness and she'd mistaken the supernatural healing power of both of them. On one hand, having a superhero mentor her made the arrangement even more amazing, but it wasn't an easy scenario to believe. This was the real world, and so far superheroes were only in the realm of fiction.

Not that this bend of reality had stopped her from thinking about the possibility. Myron having such a secret was something she'd thought long and hard about. She would have to tread carefully with one as large as being immortal. And if he found out she was digging, he could have her disposed of to protect his secret. She had to decide if she wanted to know what was going on or if it was safer to stay in the dark.

It took her less than a minute of thinking to pull out her phone and look up an internet café nearby. After going to her room and tidying up her appearance, she went to find it.

London was a big city and unfamiliar to her, but she knew she needed to get used to it. Both Sebastian and Myron were at home in every road and street. At some point, she knew Myron would want her to learn the place. Probably even memorise locations and the best way to get there, so she tried to take in the people around her and the information they gave off as well as the monuments, tube stations and bus routes she went past.

Having plenty of time, she walked, and by the time she reached the internet café her fingers were so cold she could barely feel the tips. In her haste at packing she'd forgotten her gloves.

She ordered a hot drink and sat down at the ageing computer. It took her a few more minutes to order her thoughts and decide what was best to search. There was a small chance Myron would watch her movements as well as what she did here. With that in mind, it wouldn't be good to type in anything that couldn't be explained as simple curiosity about his family.

After thinking about it, she decided to go along the route of the hotel owner and put in the name of the hotel she was staying at and Mycroft Holmes. As she scrolled through a few results that didn't tell her much she spotted a familiar name.

The Diogenes Club was where she'd interrupted him and it had also been founded by Mycroft Holmes. It was only a little more information, but after flicking through several pages of description about the club and what members had done through the ages, she found an image of the great man.

She sat back and stared, wide-eyed. It was a painting and old, but it was so similar it could have been him. A chill ran through her and made her shiver. If Myron was Mycroft, then the Holmes brothers had found a way to make themselves ageless. A thought that her mind struggled to accept.

The next twenty minutes were spent in a daze as she tried to search generically enough that no one would be able to guess what she was looking for, but specific enough the results gave her more information. Little more of interest came up. There was no family tree, and Holmes was a common enough surname that without specifying one of the family members she was overloaded with irrelevant information.

When her time ran out, Amelia decided to leave and go

back to the hotel. She could think about what it might mean and how they might have achieved a supernatural status from somewhere less out in the open. At the moment, she still didn't know for sure if Myron had summoned her to London for her safety or to learn from him.

With a sigh she pulled on her coat, paid her bill and stepped back out into the cold January air. It was dark now and even colder than before, so she huddled down into her coat, trying to keep her neck warm.

As she rounded the next corner she bumped straight into a guy coming the other way. She bounced off him but he caught her and held her upright until she was steady again. Only then did she look up.

"Sebastian!" She immediately tried to think of some way to explain her presence without giving away her secret arrangement with Myron, but her brain fogged up in response.

"Amelia, you're in London. Where are you staying?"

"The Raddison," she replied, not willing to volunteer anything else.

"Ah, so brother of mine has brought you here."

"You know about that?" Relief made her exhale and relax the muscles in her shoulders. Hiding the agreement from one of the most observant men in the world wasn't an easy task.

"Yes. I talked to Myron about taking an interest in you a few weeks ago. Do you have plans this evening? I know a particularly good seafood restaurant not too far away."

She confirmed she had no plans and allowed Sebastian to offer her his arm. A few seconds later she walked right back past the internet café she'd been sat in, and she thanked the heavens that she'd left when she had. It wouldn't have been easy to explain to him what she was doing in there, and now she was standing beside him and listening to him talk about a mysterious problem he'd solved, she couldn't believe what she'd been thinking of. Sebastian and Myron were flesh and blood, just like her. Eccentric, highly intelligent flesh and blood, but mortal.

Pleased to have some company in a new place, Amelia shook off her silly concerns and laughed at his description of his latest case. There was a very amusing conversation with the father when Sebastian had figured out he was hiding the evidence of his family's enforced diet by feeding the almost empty food wrappers to the dog.

"Was the dog all right in the end?" she asked, aware he was being a little callous in his description of the events.

"Yes. It's on a special diet and being monitored by some vet, but it will live, if that's what you mean." Sebastian waved his hands in the air as if the detail was a fly buzzing around his mind and bothering him.

They walked into the restaurant and were taken straight to a cosy table in the packed building. The waiter greeted Sebastian by name, and less than a minute after they'd sat down the chef came out, shook Sebastian's hand and promised to cook them anything they wanted to eat.

Once they'd ordered and were waiting for food, Sebastian turned his focus on her again.

"So, have you seen my brother dearest since you've been in London?" he asked.

"Yes, earlier. He was trying to teach me to observe situations and people the way you both do. I'm not very good at it yet. I think I disappointed him, and I've been instructed to practice."

"Hmmm. I didn't realise he was taking that much of an interest in matters."

"Me neither. After we argued over the possibility of Guy Thomas being my stalker, I assumed our arrangement would be over and he wouldn't teach me anymore, but here I am." She shrugged her shoulders and smiled. It was so much easier not having to hide it from him. She'd been on guard with Sebastian ever since she'd made the offer to Myron.

Sebastian asked Amelia about her books next, and they talked about plots and possible scandals she could use from real world cases and experiences of his for the rest of the meal. Since Myron had insisted she rewrite her last novel because it used real world events, she'd made Sebastian promise to tell her if anything he suggested was inspired by true cases. If it was too sensitive in nature she wouldn't use it, and she soon noticed her idea of too sensitive and Sebastian's were a world apart.

It also became apparent that Sebastian needed little encouragement to talk about the many cases he'd solved. The more convoluted and impressive the more it excited him to tell her.

By the time she pushed her knife and fork together and declared herself full, the table beside them had finished the last of their drinks and were leaving. The husband slipped a twenty pound note under the edge of his beer glass and the couple left.

Less than a minute later a man on his way back from the bathroom caught his foot on the far table leg. She looked at him as he tripped, as did Sebastian. When Amelia refocused her attention, she noticed the waiter's tip was gone.

"Sebastian, that man just stole..."

"I know," he replied, already getting to his feet. "Be right back."

She watched him hurry after and simply brush past the guy, grabbing his arm and whispering something. Sebastian then circled around to come back to their table.

"Got it," he said and held up the note between two fingers.

"You picked his pocket!"

Sebastian grinned.

"That's not all," he said as he reached for the dessert menu, opened it and handed it to her. Instantly, her eyes were drawn to the chocolate brownie picture. When she glanced back up for Sebastian to continue and explain the rest, she noticed he was still grinning at her.

As she looked at the other table, she gasped. The money was back where it had started, tucked under the empty glass. While she was sitting, wide-eyed and unable to speak, the waiter cleared the table. He then came over to them, pulling his menu device from his pocket.

"She'll have the chocolate brownie," Sebastian said before they'd even been asked. She laughed, and it broke the hold on her voice.

"That was amazing. Will you explain how you did it?" she asked when they were alone together again.

"I can teach you, if you like?"

Delight stretched her mouth into a grin as she nodded. She'd very much like to learn how to do the subtle but difficult acts he'd just performed.

She ate her dessert as quickly as she could, which wasn't particularly fast after so much food, and pulled out her purse to pay. Sebastian shook his head and pushed it back towards her.

"You need the money more than I, and this was my idea. If they even let us pay." He fished a card out from his inside jacket pocket, but as he'd suggested, they weren't allowed to pay but ushered from the building with smiles.

Excitement made Amelia's pulse race, so they took a taxi back to Baker Street. As soon as they walked in, Mrs Wintern noticed and come out of her flat.

"If you want tea this late you will have to make it yourself. Although I'm sure that's not what you two young people had in mind this late at night."

For a second, Amelia didn't know what to say. Mrs Wintern was normally so prim and proper, and she'd just insinuated that Amelia was there to sleep with Sebastian. It was even more of a surprise when Sebastian didn't deny it. Instead, he continued on to his flat as if she hadn't said anything.

"Creative minds are never good at respecting bed times," Amelia said before following him up the stairs. With her intentions firmly fixed on Myron still, she didn't want a single person to think her involved with the younger Holmes brother.

"Right, let's get started." Sebastian pulled his coat off, hung it on the coat stand and moved it to the centre of the room. After looking about the room, he picked up a pack of cards and slipped one out.

"We'll start with this. I'll teach you how to pick a pocket first. It's the easiest part. Then we can work on doing it discreetly, and after that, doing the opposite."

Amelia nodded as he came back across the room towards her, swishing the bottom of the coat tails as he did.

"You use just two fingers." He held up the first and second finger on his right hand where the card had been.

"Where is it?" she asked.

"In the pocket already." He showed her the motion she needed to do to take the card back out again. It took her several attempts at copying him before he was happy she had the basic technique right.

"Now let's make it a little harder." Sebastian took the coat back and encouraged her to pull the card from his pocket without him noticing. He closed his eyes and held still in the middle of the room.

After taking a deep breath, Amelia walked past him and reached into the pocket. Before her fingers had touched the top of the card, Sebastian grabbed her wrist.

"I could feel you," he said. "Try again."

Over the next half an hour she tried again and again, but every time Sebastian caught hold of her, and she noticed he didn't always let her go again very quickly. Deciding she wasn't completely comfortable with the situation anymore, she yawned.

"I think I'm too tired. I should go back to the hotel."

"We can continue tomorrow..."

"Perhaps," she cut him off, not wanting to hear what he might say next. "I should wait to see if your brother intends to teach me first."

After thanking him she hurried out into the night, making sure nothing else could happen. When she'd settled back into a taxi she almost hit herself. It was foolish to fear that Sebastian would be interested in her. He just wasn't looking for a relationship, and was already aware she preferred his elder brother.

The day had taken its toll on her and she wasn't thinking straight any more. With silly ideas of immortal men, and now this, she almost laughed aloud at herself. She needed sleep, and she needed it soon.

CHAPTER 5

Mycroft paced his study. Several days had passed with Amelia in London, and every day increased the possibility that she'd be found. On top of that, she'd been exhibiting some strange behaviour. The things she'd searched on the internet had him concerned, but didn't appear to have revealed any important information. It had shown her to be far more curious about him than expected. She'd also spent more time with his younger brother than he'd anticipated.

A couple of old agents were taking shifts and keeping an eye on her, but neither would be happy to do so much longer, and already they were getting suspicious about his desire to keep tabs on her. He needed to figure out what Mr Delra had said to the ruling monarch to get her to allow the Russians to leave. Twice he'd thought he was close to an answer.

There was no doubt in his mind that it was information the terrorists were using to get their way. The royal family had several secrets, as any large family in power did. Most of them had been protected by Mycroft over the years, but occasionally they made a mistake and more people found out or were involved in some sort of scandal.

Earlier in the year he'd retrieved some compromising photos of one of the young women, but they were an unlikely threat over the heads of the family. A scandal if they came out, but not a disaster. He'd investigated it anyway and those were safe.

His second line of enquiry was an illness that had been treated by a doctor not recommended by Mycroft. The medical records were still sealed and safe. It left four possibilities, and all of them had implications that could take several years to unravel. Any of the four would be enough to garner the reaction of the royal family.

Mycroft needed to know more, but his hands were tied. He couldn't pursue the Russians until he knew what they had, if they were the ones who had it, and he couldn't ask for help from his younger brother through official channels.

He sighed and called Daniels to get the car ready. He needed space to think, and that meant a trip to the Diogenes Club. It had taken them several weeks, but the members had just about forgiven him for the disturbance Amelia had made. At least, most had. None of them scowled when they saw him, but there was still an extra layer of frostiness to the usual silence. Given enough time, even that would pass.

As soon as Mycroft walked in, he felt the familiar sensation of relaxation. The threads of half-finished ideas in his head unravelled from their tangled mess and allowed him to focus on one at a time. He followed the butler to his usual room and stopped in the doorway when he noticed another occupant. A single glance let him know it was Sherlock dressed as an older man. The butler thought this was their father. Mycroft had been their father twice before that. It helped them look like a normal family to any people who knew them over a prolonged period.

He gave Sherlock a nod of acknowledgement and went to his usual seat. Right where his tea tray would be placed in a couple of minutes was a sheet of paper. On it Sherlock had written a message in their own code and the alphabet they'd made up when they were children. It required a perfect memory of the original French version of the Count of Monte

Cristo, as well as the knowledge and memory of what all the lines and squiggles meant in their personal example of an alphabet. Both of them were fluent in it.

Impressed that his brother had the sense to use it now when it was imperative their communication was confidential, Mycroft started reading.

Still no lead from boat owner. Thinking of giving him a nudge. You've been awfully quiet on the matter. Also the brandy isn't as good as it was last time I paid you a visit.

Mycroft picked up the pen and wrote out a reply, taking very little time to do something most people would struggle with.

A nudge would be a good idea. He will be trying to convince himself he lost the coin. I assume you still have it to send back with a helpful note. When he does make a move, don't go to the address until you have informed me. I will be handling the next stage personally. I think this brandy is better.

After tea arrived for both of them, Mycroft handed the note back and watched in silence as Sherlock read it. His younger brother raised his eyebrows and frowned. The reply he then furiously wrote out was not going to be a surprise to Mycroft. It was unexpected for the elder Holmes to want to attend as well, and Sherlock would want to know why.

Not like you. Has the situation changed? Is Amelia still safe?

The last question was an unanticipated one, but Mycroft paused for only a second with the pen in his hand.

Amelia in no more danger than before, and situation similar enough. I can handle it. Don't interfere. Give owner a nudge and report results to me.

When the message was passed back to Sherlock, his younger brother rolled his eyes but he didn't argue. Seconds later the piece of paper was feeding the fire in the grate, and not long after that it was gone.

They sat together in silence for a few more minutes, drinking tea and thinking. Mycroft could tell his brother wasn't happy with not being told every detail, but Mycroft knew it wasn't a secret they'd entrusted anywhere else, and that meant it was a secret he was responsible for alone. If Sherlock found out about it Mycroft would be betraying that confidence.

Half an hour later Mycroft still hadn't disclosed any more information. Finally, Sherlock gave up and left. When it came to patiently sitting through and waiting for a result, Mycroft had always been the brother best suited to the task.

Although he couldn't have predicted Sherlock's presence there, Mycroft sat back in his chair, already satisfied that his trip to the Diogenes Club was fruitful. His brother might give Mycroft's tasks the lowest priority for solving, but at some point he always ran out of cases, and even Amelia's frequent visits weren't enough to stave off the inevitable boredom. Sherlock was unpredictable for this one reason.

To keep the royal family content and oblivious to Mycroft's dealings behind the scenes, he spent the rest of the afternoon solving a security issue with their palace in Sandringham. One of the maids had compromised their system. When Mycroft had seen her CV he hadn't been surprised, but no one else had picked up on the obvious issues.

He wasn't willing to read the paperwork of every applicant to one of the royal households, so he had been ordered to detail as many indicators of a problem as he could. They'd got the notion into their minds that some young technology geek could write a computer program to do it for them. It wouldn't work, but it amused him to see them try and replace his expertise.

When he was satisfied he appeared to be working on what others wanted, he went back to his house. For now, all he could do was wait, and that wasn't a task he struggled with. He might even take a short walk.

CHAPTER 6

Amelia sat down to sip the tea Mrs Wintern had just shown up with, and Sebastian joined her, sitting opposite in his usual chair.

"You're getting much better. You'd fool the average person now," he said, and she detected the hint of smugness in his voice. He was pleased with her progress because it reflected well on his teaching capabilities, but it was a compliment and she'd take it. It was also obvious he meant that he still noticed her taking the card from the pocket of the coat rigged with bells on it. She could do it silently, but he still saw, and they hadn't got as far as doing the opposite of putting something inside a pocket or tucking it under a glass as he had the money while in the restaurant.

In the few days since being in London she'd learnt a lot and spent the entire time practising one task or another based on the directions of the Holmes brothers. It made her feel tired, but at the same time pleased. It was a taste of a more exciting life, one where she wasn't always at home by herself. The two most anti-social men in the world had let her in enough to show her she might just be able to fit into their worlds, and she didn't want it to stop.

"Has my brother given you another lesson?" Sebastian

asked a few minutes later. She shook her head.

"No. I expected him to, but only the one so far."

"Well, at least he's keeping an eye on you. You're safer under his watch than anywhere else."

At this, Amelia furrowed her brow and tried to hide the flutter of panic that took hold of her insides and gave them a squeeze.

"He didn't tell you?" Sebastian asked. It took a second for Amelia to process this out-of-the-blue question. He'd evidently read her expression and figured out she knew so little.

"No, he hasn't told me anything. I suspected that's why he brought me here, but when you mentioned our arrangement and Myron bringing me to London, I assumed that it was as innocent as that."

"Your arrangement? No, I had an arrangement with him to keep you safe after we found out who'd paid your stalker."

Amelia's mouth dropped open and she stopped processing thoughts. She'd told Sebastian about her agreement with his brother. If Myron found out, he'd refuse to ever see her again.

"There's no need to worry, you're safe when you're with either of us." Sebastian sat forward. After a few more seconds, she shook her head to clear her thoughts and concentrate on being present.

"I shouldn't have told you about my arrangement with Myron. He forbade it." She gulped and got up, knowing it could end everything she'd just been thankful for.

"Ah, yes well, I did sort of trick you into it, didn't I?"

"Your brother won't care about that."

Sebastian looked thoughtful for a moment and studied her face. At first she considered pretending to be calm, but she let him see the fear coursing through her. It would do nothing for her to hide her emotion right now.

"I won't tell him if you don't. Since it means that much to you. But at some point he'll find out, you know that, right?"

"Yes, but maybe by then he'll actually like me and consider forgiving me."

"I'm sure he likes you already."

"You're alone in that opinion. I've made him angry far too many times for him to like me, but maybe, if I try really hard, I'll get close to being as good as you and he'll decide he can tolerate having me around."

Sebastian chuckled and took the hint. He stood up again and they ran through their little scenario where she had to try and take the card out of the pocket without him noticing. An hour of walking past the coat in the middle of the room and picking her moments, she still hadn't snuck a lift past his watchful gaze.

"Enough, I think. You're getting better, and I might not notice if I wasn't expecting it now. We'll move on."

Sebastian removed the coat from the bell-rigged contraption he'd created and put it back on.

"Like before, try and put the card in without me noticing."

"All right, give me the card, then," she said and held out her hand for it.

"Left pocket." His eyes twinkled with merriment as she hesitated. When she realised he meant her left pocket, not his, she reached in and pulled the card out. A laugh bubbled out of her. She hadn't noticed, and she wondered if she ever would, when he did that.

A moment later he closed his eyes, and she knew he was expecting her to slip the card in the pocket. Just as he had the first time she'd tried to pull it out, he grabbed her wrist long before she had the card nestled in the right place. She sighed as he let her go.

It took seven attempts until she could get the card in the pocket before he noticed her and reached out for her hand or wrist. Another four tries, and she stood on the other side of him without him moving. A grin flitted across her face.

"I did it," she said, stirring him from having his eyes closed.

As soon as he opened his eyes, he checked and pulled out the queen of hearts.

"A few more times, and then we'll move on to doing it when I'm not wearing the coat."

They spent the next few hours having him teach her to slide the card into the pocket without ringing bells, and then trying to do it as she walked by. Finally, she tried to hide it from his watching eyes, but just like before, Sebastian could spot every time she slipped something into his pocket.

Before he could teach her anything else, there was a knock at the door and someone she didn't know came in. He was dressed in shabby jeans and a hoody. He didn't look very warm, and was young enough he shouldn't be out that late.

"The address you wanted," the teenager said and handed over a piece of paper.

"They didn't notice you or the others."

The kid shook his head and shrugged down a little into his hoody.

"No, we were careful like you taught us. He went there and then left again a few minutes later. No one ever sees us."

"Nope, that's what makes you invaluable," Sebastian said and handed over a shopping bag of packages sitting by the door. Amelia recognised some food, snacks and matches.

"Cheers, mate."

The kid hurried out the way he'd come, leaving behind the faint smell of unwashed sweaty body. She tried not to wrinkle her nose, suspecting it wasn't the kid's fault he had the unpleasant odour.

She watched and waited as Sebastian went to his phone and tapped out a quick message. Afterwards, he tucked the piece of paper with the address on in his pocket. She hoped he'd explain but he didn't. He simply handed her the card again and indicated that she should try once more to place it somewhere and get it past his notice.

After thinking for a few seconds, she decided she was going to try to deposit the card and then lift the address right after. The cover of the card might provide the distraction necessary to get the second action past his notice. With her nerves, he noticed almost immediately when she tried to place the card both of the next two attempts. Then an idea popped into her head.

"Sebastian?" she said, softening her voice and biting gently on her lower lip. He raised his eyebrows.

A couple of seconds later she took a few slow, deliberate, steps towards him and tilted her head down so she could look up at him through her eyelashes.

"You remember when I came over the other night and Mrs Wintern said that... well, that we were likely to not want tea?" Amelia came the rest of the way towards him. "You didn't deny it, and it got me thinking. Would you... maybe..."

She trailed off as if she couldn't finish the sentence and stepped into his personal space. He froze to the spot and she stared at his lips, trying to make it look like she was considering kissing him. As she closed her eyes and leant in a little closer, she slipped the card in and then followed it up with a quick pinch of the piece of paper.

Hoping he was still frozen and didn't entirely believe her act, she lingered but let it get awkward. Just as he pulled back, she grinned.

"Almost," he said. "Very nice try, though. I was wondering when you'd try the feminine charms. That would have worked on most men." As he pulled the card out of his pocket, she sighed.

"But not you or your brother." She didn't hide the frustration in the sentiment. When he handed the queen of hearts back to her, she realised she'd got away with the second part of the trick.

With a smug grin on her face, she pulled the address out of her own pocket and read it.

36 Galsworthy Avenue, E14

She finished before Sebastian realised what she had. He patted his pocket and laughed.

"Well done, Amelia. You're getting good at this. My brother would be pleased."

"Pleased about what?" Myron asked from the doorway. Amelia felt her heart race. She had no idea how to explain what his younger brother had just said. Thankfully, Sebastian had no problem talking.

"Amelia here, has just successfully lifted the address you need from me with nothing but her feminine charms to disguise her true intentions."

Amelia wasn't surprised that Sebastian had chosen to emphasise this point.

"She seduced you?" Myron sneered but didn't look her way.

"I didn't go that far, and I masked the lift further by placing this card in his pocket. He's been teaching me, since I'm in London with little to do."

"How appropriate," Myron replied when he'd taken in the picture on the face of the card. Not once did he look at her, and she felt her temper rise at the insinuation until she wasn't sure she could control her mouth.

"I have to keep myself busy learning something when people are trying to harm me and no one seems to think I ought to know. Every little thing I learn that might make me safer or keep me alive is worth my time." She kept her voice even but her annoyance was unmasked. "And let's face it, seducing either Holmes brother is an achievement. You can't blame a girl for wanting to try the challenge."

An awkward silence followed her outburst. It didn't take her long to regret it. Myron never liked emotional displays. When no one said anything and both of them were looking at her, she remembered she had the piece of paper with the address on. As a sort of peace offering, she held it out to Myron. He didn't thank her as he took it.

"You owe me," Sebastian said as Myron memorised it and threw it into the fire. She ran it through her head again, wondering if it would be useful to remember and deciding not to take the chance either way. "And I think we should go immediately."

Sebastian grabbed his scarf, but Myron shook his head and held his hand up.

"No, not yet."

"There will be lots of them. Whatever you're planning, you'll need my help, and you know it."

"We can't go yet. I'll inform you when I'm ready to."

"Why not?" Amelia stepped forward, aware that neither Holmes brother was going to budge without some encouragement.

"Because there's more to this problem than we've been told. What has changed, brother of mine?" Sebastian folded his arms and Myron looked furiously at him, but moved towards the door.

"They have something, don't they? Something they're not meant to."

Myron stopped in his tracks and faced his brother. He was calm, but she could see the desire to throttle his younger brother was still there.

"It's the only obvious reason for not going right now. They have something, and until you figure out what – or if you already know that part, retrieve it – you can't go and arrest them all."

Myron nodded and came back over to sit down in the armchair. A few seconds later Sebastian sat down opposite, and Amelia realised she'd been forgotten. Even when she moved closer, they didn't even glance her way.

"I started to suspect when you didn't nag me to encourage our little lead to scamper back to the main hutch, but you confirmed it when I came to see you yesterday. You wouldn't keep Amelia in danger if she didn't need to be."

"So I'm bait?" Amelia asked. Both of them looked at her and glared, making her regret the question.

"I've been asked to back off and leave the Russians and North Koreans alone," Myron finally explained to his brother.

"Surely not while London is in danger?"

"London's not in danger."

"But I am," Amelia said, finishing Myron's implication. He nodded but had the good grace to look a little guilty. "Who would want to hurt me?"

"You're a complication in the earlier encounter, an unknown and a loose end to be tied up," Sebastian said without any hint of sensitivity. It was a good thing she wasn't surprised by the news and had recently faced enough difficult situations with the Holmes brothers that she had some confidence in their ability to protect her. The panic that threatened to overwhelm her at the news was held back from her mind by the comfort of their presence but she knew it was close to showing. In front of Myron, she couldn't allow that.

"So what am I being traded for?" she asked when no one else said anything.

"These days, probably information." Sebastian looked to his brother to get him to confirm the prognosis. After a few seconds, Myron nodded.

"What information?" Amelia came a few steps closer and leant against Sebastian's desk, from where she could see both men's faces.

"That's why we aren't making our move yet; my brother doesn't know. But the order could only have come from the royal family. They're the only people Myron answers to, and there's only one thing the family care about more than their country."

"Family. It's always family." Amelia shook her head in annoyance. "So it's a secret of some kind, and we need to find out what and where they got it from before we deal with them, right?"

"Correct, Amelia." Sebastian smiled. In response, she fetched her laptop from her bag and turned it on.

"No." Myron gave her a pointed look. "I'm going to sort

this out and ensure, whatever secret these terrorists have, that it remains a secret and out of their hands."

"It's my life on the line here. I won't let you deny me the right to try and keep myself alive."

Myron looked like he might have her thrown out, but Sebastian shrugged and went to his usual case board to start building up what they knew. If Sebastian was going to include her, she knew it gave the elder brother little choice but to allow it. Now she only had to impress them both. No pressure at all. And no reason why her hands should be shaking as she started typing her first search term.

CHAPTER 7

Despite the late hour, Mycroft didn't feel tired. His mind was abuzz with information and his body was appreciating the constant supply of tea Mrs Wintern kept supplying the three workers with. He needed to keep his mind and body alert.

Sherlock and Amelia were doing their best to find the information and who had leaked it while he sat and listened. It would be a tough task to ensure they found enough to let him know what he needed to acquire back off the Russians but not enough that they worked out what the exact nature of the secret was. It was unhelpful enough that his younger brother had worked out it was the royal family, although the leap wasn't a difficult jump for sound logic. They were the only people he answered to in any shape or form.

Mycroft watched Amelia type away on her small laptop at the desk. Given how recently she'd discovered the intent of the Russians towards her, she was coping well. He'd feared tears or an emotion even worse, but she was using the threat as a channel to achieve, something not many people found easy.

He hadn't appreciated her outburst when he'd arrived, but he knew his own prickle of jealousy had caused it. He took a certain satisfaction in the statement she'd made a couple of months earlier, when assuring him that she preferred him to his younger brother. If nothing else, it showed she had taste enough to look past appearances and even social awkwardness. His brother was the more attractive of the two of them by normal standards. Although both were tall and dark-haired, and he was always the more immaculately attired of the two of them. Sherlock had the better face and the better social skills.

Finding her flirting with Sherlock and then having his younger brother delight in the attention had tugged at a nerve. She'd come to him for tuition and learning, and now Sherlock was the one she appeared to favour. Just when he'd started to feel like training her might be a task worthy of his time.

He also hadn't missed the comment of his younger brother's about her pleasing him with her progress. At some point, Sherlock had been told or worked out he had agreed to teach her. That sentence made sense in no other circumstance and he didn't think she would have missed that little detail either. Even she wasn't that stupid. His younger brother knew, and Amelia was aware of that, yet she hadn't told him.

"I think I've found something," Amelia said, disturbing both Holmes brothers from their thoughts. Sherlock beat Mycroft to her side, and she allowed him to take the laptop from her with whatever she'd learned.

"That might be it," Sherlock replied, not taking his eyes from the screen.

"It's a forum I sometimes go to when I want to check facts to do with the royal family."

"Let me see," Mycroft said and held out his hands. When Sherlock didn't respond, Amelia got up from the desk, took the device from him and brought it over to Mycroft. She perched on the arm of the chair and pointed at the forum post she'd noticed.

The royal family must have secrets, right? My sister

worked for them a while back and she said they are a close family but not perfect at all. I'm sure some people would pay for the secrets they keep. There would be such a scandal if some of them were exposed.

"It's in a thread about the similarities between the royal family members, most of which are suggesting some form of incest, but this guy posts this one comment and that's it. No posts before or since."

She then moved the cursor and clicked on his username. A profile that had a cat as the picture and only an email in the information came up. It wasn't a perfect lead, but the post was suggestive and it was better than no lead at all.

"I think it might be worth emailing him and seeing what he knows, don't you?" She gave him a smug grin as he nodded and passed the device back to her. When she didn't move, he coughed. Sherlock glanced their way and laughed.

"I don't think brother of mine knows what to do when he's forced to share a chair."

Amelia let a wry smile flicker across her face before she moved back to the desk. While she responded to the message, her fingers flew over the keyboard, typing almost as fast as his own assistant could.

"Done. I've told him I'm very interested in what he might know and want to meet as soon as possible to discuss it. I said I was doing some research for a fiction novel but wanted it to be as realistic as possible. Mostly true, but not quite."

Mycroft nodded at the information but inwardly he seethed. This wasn't how he'd wanted the situation resolved. Amelia was far too involved, and now she would have to be the one to meet this guy, assuming he agreed to talk to her.

"Now what?" Amelia said and turned to him.

"We wait." Sherlock came over from his case board and sat down again. "Are you going to stay with us, Myron, or should we just report to you when we've done the hard work for you?"

"I'll stay. The sooner this is resolved the better." Mycroft gave his brother a fake smile, which Sherlock dutifully returned. Amelia's yawning broke the awkward silence before it could get going.

"Well, if you two are going to keep awake I might take a nap. There's no knowing when we'll get a reply."

"Really? You don't want to finish up our little lesson?" Sherlock asked. "We can show my brother what you've learnt."

"I'm sure Myron has no desire to see me try to pick your pocket or anything like it, for that matter."

"On the contrary. If you're as gifted as my brother claims, Miss Jones, I'm very curious." Mycroft knew she'd felt awkward and wanted to see exactly what she'd been doing with his brother. At the least, it made her squirm, destroying the smug air she'd had for over an hour, and at most, it might prove useful in his own training of her.

Sherlock put his coat on and stood in the centre of the room with his eyes closed. After composing herself, Amelia glided towards him and tried to slip the familiar card into his pocket without him noticing. Just as she was pulling away she made a noise with one foot on a creaky floor-board. The sound gave her away, but the motion hadn't. Despite that, Sherlock grabbed for her and had her wrist locked in his grip less than a second later. She pouted in response.

"Close," he said, a sparkle in his eyes.

"If it wasn't for the floor, I'd have managed that one."

"Perhaps, but I'd have noticed," Mycroft said, interrupting their little moment. She turned her pouting expression to him.

"Care to take a wager on that?" Sherlock held out a stack of twenty pound notes. Without even working out how many were there Mycroft nodded and stood up. If Amelia objected to being put to the test, she didn't protest. Instead, she stood off to the side as Sherlock instructed him to stand in the same spot. After fixing his eyes on her for a moment and seeing the look of doubt she couldn't hide, he closed his eyes.

Instantly, his other senses took over from his sight, and he became more aware of every little breeze and scent playing across the room. Amelia's sweet but gentle perfume lingered beside less pleasant smells, but he focused on the nicest of the fragrances, knowing its strength would signal her approach. He also concentrated on the feel of air moving around him.

A few seconds later, he reached out and felt his fingers close over Amelia's wrist. He opened his eyes to see her looking up at him. The card was in his pocket but he'd stopped her with her hand only inches away.

"It seems you've won, Myron," she said and he caught a slight flicker of an emotion he wasn't expecting in her eyes before she went back to her usual self.

As Sherlock was counting out the money into his hand, Amelia's laptop let out a shrill sound. Instantly, her booted feet hurried across the carpet towards the device.

"That was quick," she said after scanning a few lines. "He is willing to meet. He's specified the location. At a fast food place not far from here, but he's left the time up to me. Says it's open all the time."

Sherlock hurried over to read the message and handed her the jacket she'd placed over the arm of the nearest chair.

"Tell him you'll see him there in fifteen minutes and give him something to identify you by. We'll go now."

Less than a minute later all three of them were going down the stairs, and Mycroft found himself unhappy about the arrangement. It couldn't be helped that Amelia was meeting the informant. Given the circumstances and the little they knew, she was the best suited to the task, but it annoyed him that his younger brother was joining them. He could have instructed her to complete this part of the task for him.

"I'll get a taxi. See you there," Sherlock said as soon as they were in the cold night air. Amelia looked to Mycroft and shrugged. When Daniels opened the door to his car, he motioned for her to go first. At least she was cooperating, and he knew she had a point. It was her life being threatened, so while she was useful he might as well let her help.

"I'll sit near you when you meet this guy, but you can wear this," he said, and handed her a little microphone. She pinned it to the top of her corset waistcoat, where only her eyes would be able to see it, as he placed the counterpart technology in his ear.

"So you can hear what I'm saying?" she asked. He nodded.

"Get him to say what little he knows and if he's already passed the information on to another, find out who, and if you can, with what device."

"All right, I think I can do that." She exhaled and gave him a small smile. Mycroft then told Daniels where to go.

They travelled in silence, mostly because he had no interest in talking to her. Once this part of the job was over, she would go back to the hotel, where she would be safe until he'd completed his task.

She hurried out of the car ahead of him, and he hung back as she walked the few hundred metres to the corner and then around it, into the building. She ordered a drink and some chips before heading to a seat in one corner. Despite not being prepared as much as a trained agent, Amelia had the sense to sit with her back to the wall, where she could see the rest of the building. He saw her gaze flick to each of the exits and trace her possible routes to all of them before she settled back to focus on her food.

He took a seat with Daniels on the other side of the area, also making sure he could survey as much of the room as possible. When the informant approached, Mycroft wanted to see where he came from. Sherlock was nowhere to be seen, and Mycroft could only hope that it stayed that way. The less his brother knew about the situation the better.

Daniels got them food and drink to help make them blend in, and sat eating the junk the establishment called food while Mycroft sipped tea from a cardboard cup and tried not to grimace at the taste.

They had been there less than five minutes when a young male who barely looked old enough to shave, wearing a long wool coat and corduroy trousers, walked in. He didn't appear to be struggling for money, but that might not mean he wasn't. Often it was middle class and upper class people who were riddled with debt and unable to stop spending. Looking like a recently finished public school boy made him a more likely candidate for the role.

His eyes roved over the tables until he saw Amelia sitting alone. Immediately his eyes lit up with recognition, and she gave him a quick nod.

"Amelia Jones?" Mycroft heard him ask when he was closer to him. She nodded and he sat down.

"So what's your name?" she asked when neither spoke.

"I think it's best if I keep that to myself. At least until I know where this conversation is going."

"You made me curious, very curious. At the moment, where this conversation goes is up to you, but I would like to know what you've found and I am sure I can make it worth your time."

Amelia's response was a good one, but not perfect. She'd left the conversation open for the kid to demand she show him money, or even hand it over before he gave her any useful information. He hadn't given her anything and had no intention of reimbursing her if she did have to pay to get them a lead.

While they were waiting for a response to this, Mycroft noticed the swish of a familiar coat as it came rushing by. Before he could react, Sherlock was right beside the kid and pushing him farther over in the booth to sit down beside and trap the boy in place.

"Let's get right to the information we need," Sherlock said, followed by the rattle of something metal dropping onto the table. The kid gasped. "You've seen one of these before, haven't you?"

Mycroft gritted his teeth, knowing Sherlock had just shown the kid the Russian coin. The boy nodded.

"We're with a particular branch of the government. I think it's really important right now that you tell us what you know."

Mycroft rolled his eyes. One way his younger brother was always predictable. He loved drama.

"You won't be in any trouble if you tell us what you know," Amelia said as she leant forward and patted the boy's arm. "Where did you get the information?"

"My sister," he gulped again. "Is she going to be in trouble?"

"Well, some people might have to talk to her as well, but as long as she cooperates with us, I'm sure the situation can be sorted out." Amelia smiled.

"Who else knows?" Sherlock cut across the conversation, and Mycroft wished he'd shut up. Amelia's tactic had appeared to be working, even if it wasn't completely accurate.

"Your sister told you, but that wouldn't have been enough to get paid, would it? Where did you get the evidence to sell?"

"When Margaret said about it I hacked into the database she said she'd seen it on. Stuck it on a memory stick, and these two men came forward and told me they'd pay well for it. Gave me a whole bunch of those coins."

"Can you describe the stick?" Amelia asked before Sherlock could speak.

"Yeah, it was silver, with 64 gigabytes on one side. Has a clear cap and a cream string to attach it to something. About this big."

From where he was sitting Mycroft couldn't see the dimensions, but both Sherlock and Amelia watched as the boy held out his fingers to show them the size.

"How long ago did you sell them this?"

"Only a few days ago. They expressed an interest in it a

couple of months before Christmas, but they only paid and picked it up when I threatened to sell it elsewhere about two days ago."

"And your sister and you haven't mentioned a word of it to anyone else?" Amelia asked.

The boy shook his head.

"Right then, one last thing. I want you to write down your name and address for me," Amelia passed over her notebook and a pen. "And don't give me anything fake. It won't take us long to verify it, and if you've not supplied the correct information we will have to take matters further."

After scribbling furiously, the boy passed the details back to Amelia and looked hopefully at Sherlock. Mycroft glanced away as they let the kid walk out. The enquiry would need to go further, but it could wait. Right now, he had to make sure the information was only held by the terrorists and hadn't been passed to Mr Delra. That meant taking a trip to the address Sherlock had found for him.

Not waiting for Amelia or Sherlock to follow, Mycroft got up and headed for the car, leaving the almost untouched drink and making Daniels jog to keep up. He knew Amelia wouldn't allow herself to be ordered back to the hotel, so he intended to leave her behind.

As he got into his car, his brother followed in behind and slammed the car door shut. Daniels pulled off before Amelia could do more than walk around the corner.

"Myron!" he heard her yell in his ear. He yanked the earpiece out before she could make any more of a fuss and tucked it into the car's ashtray.

Sherlock laughed and sat back next to him.

"She is going to be mad at you for weeks."

"She's safer being left behind," Mycroft replied.

"I agree, and would have done the same thing. She's still angry."

"It's you she'll be angry at. I'm just paying for her hotel. You're the one teaching her." Mycroft looked out the window. His brother would know this wasn't true and get the hint.

"You worked out I know you have an arrangement with Amelia."

"Not any longer, I don't."

"Yes. You do." He raised his eyebrows at his younger brother. "I know it's safe to assume you made it a condition that she didn't tell anyone. She didn't tell me. I worked it out and then used my knowledge of our own little agreement to keep her safe to get her to slip up and admit she had a separate deal with you."

"So she still said something." Mycroft sneered.

"Only because I made it clear I already knew. She'd never have betrayed you otherwise. I thought that would be obvious after she let you notice her slipping the card into your pocket."

"I assure you she didn't let me notice something I wouldn't have." Mycroft lifted his chin a little higher. "However, to the task at hand. I want you to stay out of the way on this one. We need to find that information before anything else."

CHAPTER 8

Fury ran through Amelia as she stomped her feet on the side of the road. Myron and Sebastian had abandoned her in the middle of the night. She knew the logic that had led to the decision, but it didn't lessen her anger. Both of them would expect her to go back to the hotel and wait for one of them to let her know their mission was a success.

As a taxi came up the road towards her, she knew she wasn't going to listen to them. The fear that Myron had instilled in her less than a week earlier about memorising an address had paid off. She could still remember the location Sebastian had found for him. Whether they wanted her to or not, she could follow them there and help. Knowing the London traffic, she'd only be a couple of minutes behind them.

After giving the driver the address, she urged him to get there as swiftly as the traffic would allow. She had enough cash to pay him double if he managed it.

The whole way over to the address she kept an eye out for Myron's car and where they were going. As of an hour ago, she was on duty helping the Holmes boys. She couldn't make a mistake, and that meant taking in and remembering the massive amounts of information they regularly processed.

Only when the taxi pulled up a couple of streets away, as she'd asked the driver to do, did she wonder if she'd done the right thing. For some reason these terrorists were after her, and she had travelled right to them. The first tendrils of fear crept up into her mid-section as she stepped out onto the pavement. She needed to stay in the shadows and find Myron or Sebastian before anyone noticed her.

Not long after walking in the right direction she spotted the familiar black car, and Daniels stepped out of a shadow to confront her.

"Miss Jones, you shouldn't be here. Go back to the hotel," Daniels said as he pulled her into the dark alleyway.

"I'm not going to sit and wait for this to be over while the two people I like most are wading into danger on my behalf. Myron has been training me for combat and Sebastian for the sneaky stuff. I know I can help them," she replied, as much to convince her own mind as Daniels.

"Myron is going to be angry."

"He might, but I'm safer with them. Which way did Sebastian go?" At this question of hers, Daniels grinned. He understood her logic. Sebastian would let her help if she wanted to, whereas Myron would probably try and send her back to the hotel still.

"He went around the back. Go down there until you reach the next road. You'll find a back gate ajar and Sebastian preparing to jump a fence. You'll have to hurry."

She patted his arm to thank him for the information and jogged off down the alley, pleased she'd worn trousers that day rather than a skirt, and extra pleased the knives Myron gave her were tucked up against her back.

As Daniels had described, she noticed the gate to a back garden was left open by a small fraction, so she snuck through it and hurried down the little alleyway beside the house, keeping her footfalls light to hide any noise. She paused at the end of the house to see if she could spot Sebastian, but the trees around the edge of the garden blocked out too much light. The shadows at the end could have hidden an army of grown men.

Focusing on her breathing and moving quietly, Amelia crept closer to the fence. When she was almost there, a hand reached out and tugged her into the shadows at the side. Panic almost made her scream before her brain let her know the grip was familiar.

"Sometimes I think you're far too clever for your own good," Sebastian whispered in her ear.

"Everything I know, you or your elder brother taught me," she whispered back. The sound of a low chuckle came to her ears. It was true. She'd never have been this bold if they hadn't taught her.

"We need to get over the fence in exactly one minute."

"You can go first," she said.

"Are you sure?"

"Yes. I can copy your movements if you go first."

"All right." Sebastian moved forward to use the tree as a platform over the fence and she came up behind, watching every foot and hand placement in the dim light as he hauled himself up. He moved slowly to minimise the movement of the branches, but it was a good thing it was mid-winter and there were no leaves to rustle.

Amelia tried to count out a minute in her head, but Sebastian moved before she got there and she had no choice but to follow. Being second, she couldn't move as slowly as he had done, but she didn't need to. Her body was so much lighter the branches moved less for her and allowed her an easy passage.

As she lowered herself down the other side, Sebastian reached up to steady her.

"Stay close," he whispered as they rushed across the back garden to the back door of the house. As they got closer, a movement-sensitive light came on. He grabbed her hand and sprinted to the house. Less than two seconds later they stood with their backs pressed against the brick wall to one side of the patio doors.

As the light went out again, it revealed a thin strip of light from the patio window, and she could see the outline of a person looking through a gap in the curtains. Her pulse raced and her body shook as she tried to stay calm.

After what seemed like an age, the curtains flapped shut again and she exhaled. Not daring to move in case she triggered the light again, she waited for Sebastian to move.

Slower than she'd thought possible, he slid his body across the wall towards the kitchen door and away from the patio with the sensitive light, leaving her closest to danger and not sure she could match his slow, steady movement. She turned her head slightly, to keep an eye on him, and realised she was going to need to follow.

She took a couple of deep breaths and inched her body along the wall, feeling the scrape of fabric against brick. A few seconds later the string on the back of her corset caught on something, and she found herself stuck, unable to move further. Sebastian wasn't paying her any attention, so she had to try and get herself unsnagged without help.

Just as she was almost there, the string coming loose made her jolt. Instantly, the light went on. She froze and pulled an apologetic face at Sebastian when he turned to look at her.

From where she now stood, she couldn't see the patch of grass the living room light had shone out onto, so she could only keep still and hope no one inside noticed the disturbance again.

Amelia tried to count the seconds while they waited, and she hoped nothing bad happened. Neither Holmes brother would forgive her if they were discovered because of her. After a minute, darkness enveloped them once more. This time she decided not to move. She would wait until Sebastian was inside before risking setting off the light again.

An agonising amount of time later he was by the back door and reaching out with one hand to find the lock and handle. At the same slow speed, he then turned to face the back door and crouched in front of it. Several more minutes after that, he had a lock pick in his hands and was about to start work on the door.

The sound of a loud crash sounded from inside the house, followed by loud voices and running people.

"Crap," Sebastian said and gave up on being stealthy. He threw his body weight at the door, but it didn't do more than give a few millimetres. After a second impact into it, the door flew open and Sebastian rushed inwards. Amelia followed.

It didn't take long for someone to notice them, and an Asian-looking man came through the kitchen door in time for Sebastian's fist to connect with his nose. The unfortunate guy went flying backwards into someone else.

Before Amelia could get close enough to even consider helping, two Russians came into the room from a separate door. Both had guns, and they were pointed right at them. Sebastian put his hands in the air, and Amelia didn't hesitate to copy him.

This had managed to go horribly wrong in less than ten minutes. Myron was ushered into the room only a few seconds later. Blood dripped from his nose, and he gave Amelia an angry look when he saw her, but otherwise remained his expressionless self.

The men around them talked in languages she didn't understand, but some plan must have been made because they were then ushered towards the front of the house, through the living room, and then up the stairs. Two Russians went first, then Myron and Amelia, before Sebastian came up behind them all. It didn't surprise her that the two men were already trying to protect her in the limited capacity left open to them.

Once on the next floor, Amelia noticed there were four doors off the landing, and they were ushered through to one of the rooms at the back. She tried to scan the others as they walked past the doors but she only got a glimpse into one which showed a pile of beds arranged across the floor.

The room they were taken into had a similarly covered floor, and she noticed there were enough sleeping places for nine men. So far they'd only seen seven, five Russians and two North-Koreans.

The men pushed the beds out of the way to one side and used twine to tie their hands together in front of them. Amelia tried not to wince as it dug into her wrists. Unlike the last time they'd captured her and Myron, they weren't gentle with her. They'd learnt that she was also a potential threat.

Once they were bound, all three were encouraged to sit with gun-aided gesticulations. All but two of the men then left. She let a sigh escape her lips at finding herself in such a position. This time it wouldn't be so easy to escape.

No one spoke, and Amelia was left to wonder what had happened for them to get caught. Myron appeared the worst off, of the three of them. His nose looked swollen where it had been hit, and it still dripped blood for several minutes after they had sat down.

It didn't take her long to work out that Sebastian was annoyed with Myron. He sat with his body turned slightly away from him, and his fists were clenched into white-knuckled balls. Myron sat with his chin high, as he often did when he was annoyed with something but unwilling to explain, and didn't even glance at either of them. The atmosphere of anger and silence grew worse with each long minute that passed.

Eventually the Russian guards picked up on it as well, and Amelia noticed they looked back and forth between the two Holmes brothers to see who was going to say something first. It wasn't long before Amelia was doing the same, but neither spoke, and after an hour she wondered if either were ever going to.

Despite the men who sat opposite, Amelia felt herself calming down. She was a prisoner, but she was with the two smartest men in the world, and the Russians had holstered their guns. For now, there was time to think of a way out, or wait for a rescue. Daniels would know something had gone wrong by now as well.

When another hour had ticked by, she found her mind churning over ideas without waiting for the men either side of her to come up with something. They were either waiting for an opportunity, or not able to think of something if nothing had happened in the hour or so that had already passed. It was important that she try to follow their line of thoughts. If the right opening came along, she might need to see it and act without instructions, as well.

It took her several minutes to come up with a few sensible ideas of what might provide an escape attempt. At some point the guards would need to change, and there was also the possibility that the rest of the terrorists arriving back might create a distraction. For scope, that wasn't much to go on, and she felt her heart sink when the two North Koreans came into the room and switched with the Russians without there being a single potential moment for escape.

She spent the next few minutes fighting the despair that wanted to overwhelm her emotions and rubbing feeling back into her fingers. The twine was mercilessly tight, and she knew it wouldn't be loosened, even if she did her best at being charming. A small smile crept across her lips at her line of thought. Sebastian and Myron wouldn't be surprised that her thinking had gone in that direction. They knew she liked to use her female nature to aide her cause.

A few seconds later she had to wipe the larger smile that threatened to show from her face and try to look like nothing had occurred in her mind. She'd just had the perfect idea to create an opportunity and help the men either side of her. It might even be enough to make Myron forgive her for a whole array of grievances.

After planning out exactly what she'd do, Amelia waited for the right moment. It would need to be done well, or she'd only make things worse.

CHAPTER 9

Anger and pain were the focus points in Mycroft's mind. The pain would keep him awake and his body running on adrenaline, and the anger would fuel his resolve to get out of the mess they were in. Both would be needed before the night was over.

Ever since arriving at the terrorists' house, nothing had gone according to plan. Sherlock had been late through from his location, giving Mycroft too many men to handle alone, and he'd caught his foot on the fabric of the first terrorist's trousers and knocked a vase off a small table by the front door. Instead of going down quietly, the Russian had made a loud noise and alerted everyone in the building to his presence.

Although they might have coped had Sherlock been on schedule for his half of the plan, Mycroft knew it was his fault they'd been caught. He'd been clumsy, something practice would have avoided. It resulted in his anger being directed partially at himself, but plenty more had flared when he'd seen Amelia emerge with Sherlock. The stupid girl hadn't gone back to the hotel, where she'd have been safe.

Now he was sat in the middle of a room that stunk of male body-odour with both Amelia and Sherlock and no easy route out that didn't risk her getting hurt. And he still didn't know where the information that the terrorists were blackmailing the royal family with was. This was exactly the sort of scenario he'd intended to avoid.

Over the last few hours he'd run every possible plan for escape through his mind, and he knew Sherlock would have done as well. The fact that both were still sat there patiently waiting was confirmation that both knew it was best to wait to act. Protecting Amelia would need to be Sherlock's main goal, while his needed to be finding the information and acquiring it before it could be taken somewhere safer. He hoped Sherlock would see that and know what to do when the time came.

Meanwhile, Daniels would be waiting for them. His chauffeur knew better than to do anything else on this mission. It wasn't approved, and therefore no help could be called for. At best, the pair of retired agents who were following Amelia around might decide to help, but that was so unlikely it was better off being discounted. Watching a girl move about London was one matter, performing a rescue mission when outnumbered was far more. This wasn't their fight, and hadn't been for several years. Both had already sacrificed a lot for the survival of their country. Neither would want to risk more.

Knowing their chance would need to come shortly before dawn, as the hours and minutes ticked by, Mycroft grew more tense. By morning, they would lose the information for good.

When the first light of the morning was still over an hour away, Amelia grew restless beside him. For several minutes she fidgeted back and forth, until every eye was on her.

"Sorry," she said when she noticed the attention. After glancing at them all, she looked at the two Korean men sitting opposite. "Do you think I could go to the bathroom?"

Mycroft groaned and the men ignored her. Yet another reason why he didn't like having a woman to work with.

They never seemed to be able to hold their bladder. Women and needing the toilet was an art form he would never understand, and it seemed the Koreans didn't, either. They told her to be silent in their language and ignored her.

"Myron, I don't think they understand. Will you ask..."

"Silence," the left one yelled again. Amelia bit down on the last few words of the sentence, but she fidgeted some more and gave him a pleading look. Before he could get annoyed enough with her to consider translating, his younger brother did the honour.

As soon as Sherlock had finished speaking in Korean Amelia pulled a pleading desperate look at both men. At first it didn't look like it would work, but after talking amongst themselves in low whispers, they agreed to take her and motioned for her to get to her feet.

It took her a few awkward shuffles to get the momentum to lift her body up, as most of her limbs appeared to have gone to sleep, but she eventually managed it and smiled gratefully as the smaller of the two men took hold of her arm, just above the elbow, and led her out to the landing.

The door closed before Mycroft could see which way the bathroom lay, but he'd caught enough of a glimpse to know another of the doors off the landing was open and someone was in there doing something while sat on an old dining chair.

Over the next few minutes he heard the usual sounds one might expect when someone was using a bathroom, ending with a flush and the patter of feet towards the sink. Mycroft doubted they'd let her wash her hands, but found himself wrong when the tap turned on and water gurgling through pipes sounded from above.

A few seconds later, a loud thud let him know that someone's head had connected with solid wood and come off the worse. A few more yells came from just outside the door, and their own guard got to his feet, caught between the dilemma of being needed outside and in there. It only took him a couple of seconds to decide to watch them.

Mycroft closed his eyes, internalising his groan of despair. For some unknown reason Amelia had decided to try and free herself, but he knew she wouldn't succeed and now their own guard was doing exactly the right thing in the situation. Even though Mycroft and Sherlock could probably overpower him while Amelia was distracting the others, they wouldn't get more than a couple of feet outside the room without someone shooting, and it was likely to be Amelia who took the bullet. If the guard had left them to try and get her back, they might have got further and evened the fight well enough to protect her, but that wouldn't happen now.

To add even more stupidity to her decision, it would also make them more alert to their actions. Once one tried to escape, the terrorists would be more aware of a second attempt. She'd just ruined their chances of getting away with the information and her unharmed.

A few more thuds and a cut-off squeal of pain followed this process in Mycroft's mind and confirmed his suspicions. Already she'd been stopped, and for nothing. The only relief was the lack of gunshot noises, silenced or otherwise.

The brief attempt at escape ended with the door opening and Amelia being thrown onto the floor at his feet. She groaned in pain as it wrenched her shoulder, and he could already see the swelling around her eye and right cheek bone from the punch that must have landed there. From all the movement, the twine had also rubbed through the final few layers of skin around her wrists, and it was turning red before his eyes.

He ignored her and turned his head away, unable to keep the anger from his eyes, but not wanting the Koreans to see it. After a few seconds, Sherlock leant forward and helped her lift herself into a sitting position between them. As soon as he let go of her, she slumped against the wall.

When she tilted her own head back and closed her eyes he risked glancing at her again. Her breath came in quick gasps through clenched teeth as she tried to block out the pain she was in. Most of it would fade as she sat there, but he found himself hoping she hadn't broken anything. He still wanted to get her out of this alive, even if she'd been stupid enough to make it harder on them. He could only hope the pain she was in now was enough to make her learn her lesson.

The Korean terrorist who had gone out with her to the bathroom didn't come back. Instead, one of the Russians who hadn't yet been their guard came and took his place. Mycroft recognised this man. He'd been one of the Russians on the boat.

He counted another twenty minutes going by before the door opened and two more men came in. The motioned for him and his two companions to get to their feet. This time Amelia needed help, and she grunted in pain a couple of times before the three of them stood. It was time for them to be moved to yet another safe-house.

They were ushered down the stairs one at a time, with a gun in their backs encouraging them to cooperate. Once they were in the hallway, Mycroft heard the sound of a van pulling up outside and each of them were gagged with tape to keep them quiet.

Sherlock would also know that this was the only moment they had to escape, and Mycroft needed to be last out of the house to go back for the information. Heading up the group of three, the younger Holmes brother stepped out of the door first, followed by Amelia, putting him exactly where he needed to be. The familiar Russian with a gun came up behind them. Sherlock needed to be the one to make the first move when he had a gun so close to his back. He would need to cover Amelia long enough to get her out of there.

The back door of the van was open and Sherlock had his foot on the back bumper before he made a move. He pushed sideways with his foot and threw his whole body into the nearest terrorist. Immediately Mycroft pushed Amelia down to the ground and spun himself around to face the Russian holding a pistol.

He didn't shoot, but pointed it at Mycroft and threatened to. This was a problem. Of all the tests his brother and he had done, surviving a bullet at close range wasn't one of them. Mycroft hadn't moved fast enough, once again.

As his mind was running through the possibilities, Sherlock grabbed Amelia's arm and tried to pull her away from the van and the house, but she wouldn't go. Instead, she came up beside him. It seemed she wasn't leaving without him. The sentiment was foolish at best.

Before he could push her away and get her and his brother out of there, a darting body came from the side and tackled the terrorist. The gun went off as he hit the ground, but the bullet whistled past his ear without causing harm.

"Run," a familiar voice said as its owner got back to his feet. More guns were fired from the direction of the house, and the four of them took off down the road towards Mycroft's car. While running, he pulled off the tape that kept him silent, and noticed Amelia do the same, although their hands remained bound in front of them. Sherlock had already freed his mouth.

Daniels must have been prepared, because the vehicle came down the road towards them as they sprinted. Sherlock got there first, yanked the door open and pushed their extra helper inside the car. Amelia followed only a few seconds later.

Knowing everyone who needed to be was safe, Mycroft stopped running and turned to go back for the information, but his younger brother grabbed his arm.

"It's too late. It would be suicide, even for us," Sherlock said in a low voice.

As two of the Russian men came forward to try and get a better aim, he knew his younger brother was right. They got into the car and he ordered Daniels to drive off.

"Just drop me off here," Jeremy said when they were a few blocks away. "My work is done."

"Tha—"

Jeremy put up his hand.

"We're even now. We'll leave it at that." The retired agent got out of the car and Mycroft knew he'd never see him again. The job was done, and they had completed the final business arrangement between them.

"Got anything to undo these?" Sherlock asked as soon as the three of them were alone. He held his hands up to emphasise the twine still holding them together.

"I have," Amelia replied before he could. She turned to one side, but his younger brother didn't know what she meant. After expressing an exasperated sigh, Mycroft reached towards her and pulled one of her knives from the sheath at the bottom of her corset.

"At least that's something you can help with," Mycroft said, unleashing the anger and frustration he felt. If Amelia hadn't interfered he'd have the information, and the royal family, country, and her would be safe. "You should have gone back to the hotel."

"I came to help, like I've been training to," she said as Mycroft cut Sherlock's bonds and then handed his brother the blade to return the favour. When both of them were free, she held out her hands to be cut free as well.

"You're an amateur who thinks you are a lot better than you are. Because of your actions, our country and royal family aren't safe. They still have the information." Mycroft vented his frustration on Amelia, and although he knew he'd made a mistake or two of his own, it would have been rectified had she not acted out herself.

"Brother, it's not—" Sherlock tried to speak, but Amelia cut him off.

"It's okay, you don't need to defend my actions." She reached into the top of her corset with two fingers and pulled out a small data stick that matched the description they'd been given many hours earlier. With a calm but focused look, she held it out to him. "Your secrets are safe. They have been for hours."

A chuckle started deep in Sherlock's chest and soon turned into a full blown laugh as Mycroft took the stick from her. "It seems our invisible amateur has done what we couldn't, brother of mine. Did you get it on your eventful trip to the bathroom?" Sherlock smiled at her and she nodded.

"I saw one of them wiping the computer hard drive clean, and an envelope was beside it, about the right sort of size for this, on the way to the bathroom. I took the Korean by surprise, and then the Russian. Once I'd got the stick and switched in the small magnet they were using to scramble the hard drive, I made a run for the window as if I'd just been trying to get out of the house all along. They never even noticed. Although they gave me a good beating for my trouble."

She ran her fingers lightly over the right side of her face, feeling the swollen area, and a few flecks of pain appeared in her eyes, eyes that never left his face. Mycroft didn't know what to say. Somehow, this girl had saved his job and completed his task, and she'd done it all with the little they'd taught her.

The earlier words his brother had said came back to his mind. He had her loyalty, and as of now he knew she had his respect.

"I think we should all get some rest and heal," Mycroft said.

"Some of Mrs Wintern's tea would be very welcome." Sherlock smiled and Amelia nodded.

"Yes, to Baker Street."

CHAPTER 10

The midday sun shone in Mycroft's eyes as he looked out the car window. Daniels was taking him to Buckingham palace, where the butler would be waiting for him in the same room as a week ago.

He'd just left Amelia and Sherlock in the living room at Baker Street filling Mrs Wintern in on their night's adventure. Amelia hadn't broken anything, but she'd sprained one wrist, both wrists were bloodied, and there were bruises and swellings on her face, thighs and torso. It would be painful for a few days but leave no lasting marks.

The information about the royal family was tucked in his pocket, and Amelia was confident the terrorists hadn't got another copy in the house. No one could be sure, but it would be surprising for the royal family not to know if another copy was held somewhere by Mr Delra. It would have been leaked to the papers already.

An agent of his had already been to the original informant and her brother to ensure they were silenced on the matter, but it was yet another worker for the palace who hadn't lived up to expectations. Mycroft found himself wondering if he was going to need to read the CV of every person who applied for a job. There seemed to be no other way to keep the family safe, and Sherlock was unlikely to want the task.

Mycroft had also sent a team to round up the terrorists. All but two of them had been arrested and moved to a secure location for him to interrogate later. The remaining two were suspected to have left London and be on their way to Europe. Catching them would be difficult, given how far they'd already managed to get, but not impossible. It depended on the attitude of the royal family in response to the current situation. He'd overstepped their opinion of his role too much to do so again so soon.

The same two men were awaiting him in the courtyard of the palace as had brought him there a week earlier, and they had similar expressions. Not everything about this meeting was going to go well.

He frowned as they walked him to the same room, but forced his face into a more neutral expression when he saw the butler already sitting there with a steaming teapot. Tea was a positive sign.

"Good morning, Mr Holmes. Tea?" the butler asked, and motioned for him to sit opposite. He nodded, knowing this meeting would be longer than the last.

As he came closer to sit down, he saw the standard information folders and knew it would contain his report of the night's events. His assistant had typed it up already and filed it. Without waiting to be asked for it, Mycroft retrieved the data stick and placed it on top of the folder.

"My recommendation is that this is looked at to see the sources of the information, and then both source and copy are destroyed," Mycroft said.

"I will pass it on to Her Majesty." The butler finished pouring them both tea and sat back. "She wishes me to express her displeasure that you felt it necessary to interfere in this matter after she commanded you not to, despite your *token* of reparation."

Mycroft gave a brief fake smile. The token was the retrieved information, but he hadn't given it back to repair any loss of reputation. If they had the brains he did, they would know he'd lost none.

"The royal family have been put at great risk."

"The risk is now at least over," Mycroft interrupted, not able to sit there any longer without defending his decision.

"They will decide when the risk is over. We only have a vague promise from a young woman you were with that there were no other copies, and it is hardly backed up by the word of the boy who sold it in the first place. We are in contact with our *friend*, Mr Delra, to ascertain the legitimacy of your claim."

Mycroft fought back the temptation to roll his eyes. They wouldn't get an honest answer from the puppet behind the scenes. A man like him would deny having another copy to melt back out of sight and be the mysterious benefactor behind another project years later. Whatever he said, it couldn't be trusted.

"If Her Majesty is satisfied that her family is safe, we will allow this matter to slide and move on to other issues. As such, she has recommended that you don't interfere with the process to catch the remaining two members of the gang you encountered last night. It would be better if they made it home to report on the effectiveness of our agents."

"As you wish," Mycroft replied. There was no point going over his recommendation again. They had it in writing on the table in front of him that he thought his brother should be tasked to go after the errant pair. Nothing he said would convince them otherwise. At least there was a chance Sherlock would decide to do it anyway. Having a bored younger brother had its merits.

"We understand the immediate threat is now over, however?"

"It is. For now, at least, London is safe."

"For that, you have our thanks."

Mycroft nodded his acknowledgement of the gratitude and picked up the teacup nearest him. The telling off was done.

He still had his job, and they were pleased enough with his work that they didn't want the meeting to end badly. With every event considered, it was the expected result. They would always need him, even if they didn't always appreciate his genius.

"There is also one last matter that has caused concern."

"And what is that?" Mycroft sipped his tea to cover any surprise on his part. They should be done.

"This Miss Jones. She appears to have cropped up several times now in relation to recent events. We understand she seems to hold some *appeal* to yourself, or possibly your younger brother."

"And if she does?"

"While we have made use of your family for several generations and recognise that, for it to continue, acquiring a wife is necessary, we would ask that you ensure any additions to your family are adequately protected and trained for the role they are to fulfil."

"You're making a big assumption." Mycroft smiled his usual fake smile. Not even Sherlock told him how to handle his own private life.

"Are we? You chose to protect her over Her Majesty and the rest of the royal family. She must be very important to *your* family."

Mycroft gave the briefest of nods but didn't even add a smile to the look. He wanted this part of the conversation over as soon as possible.

"Then see to it she gets training or is kept out of the affairs and safe at home. We wouldn't want the ties between our two families dissolving over one errant member, now, would we?"

"Of course not. I'm sure adequate measures can be arranged."

"Good. Then here is to the continued survival and success of our great nation and its chief families." The butler raised his cup and Mycroft copied the motion.

"To our success."

As soon as it was polite to do so, Mycroft excused himself and made his way back to his car and the familiarity of his own chauffeur.

"Home, sir?" Daniels asked when they were both sat in their usual seats.

"No, the Diogenes Club. I have some thinking to do."

"Right you are, sir."

Every minute of the half-an-hour journey, Mycroft allowed himself to stew in the anger he felt. London might well be safe, as well as Amelia and the royal family, but he had been given little of the credit, and the job felt incomplete.

Mr Delra was still an unknown force, hiding in the shadows and able to show himself at a later date. Mycroft knew it wouldn't be the last time he or his younger brother encountered the man, either. Men like Mr Delra didn't stay friends with royal families for long without doing something to upset them.

Having terrorists escape the United Kingdom also did nothing to benefit them. It would show the exact opposite of the image the butler suggested. Instead of looking effective, they would look sloppy. Two men had slipped through the net, and that meant their net had holes.

And finally there was Amelia. The butler had hinted that Mycroft's priorities were ill-placed before, when acting to protect Sherlock in the past, but he'd heard what hadn't been said concerning Amelia.

They wanted her out of the way and shut up in one of the Holmes residences to organise dinners and clean their clothes. On top of that, they assumed because she was female that one of the two brothers must wish to wed her and bed her. Both points were offensive for several reasons. Mycroft and Sherlock were quick to admit that most women were weaker and inferior in mind due to their emotions, but that didn't mean they should be used for only one thing and kept at the whim of the men in their lives. It also didn't entail that either of them would wish to be so sentimental as to marry someone for compassionate reasons, either. On Amelia's behalf, and for the very few women who'd impressed him before her, he was angered by the insinuations.

With all these annoyed thoughts, Mycroft walked into the Diogenes Club and made his way to his usual room. Once settled behind his desk, he found himself reminded of Amelia's presence there. He pushed it from his mind for the moment, to focus on other matters. He could decide what to do with her once he'd sorted out Mr Delra, and the rest of the business with him.

Mycroft had one more retired agent who owed him a favour and would happily keep an eye on Mr Delra for him in exchange for some holiday time. The agent had often preferred to be stationed in warm countries, and Mr Delra seemed to like the same sort of climate.

The next order of business was the two escaping terrorists. Mycroft couldn't let them leave without at least trying to catch them, but he couldn't use government resources for that either. He would need to borrow his brother, but before he could write a note in their familiar code, his extra phone buzzed to let him know it had received a message.

Ever since Amelia's incident with a stalker, he had kept it on him at all times rather than in the desk drawer in his library. Wondering what on earth she could want, he pulled the phone from his pocket.

How did the meeting go? Are they knighting you for being a hero?

He snorted at her curiosity intermingled with flattery before tapping out a reply.

No. I had my knuckles rapped for misbehaving. Shouldn't you be resting?

Not wanting to disturb his fellow club members, Mycroft tucked the phone deep in a pocket so when she replied the buzz would only disturb him. In the meantime, he sipped more tea and thought about the best way to persuade Sherlock to help him with this last part of the situation. Once more, Amelia's messages disturbed him before he could act.

Your brother is restless, which makes it rather hard to nap. Do you need any more help?

Relief spread through Mycroft as she solved his problem for him.

No. I'm trying to obey my orders and not pursue the two Russians who got away. Perhaps you should send my brother out on an errand?

Mycroft pushed the pen and paper away from himself after sending this message. If Amelia didn't understand his meaning, she would read it out to Sherlock and his younger brother would know what it meant. A minute later, another vibrating feeling came from his pocket and caused him to reach for the phone again.

Wonderful. Now I can rest. Your brother is suitably occupied.

As he put the phone back in his pocket, he exhaled in relief. For the second time in less than a day, Amelia had helped him out of a difficult situation with her own unique style of business.

She was a very distinct woman. Not afraid of her emotions, but not ruled by them either. At least for the most part. She'd shown some weakness when scared, but only in her judgement to run to him at all costs. But as Sherlock had pointed out, she'd shown him great loyalty. More so than even his younger brother did, and something about that pleased him more than he'd expected it to. Loyalty was not easily bought these days.

If Sherlock had retrieved that information, he wouldn't have been assured to get it back, but she'd handed it over to him at the first opportunity and faced a considerable amount of pain to get it. It showed bravery and courage on top of a reasonable amount of skill.

The pain she'd endured was one of Mycroft's sticking points. Four times now a doctor had tended to her wounds because of something related to him. The first and the most recent time, at the hands of the Russians, were due to his lack of care, and he felt uncomfortable about it. Thankfully, neither of those occasions had led to scarring, but one other had.

The scar through her eyebrow was a constant reminder that he'd ignored her when she'd turned up in the Diogenes Club. Instead of trusting her judgement, he'd thrown her out that day, and it had resulted in her going through yet another situation where she was left hurt and emotionally vulnerable.

Of the four occasions, only her stalker hurting her had been entirely unrelated to him, and he'd saved her from far worse by helping his brother get to her. It mitigated a little of his guilt towards her, but the royal family were right about one thing. He needed to do a better job of keeping her safe if she was going to be a part of his future.

If he could, he'd have given her the healing ability that Sherlock and he shared, but they'd never been able to replicate it for others, and neither knew where it had come from. One day a gene within the brothers had activated, and they found themselves able to heal and live longer. By nature of being involved with them, Amelia would be the most likely to be hurt. She was the weakest, the least skilled, and she couldn't heal as fast. If he taught her more, she would need to understand it would lead to more pain.

Mycroft didn't need to ask Amelia to know what she

wanted. In going to the bathroom and attacking the Korean she'd made it clear. Pain didn't bother her if it was part of the task and necessary to achieve the goal set before her. She knew when she'd decided to retrieve the information for him that it would be dangerous, and still done it anyway.

That meant the decision came down to how he felt. He needed to decide if he wanted Amelia in his future or not. As he thought about the last week, he rubbed his hand across his chin. She'd gained his respect, and when he pictured her face as she handed over the data stick, he knew he liked her. There had been no boast in her eyes. Just a gentle confidence and appreciation for getting the task complete, along with a small amount of relief.

It only took him a few more seconds to fix on what he wanted to do. He reached into his pocket one final time and tapped out a message to her.

Tea, 4pm. Same place as last time.

With that sent, he got to work arranging her training for the future. He had three hours before their meeting, and plenty to organise.

EPILOGUE

As Amelia hurried down from her hotel room into the reception area, she hoped she wasn't late. It had taken her most of the afternoon to wash, dress and make herself presentable with all the cuts and bruises she had.

The bruises and swollen areas of her face were covered up as best as she could manage with make-up, and she wore her longer set of fingerless gloves to cover the awful scabs around her wrists. Myron would still notice she was hurt, but few others would. It was a relief the winter gave her an excuse to cover up so much.

Before she could go through to the terrace she noticed a familiar figure come striding through the hotel entrance. She smiled as he nodded his acknowledgement of her, and they walked through to the terrace café together.

As soon as he'd ordered drinks for the both of them, he fixed his eyes on her. She saw him concentrate on the area around her left eye.

"It barely hurts now," she said, as much to break the silence as to answer the query in his look.

"Good. Are you ready to attempt this lesson again?"

She smiled and nodded; already her eyes had been tempted to flick towards the people on the nearby green and give herself an extra edge on describing them, but she knew he would get the lesson underway swiftly.

Taking a deep breath, she turned her head and her eyes found an elderly woman and child near the duck pond. The child had the same dimple in her chin as the woman, but her hair was too grey and her skin too wrinkled to be the mother of such a young girl. It was a grandparent with her granddaughter, but Myron would expect her to see way more than that. She studied them for a minute or two more.

"There, grandmother and granddaughter. They come here often. The man with the small stand knows them, but they're not here for a good reason today. I think someone died and she's taking the child out to occupy her."

"Who died?" Myron asked.

"The father," she said after pausing a moment.

"Why?"

"It's not the mother. The young girl wouldn't have snacks in her little backpack if the mother was dead."

"Correct. Another," Myron commanded, his face remaining impassive.

She surveyed the area again and picked out a lone male dressed in denim jeans and jacket. He had a digital camera fixed to his face and was pointing it at something on a tree near the edge of the park. He'd been like that several minutes before she could gather enough information about him.

"Single guy, there. Amateur photographer. Is some sort of programmer as a day job. Here on holiday and in his low thirties."

"Explain, why?"

"Well, amateur photographer because he's spent over two minutes fiddling with settings on the camera for just one shot, but it's not an expensive camera. If he wanted to be paid, he'd have something better. Single because no woman would let her boyfriend wear those two colours together, and programmer because of the glasses. Low thirties is a guess based on his haircut."

Myron nodded.

"Correct again, although you missed that he was staying with his sister."

"Really?"

"He also has food a woman packed for him."

Amelia sighed. She had been so close. Before she could pick out another target Myron's phone went off.

"It's my brother," he said a moment later.

"Answer it, then. I need to use the bathroom anyway." She smiled and left the table, trying not to listen as she walked towards the café toilets. It would be an update on the remaining elements of the terrorist threat, and she was sure Sebastian would tell her what she missed if it was anything of interest.

When she came back Myron was still on the phone, and so intent on the conversation that he didn't notice her approaching from behind.

"No, Sherlock, come back to London. You couldn't have done anything else, and we don't want anyone learning that it hasn't hurt you."

Amelia hung back for a moment, her eyes going wide and her pulse beginning to race. Myron had just called someone Sherlock, and it definitely sounded like it was his younger brother. Afraid he would notice her, she waited for a few seconds and then hurried forward, clipping her boots on the leg of a table so he'd notice her and not realise she'd heard anything.

"All right, brother of mine. I'll see you at Baker Street later." Myron hung up, and she smiled at him and sat down, pushing the implications of what she'd just heard from her mind. She couldn't dwell on the man in front of her being well over a hundred years old. It would paralyse her mind, and she couldn't let him see she suspected something like that.

"Did he succeed?" she asked when neither of them spoke.

"Almost. He's apprehended one, but the other got away.

Most importantly, he's unharmed and on his way back home."

"Does that mean you have to rush off?"

"No. He will be several hours, and we haven't finished our lesson."

She nodded and spent another fifteen minutes telling him what she saw in the people around them. On only two more occasions did she miss something that Myron pointed out to her.

"Well done," he said when she finished telling him the waiter's family history. "You've improved."

"I have a good teacher," she said and gave him a lopsided grin. He didn't respond but stared at her for a moment. The hint of a frown passed across his face before it went back to the usual impassive look.

"What?" she asked. Hoping he hadn't seen something in her that might give away the emotions coursing through her. Despite her best intentions, she was struggling not to think about him possibly being Mycroft Holmes, a man who should have died long ago, let alone look so young.

"Your hair is up. Down is better. Like the last time we were here," he said a few seconds later.

"You think so?" She raised her eyebrows and tried not to look even more shocked. He nodded. "Then down it is."

She lifted her fingers to pull out the pins holding her bun in place. Less than five seconds later her hair was cascading around her shoulders the way it had the first time she'd walked out onto the terrace. Myron blinked rapidly at her.

"It wasn't a command."

"I know, but I'm getting a second date; the least I can do is make a little effort for you." She gave him her most mischievous look to let him know she was teasing, even if she hoped her words would be true.

"This isn't a date."

"Maybe not, but this is probably the closest thing to a date a woman has ever managed to get with you." Amelia looked up at him through her eyelashes and grinned. A few seconds later a smile flickered across his face, the first genuine one she'd ever seen him make.

THE END

ABOUT THE AUTHOR

Jess was born in the quaint village of Woodbridge in the UK, has spent some of her childhood in the States and now resides in the beautiful Roman city of Bath. She lives with her husband, Phil, and her very dapsy cat, Pleaides. During her still relatively short life Jess has displayed an innate curiosity for learning new things and has, therefore, studied many subjects, from maths and the sciences, to history and drama. Jess now works full time as a writer, incorporating many of the subjects she has an interest in within her plots and characters.

You can find Jess on many social media platforms such as facebook and twitter as well as having her own website and blog at www.jessmountifield.co.uk. If you also wish to contact the author you can do so at books@jessmountifield.co.uk

LIST OF PRINTED WORKS

Historical Adventure:
With Proud Humility (Hearts of the Seas: 1)
Chains of Freedom (Hearts of the Seas: 4)

Fantasy:
Tales of Ethanar: An Anthology (Containing the first six
Tales of Ethanar - Wandering to Belong, Innocent Hearts,
For Such a Time as This, A Fire's Sacrifice and The Hope of
Winter) - Coming Spring 2016
The Fire of Winter (Winter: 1) – Coming Summer 2016

Sci-Fi:
Sherdan's Prophecy (Sherdan: 1)
Sherdan's Legacy (Sherdan: 2)
Sherdan's Country (Sherdan: 3)

As Amelia Price:

The First Lesson: The first three stories in the Mycroft
Holmes Adventures series (Containing The Hundred Year
Wait, The Unexpected Coincidence, and The Invisible
Amateur)

19517397R10169

Printed in Great Britain
by Amazon